TAME

CARTER KIDS #3

CHLOE WALSH

Tame,
Carter Kids #3,
First published, September 2016
All rights reserved. ©
Cover designed by Bee @ Bitter Sage Designs.
Edited by Aleesha Davis.
Proofread by Brooke Bowen Hebert.

DISCLAIMER

This book is a work of fiction. All names, characters, places and incidents either are products of the author's imagination or are used fictitiously. Any resemblance to events, locales, or persons, living or dead, is coincidental.

1

NOAH

*I*f the asshole in the Armani suit stopped by our seat to look down my girlfriend's top one more fucking time, I was going to lose it.

How many times did a man have to take a piss?

Every five minutes?

Dammit to hell, even thinking about his blond head walking up and down the aisle for the past twenty minutes made me want to break something.

I *would* be breaking something – his fucking nose if he looked at Thorn's tits one more goddamn time.

These pricks in first class clearly have issues with staring.

Well, I have issues with controlling my temper and he was pushing me.

If he kept it up, I would have no problem pushing back.

Teagan was sitting beside me, on her own free will, completely unaware of how tempting she looked, oblivious to the stares she was receiving.

We'd come straight from the hotel and she was dressed in a pair of my sweat pants and a white wife-beater, giving me – and the prick in a suit – a fucking perfect side view of her bare breasts.

Thankfully my sweats covered her legs, because knowing my boxers were all she had on underneath was driving me out of my mind. The visual would be my undoing.

She had a huge, white, megawatt smile on her face, clearly engrossed in the paperback she'd picked up in duty-free before boarding.

Watching the emotions play out on Thorn's face as she read was a beautiful sight.

My girl had brains...

"Noah, quick, give me your iPod," Teagan squealed, startling me.

"Christ," I muttered, jerking in my seat. I passed her the iPod and watched as she tapped the screen furiously. "What's wrong?"

"I need a song," she growled, scrawling through a playlist she had already created. "There's this scene. It needs a song..." her voice trailed off as she searched. "Yes!" She screeched, cackling with excitement before handing the iPod back to me. "Perfect."

I cocked a brow, mildly amused. "What did you choose?"

"Shh!" She snapped, head back down. "I'm reading."

What the hell?

Shaking my head, I decided not to ask any more questions.

Women were a complex species.

I was way out of my league with this particular one.

I knew my team thought I was insane, chasing a woman to Ireland; not to mention bringing her back with me. But they didn't get it. No one did. Well, Lucky kind of understood, but Tommy certainly didn't. Hell, Tommy thought I had a death wish, bringing Thorn on the MFA tour with me. His irate phone call this afternoon assured me of that.

"She's been back in your life five minutes, man, and you're in trouble again," Tommy roared down the line. "God-damn, Noah, this is your career we're talking about. You've worked too hard and overcame too much to let it all slip through your fingers now."

"It has nothing to do with her," I snarled, forcing myself to keep my voice down. I was in the middle of the airport and Teagan was less than three feet away. She didn't need to be hearing any of this shit.

"Oh, because it never has anything to do with her?" Tommy shot back, his tone laced with disgust. "Like you getting arrested had nothing to do with her? Or you breaking your bail conditions to chase her down had nothing to do with her? Or her uncle adding an extra eighteen months onto your sentencing? I suppose getting into that fight last night had nothing to do with her either?"

I wasn't stupid. It wasn't like I'd woken up this morning and decided everything was rosy in the garden between us. I was still hurting. I still felt betrayed and angry and fucking bitter.

Fear of the future and uncertainty about Teagan's feelings for me still crippled me. But fear or not, nothing was going to drag me away from her again.

Besides, I wasn't looking for Tommy's approval.

I wasn't seeking any damn person's acceptance. All I wanted was her. Everyone else and their opinions could go to hell.

The moment the flight attendant stood in the middle of the aisle and began to call out the usual safety instructions, I tightened the strap of my seatbelt as tight as physically possible.

Shoving my headphones on, I pumped the volume on my iPod to the max and held onto the metal armrests like they were my saving grace.

I felt the plane move slowly and my stomach twisted inside.

A soft hand touched my neck, pulling my headphones away, and then Teagan's voice was in my ear.

"What's up?"

"I fucking hate flying, baby," I mumbled, keeping my eyes focused on the seat in front of me, desperately ignoring the window to my right.

"Big, bad Noah Messina afraid of flying?" Her soft laugh filled my ears. "We haven't taken off yet."

I didn't respond.

There was nothing I could say.

I wasn't afraid of flying; I was fucking petrified.

"Don't worry," Thorn purred, covering my hand with hers. "I'll protect you."

"Might hold you to that."

"Take off is the worst," Teagan soothed. "You'll be grand once we're up in the air."

Jesus fucking Christ.

I had seven hours on this mother fucking death trap.

The plane picked up speed, causing my head to spin and my ears to pop.

My breakfast tried to make a reappearance.

I was fucking pathetic.

"Hold my hand." Reaching out blindly, I thankfully caught a hold of Teagan's hand and squeezed. "What the fuck is happening to my ears?"

"Chew," Teagan instructed before popping a stick of gum into my mouth. "It'll help with the popping sensation."

Ignoring Lucky and Quincy as they laughed and

pointed their phones at me from two rows ahead, I clenched my eyes shut, held my breath, chewed like a maniac, and fought back the overwhelming urge to spew my guts out.

I managed to remain calm until an hour in when the pilot decided it would be a fun idea to turn the plane on its side.

"We're going to die," I screamed out, arms and legs flailing. "Thorn!"

I was literally putting myself through fucking torture.

"Noah!" Teagan chuckled in between fits of laughter. "You're a backstreet fighter turned MFA superstar. You've got this. Stop being a baby."

"Flying is safer than driving," I muttered, more to myself than to Teagan, ignoring her words.

My fists couldn't fucking make me fly...

"You could get killed crossing the road."

"That's right," she cooed, stroking the back of my hand with the tips of her fingers. "And we're already over the ocean," she added. "It's a better way to die if we crash."

My eyes flew open.

"What the fuck?" My voice was higher than when it broke when I was twelve. "What the fuck kind of thing is that to say, Thorn?"

"I'm just saying," she argued lightheartedly, hazel eyes dancing with amusement. "If we were to crash, I would rather go down in the ocean. Less messy."

"I need to get off this thing," I growled.

Looking around for someone to help me, I spotted a flight attendant and flagged her over. "Let me off this fucking death trap."

"Why don't you go for a walk down the aisle, Mr. Messina?" The hostess offered, trying and failing to hide her smile. "The seatbelt light is off, so go ahead and stretch your legs."

"And take off the one thing that has the potential to save my life?" I shook my head in disgust. "You're fucking crazy."

Frightened as I was, I couldn't help but notice the protective way Teagan covered my thigh with her small hand.

"Can we have some alcohol?" She asked the hostess.

"Of course," the hostess replied, a smile fading as she eyed Teagan's hand. "Gin, Bourbon –"

"Brandy. And we'll take a bottle," Teagan answered for the both of us. "A large one."

The attendant returned a few moments later with a large bottle of Hennessy and two disposable foam cups.

"Thank you," Teagan said, offering a small wad of cash to the hostess before taking the bottle and twisting the cap off.

"Here," she muttered, pouring a large dollop of brandy into one of the foam cups before thrusting it into my hand. "Drink."

I didn't need to be told twice.

Tossing the brandy down my throat, I swallowed it in one gulp, hissing when the burn hit just the right spot.

Teagan quickly refilled my cup and I downed that one and the one after that, too.

Out of the corner of my eye, I spotted a couple of kids sitting opposite us laughing at me.

"You'll be laughing," I snarled before tossing back my fifth cup. "When we nose dive into the fucking Atlantic."

Their laughs soon died and were quickly replaced with soft cries and keening noises.

"Noah," Teagan scowled. "Cop on, will you. They're only kids."

"Dead kids," I muttered under my breath, glaring across the aisle at the little shits.

Catching my chin between her thumb and index finger, Teagan tugged hard, forcing me to look at her. "You are safe," she said slowly. "Nothing bad is going to happen to you. I promise. Okay?"

Even though I didn't truly believe it, I found myself nodding like a child, all my earlier fear and anxiety simmering down as another feeling inside of me grew at a rapid pace.

Comfort.

Reaching out with her other hand, she took my cup from me before cupping my face in her small hands, her brown eyes snaring me.

"Keep your eyes on me," she whispered.

"I'm trying," I said, pressing my forehead to hers, seeking something from this woman that I'd never been given before.

Reassurance.

Leaning forward, Teagan pressed her rosy plump lips against mine – the very lips I'd spent the best part of a decade dreaming about.

She had her eyes open and locked on mine and I felt weirdly exposed.

Like this was more intimate than being inside her.

Like she was giving me something by just pressing her mouth to mine.

My heartbeat rocketed in my chest.

It was too much.

She was too much.

I was so stunned by her move that I could do nothing but sit there like a fucking idiot, eyes wide open, hands glued to the armrests of my seat, and my focus entirely on her face.

My skin was on fire and the more she stroked and touched my face, the more I burned.

"I think I know a way you can work out all this tension." Thorn rubbed her nose against mine before pulling back and smiling.

Running her hands up my chest, she rested them on my shoulders. "How would you feel about joining the mile-high club?"

What the...

My brows shot up in surprise. "You fucking with me, Thorn?" My dick was instantly hard. "You're fucking with me, aren't you?"

She wasn't serious.

No way in hell.

"No. I'm not fucking with you, Noah." Teagan inclined her head in the direction of the bathroom, climbed out of her seat ever so slowly, and winked. "But I will be," she purred before skipping down the aisle toward the bathroom.

The brandy must have done the trick, giving me some serious Dutch courage, because I was out of that seat and halfway down the aisle before my brain caught up with my dick.

The air left my lungs the moment I stepped inside the poky airplane toilet and locked eyes on my girlfriend who was already naked and straddling the sink.

"Fuck me," I growled, dropping my hands to the fly of my suit pants. "And you call *me* treacherous."

"Hurry up and get your cock out," Teagan hissed, "I'm freezing my ass off in here."

I cocked a brow and smirked.

Shoving my pants and boxers down, I closed the small

space between us, and grabbed her hips. "You trying to seduce me with your sexy talk, Thorn?"

"I'm not trying to be sexy," she growled, clawing underneath my t-shirt, desperate for skin on skin. "I'm trying to get laid."

Pulling her hips roughly toward me, I guided my dick slowly inside her, hissing when her tight pussy sucked me in deeper.

Teagan's head fell back, smacking against the wall with a thud.

"Shit," I grunted, pausing mid thrust to check her over. "Are you okay?"

"Don't stop," she snapped, interrupting me. "Concussion or not, don't you dare stop." She trailed her fingernails against my chest as she ground her tight pussy against my dick. "I need you inside me."

Jesus Christ...

I slammed myself further inside her, groaning loudly, reveling in being buried to the hilt inside the only woman I wanted to fall into.

"Fuck me, Noah," Teagan cried out as she leaned back, giving me more access to that perfect pussy of hers.

Using her hands to hold her weight up, Thorn clung to the narrow metal fixture behind her back while I held her hips in my hands and buried myself between her legs.

I wanted to make a mark on her so permanent she would never shake me off.

This woman owned me.

I wanted to own her just as hard.

Just as fucking much.

"Harder," she hissed, bringing her hips up, meeting me thrust for thrust. "I can take it."

She didn't have to tell me twice.

Tightening my grip on her hips so hard I knew I would leave marks, I pounded myself into her, enjoying the loud mewling sounds coming from her throat.

I was violating her body, and she was enjoying every second of it.

Thoughts of another man being where I was currently buried caused the rage inside of me to roar to the surface.

Knowing it was my own damn fault only pissed me off more.

I was a fucking hypocrite...

"Only you, Noah," Teagan cried out, as if she could hear my thoughts. "Just you."

Her skin was so soft, and the smell of coconut shampoo flooded my senses, making me hard as die cast metal. Fuck me.

This woman. Taking me deep, pulling me in further, trapping me in all that she was. I wanted to be trapped. Captured.

I wanted to be fucking possessed by her.

"Damn straight," I hissed.

Passion and lust overrode all other thoughts in my mind and I lost control. Her pale, milky skin was flushed, slick with a fine sheen of sweat, and was all I could see.

Teagan was trembling beneath me, the same way she'd trembled when she was seventeen and I'd taken her virginity. She was breathing hard, her pussy tightening around me with every thrust.

Moving inside her, feeling her heat tightening around me, the wetness of her, it was too much. I wanted to bury my dick inside her and never come back out again. This was all I wanted for the rest of my life. I was tired of fighting.

I just wanted a home and with Teagan, I'd found it.

"Thorn, simmer down," I grunted, dropping a hand between our bodies to finger her clit.

I watched as Thorn bit down hard on her plump bottom lip, though it didn't make her moans any quieter.

"Shh, Teegs," I hissed out through clenched teeth. "The whole plane's gonna hear you."

"I don't care," she screamed, voice rising with every thrust. "Let them hear.... ah fuck...let them hear what you do to me."

The harder I fucked her, the louder she screamed.

She was getting close.

I could feel it.

Seven years apart or not, I knew her pussy well enough to know the signs. The tightening sensation. The dragging feeling on my dick. The catch in her breath. The way her eyes rolled back in her head. The trembling. The tiny jerks her body made as raw pleasure jolted through her.

Ripples of pleasure shot through me, jolting my cock, making me pulse hard, throb inside her.

Yeah, Thorn was coming hard on my dick.

I would never get tired of watching this woman come. Fuck, her facial expressions set me off more times than not.

Slinging herself forward, Teagan wrapped her arm around my neck and dragged my face toward her, pressing her forehead to mine.

Her eyes were open, her gaze locked on mine.

It was too much.

She was screaming this fucking room down and I'd lost every ounce of self-control.

I felt myself come, and allowed myself to spill into her, thrusting until every last drop of my orgasm had emptied into her.

2

TEAGAN

I was back in the States.

Back in the land I had once fled and vowed I would never return to.

And I was back here with the man I had run from all those years ago. Ready to go on tour, moving from city to city, passing through a different state each week, with my MFA superstar boyfriend.

Noah sat beside me in the back seat of a shiny, black limousine.

He was all bulging muscles under his black shirt with his sleeves rolled up, tatts, and messy hair.

I swear to god the man had the best forearm porn ever. The veins, the tan, the fucking strength in his arms were something else.

With his Ray Bans on, his legs stretched out in front of him, one hand on mine and the other hanging loosely over the back of the seat, Noah looked like a fallen angel.

Someone dangerous.

Someone lethal.

When he turned his face toward me and cocked a brow, I

was immediately transported back in time – back to my youth.

Back to the nights when we were young and stupid. The nights I sat beside him in his hot as hell Lexus, feeling totally badass and unbreakable. Driving around town in his car, skipping school, breaking all of my uncle's rules – not to mention the law – to be with him.

Back then, Noah had been involved with some seriously dark and shady men, and the worst type of illegal activities an eighteen-year-old boy could be involved in.

He'd dabbled in a violent underworld full of drugs, prostitution, and gangland murder, and I, in turn, had been dragged into said underworld.

That was a world Noah had turned his back on for me years ago, but in that twisted old fashioned gangster way, the underworld wasn't ready – or willing – to let go of Noah. His so-called defection had set in motion a wrecking ball of events and repercussions that had destroyed our relationship and landed Noah behind bars for five years.

But apparently destroying us and taking years of Noah's life away wasn't good enough revenge for the sadistic mob boss, Noah's former stepbrother to be exact. Because now, almost a decade later, JD's thirst for revenge was as intense as ever, and their preferred meat came in the form of yours truly.

Yep, I was being stalked by my boyfriend's freak of a stepbrother who was determined to kill me and make it blissfully painful.

I had no idea what I was doing, skipping halfway across the world when a war of epic proportions was brewing between a freaking mob – it felt like I was jumping from the frying pan straight into the fire – but I couldn't stay away from him a minute longer. Not one incriminating piece of evidence or red flag warning was scary enough to make me run twice...

"You awake, Thorn?" Noah asked in his deep, gravelly voice. He squeezed my hand gently and just like that, all thoughts of JD Dennis evaporated from my mind.

"Yeah," I replied, fighting back a yawn. "Do we have much further to go?" I asked, making a half-assed effort to twist my body toward him.

Noah had a meeting with the disciplinary board of the MFA in about forty-five minutes.

We'd been traveling for almost sixteen hours straight, leaving Ireland yesterday afternoon to get to the damn meeting on time.

Now that we were almost there, anxiety was gnawing at my gut.

If Noah ended up with a suspension, then it would be my fault.

"Another twenty minutes?" Noah drawled lazily.

"So, what am I supposed to do when you're in the meeting?" I asked, feeling uncertain.

I didn't have a job to go to or any long-term plans – I'd left it all behind me.

My entire life was back in Ireland and I had bailed on it for Noah.

"Should I just wait in the car...uh, limo?"

"Not a chance," he shot back. "Wherever I am, you'll be, too."

"And when you're training?" Swiping the bottle of water out of the cup holder, I removed the cap and took a sip, before backwashing it back into the bottle. Hot water... "Ugh. That's disgusting."

"Be with me?" He offered with a knowing smirk, his gaze

flickering between my face and the car window beside him. "I don't know, Thorn... You could shop? Relax. Have fun."

"I'm not going shopping all day, every day." Shifting closer to Noah, I rested my head against his shoulder and the bottle on his thigh. "You don't know me at all if you think that's something I would actually enjoy."

Letting out a grunt when the hot plastic touched his thigh, Noah's hand shot out and swiped the bottle out of mine.

"Then work for me," he grumbled, slipping the bottle back into the cup holder.

I scrunched my nose up in distaste. "And take a pity wage from you for doing nothing?" I shook my head in disgust. "That's not me. I'm my own woman."

"Then help me train. Take care of my money. Spend my money. Shit, Thorn, I don't care –"

"Excuse me, Noah Messina. I am a qualified, not to mention well experienced, gym instructor." Jerking away from his body, I turned my body sideways and glared at his side profile. "I'm far from a China doll. Don't be so sexist."

"For fuck's sake," Noah grumbled, running a hand through his fuck-me hair before claiming mine once more and pressing a kiss to my knuckles. "I chased you halfway across the world to be bitched at?"

"You most certainly did."

"Well, my leg of the tour doesn't officially start for two weeks." Smirking, he added, "Let's just leave all the worrying until then and enjoy this time together."

"What about training?"

Men didn't look like Noah without sweating their asses off in a gym daily.

"Don't you have some sort of regiment to stick to?"

"It doesn't matter," he replied gruffly. "I want time alone with you. Everything else can wait."

Sighing in contentment, I turned and stared at him shamelessly, thoroughly enjoying the electrical feeling surging through my body from the physical contact of having Noah's rough, calloused hand covering mine.

"You know; I don't think I've ever been in a limousine before." Waggling my brows, I smirked. "Posh much?"

Noah barked out a laugh. "You think I'm posh?" Shaking his head in amusement, he said, "I'm used to being transported in the back of a prison van in chains, Thorn. I'm about the furthest from posh you could get."

"Speaking of prison vans." I lazily traced circles on Noah's thigh with my finger. "How long did Lucky serve in prison?"

Since Noah and Lucky told me about them sharing a cell together, I'd been curious. I'd wanted to ask, but I didn't want to bring it up around Lucky.

Noah shifted in his seat. "Eleven years."

My jaw fell open and he quickly pushed it shut with his finger.

"Lucky's one of the good ones," he told me with a knowing smirk. "He got in over his head when he was barely more than a kid. The guy has long paid his dues."

"What did he do?" I asked, wondering how any man that served eleven years in prison could be one of the good guys. Shifting closer to Noah, I rested my head against his shoulder. "You guys never talk about it. Is it bad?"

"Manslaughter."

Lucky killed a man? "How lovely," I muttered in disgust.

I was hanging around with some colorful characters, that was for sure.

"Babe, stem the judgment," Noah reproved, tipping my chin up with his finger. "You don't know his reasons."

"There's a good enough reason to validate murdering a man nowadays?" I scrunched my nose up in disgust. "I highly doubt it."

"When the man rapes and murders your girlfriend, then yeah," Noah growled, turning his face to look at me pointedly. "I'd say abso-fucking-lutely, that's a good enough reason to take his life."

"Oh." My cheeks flamed in shame and embarrassment. "I didn't know that."

"Things aren't always how they seem on the outside, Teagan," Noah replied quietly and just like that, the atmosphere around us changed. It darkened. "Not everything is black and white."

"What's his real name?" I asked, trying to steer the conversation away from the shit storm it was heading into.

"Whose?"

"Lucky's?"

The question seemed to throw Noah and his brows furrowed in confusion. "I don't know," he replied thoughtfully. "Never asked."

"You shared a cell with him for half a decade and never once thought to ask him his real name?"

"You've met the guy," he shot back. "Why didn't *you* ask him, *Jessica Fletcher*?"

"Because...he's your Lucky." I shifted uncomfortably on my seat. "And honestly, that guy comes across as a closed book."

Lucky seemed friendly enough.

He smiled whenever our paths had crossed, but I had a feeling he kept to himself.

One look at the man and it was obvious that he wasn't the type of person you could pump information from.

Shrugging, Noah smiled sheepishly. "Well I know his last name is Casarazzi."

I frowned. "You do realize that's going to bug me until I find out?"

Sliding his phone out of his pants pocket, Noah swiped the screen before putting it to his ear.

"Hey man," he said after a moment, keeping his eyes on the road. "What's your real name?" He paused and said, "Cool," before hanging up and dropping his phone back in his pocket.

"It's Hunter."

"Hunter." I pondered it for a moment before nodding in agreement. It suited him. "I can't believe you never told me that you and Lucky were cellmates."

"When was I supposed to tell you, Thorn?" Noah turned to face me. His tone of voice was soft, but the meaning behind his words stung. "During one of our many phone calls, or prison visits these past seven years?"

I flinched like he slapped me across the face. "Are you ever going to get over it?"

"I am over it." His tone was abrupt and strained.

He wasn't over it.

He pretended to be, and sure, Noah could be a pretty good liar, but he couldn't fool me.

It was still there between us, the pain and betrayal buried deep down inside – like an elephant in the room, or a ticking time bomb just waiting to explode...

"Sure you are," I grumbled, choosing to bow out of this argument.

It was pointless.

Neither of us were going to win and I didn't have the

energy to go another round with him. I also knew that I had wronged him on so many levels that I wasn't sure if we could ever get past it.

"...I MEMORIZED EVERY INCH OF YOU. I FUCKING LOVED YOU EVEN when I hated you most," he roared hoarsely. "You broke my trust, Thorn. You ripped my goddamn heart out of my chest, but you're still the only one I want by my side. At my lowest point, all I wanted was you. At my highest point, all I want is you. I must be a masochistic bastard because after all these years and all this pain, I still want to halve my soul with you. Split myself down the center and give you ownership of me..."

"...I loved you," I called out, voice breaking, as I watched him walk away from me, knocking over every piece of equipment he passed.

"You didn't love me enough!" he roared, slamming both his hands against the door before he walked out..."

"NOAH, I'M SORRY," I WHISPERED, KEEPING MY EYES SHUT, MY eyelids burning.

"What for?"

"You know what for," I muttered, biting down hard on my bottom lip.

I was a stubborn woman, and admitting I was wrong wasn't an easy thing for me – apologizing was even harder.

"For not staying." God, would it ever get easier? "For leaving you." To rot alone in a prison cell.

"Open your legs, Thorn."

My eyes flew open. "W-what?"

"Your legs, Teagan," he repeated slowly. "Spread them. Now."

Shocked, I opened my mouth to say something, anything, but the look on Noah's face caused my words to shrivel up and evaporate.

Surprisingly, I did as I was told and let my legs fall open, quivering when his warm hand slipped beneath the waistband of the oversized sweatpants I had on and cupped me.

"I'm not gonna lie," he told me as he slipped his fingers underneath the fabric of the boxer shorts I had on. "You broke me."

Sliding two fingers inside me, Noah traced his thumb over my throbbing clit.

"It still hurts," he admitted quietly. "You took everything from me and you didn't even know it." His words were so hard, a contrast to his tender touch. "When you walked away from me, you took my future with you because that's what you represented to me. My future."

He kept two fingers in my slick heat and then added a third, all while massaging my clit with his thumb. "My fucking everything."

"I'm sorry," I moaned shamelessly, thrusting my hips against his hand.

Noah's fingers moved inside me, making me wet, making me ache so hard for him. He was mentally draining me, emotionally ruining me, and still, I wanted to let him take it all.

I owed this to him.

"All those things I've done to you," I moaned, rocking my hips upward. "I would give anything to make them go away....to erase them from your memory, but I can't."

My breath caught in my throat when Noah's fingers stroked a spot inside of my pussy that caused my whole body to shudder.

"I can't change the past, Noah," I cried out, fighting to

make sense of my words as my body reveled in ecstasy. "So we can either move forward from here...mmm...or we can argue...ah...but we cannot be apart. I won't do it. Never again."

"DID HE MAKE YOU FEEL LIKE THIS?" PINCHING MY CLIT BETWEEN his fingers, he pressed his fingers deeper into me, adding pressure to my clit, making me cry out loudly. "Did he make you come?"

"...Liam was safe; he couldn't hurt me because I didn't have any room left inside of me to store the pain. You say you want me, Noah, but I didn't know that back then...so I tried to move on from you. I tried to force myself into believing Liam was what was right for me —"

"He's not what's right for you, Teagan," Noah hissed. His eyes never left mine as he took a step back and said, "he's what's safe for you. I'm what's right for you. Me..."

I COULD NEVER HAVE ANOTHER MAN INSIDE MY BODY.

Never again.

Shaking the image of Liam's face out of my mind, I cried out, "No," as I thrashed against Noah's touch, feeling the burning sensation building up inside of me, desperate to reach it.

I was panting, groaning, and pretty much thrashing like a demented lunatic, craving release as the limousine ate up the miles and his fingers fucked me into submission.

"I don't trust easily and I don't love," he grunted. "Never have." His fingers fucked me to the rhythm of our relationship; hard, fast, and merciless. "But I did both of those with you."

"I know." My breathless pants and moans of encouragement only pushed him on as he set alight every nerve ending in my body. "Oh god, I know..."

Urging him harder, deeper...

A thousand thoughts flushed through my mind in that moment, every one of him, but I let sensation guide me.

More... harder...

"I was always coming back for you." Noah's words – his beautiful, harsh words – were like music to my ears and I covered his hand with mine, squeezing my thighs together just as my orgasm rushed through me.

Sighing, he slid his hand out of me and whispered, "I'm not blaming you for everything, Thorn. I'm just trying to explain how I feel. I need to believe you're not going to walk away from me again. Just give me some time."

There were only so many ways I could tell him – show him that I was here to stay.

I needed him to believe me. My big, bruised, and beautifully broken man.

"I can do that," I whispered. "Give you time, that is."

Loving Noah Messina wasn't a choice for me.

It was something that had been instilled inside my heart without my brain's permission. I couldn't stop it. I couldn't change it. All I could do was roll with the punches and pray I made it out in one piece.

Either way, there wasn't another person on this planet I would rather break my own heart loving.

3

TEAGAN

I was shuffled into the fanciest looking boardroom on this side of the hemisphere with Noah right behind me.

Nine pairs of eyes immediately flew to my face and I flamed in embarrassment.

"I...uh...I can wait outside," I started to say, but Noah quickly shut me down.

"This is Teagan," he announced to the room full of suits. "My girlfriend. Get used to seeing her around the place because she goes where I go."

His girlfriend!

A few members of the board cleared their throats, others looked dispassionately in my direction, but no one argued with Noah, and to be fair, I didn't blame them.

Noah wasn't an easy man to challenge. In any aspect of life.

With that, Noah pulled out a chair at the huge oak table and gestured for me to sit.

I practically fell into the chair, feeling totally out of my element.

Taking the seat beside me, Noah leaned forward and rested his elbows on the expensive table in front of us. Meanwhile, I shriveled up in my chair, praying for this to end quickly.

Through hooded eyes, I watched as Noah flicked through the neat pile of paperwork in front of him. Tension was emanating from him as he stared hard at each sheet.

Letting out a low growl, he ran a hand through his hair before rolling his shirt sleeves back up to his elbows and refocusing on the paperwork.

"My name is Judith Rembrandt, head of the disciplinary board. Shall we commence, Mr. Messina?" A low sized, middle-aged woman asked in a snotty tone.

Judith had her graying brown hair pulled back in a severe bun and she kind of reminded me of one of our old school teachers in the convents back home.

I bet she was a crack the whip kind of woman.

"Where's Nick?" Was all Noah replied.

Nick Leversteen was the owner and CEO of the MFA. I was more than surprised not to see him here.

Obviously, Noah was, too.

"Unfortunately, Mr. Leversteen was unavailable this morning," the old shrew replied. "Shall we proceed?"

"Go for it." Leaning back in his chair, Noah shoved the paperwork away from him, not far, but enough to let everyone in the room know he wasn't happy.

With a nod of her head, Judith wasted no time in chastising Noah.

"Your actions in Ireland were completely unacceptable, Mr. Messina, not to mention illegal. Do I need to remind you that you are a representative of our brand, and when you behave badly, it reflects badly on the MFA?"

Nodding stiffly, Noah drummed his fingers against the

desk, but he didn't respond. I was really proud of his self-restraint at that moment because I wanted to cut the bitch for talking to him like that.

My fingernails were making tiny, burrowing holes in the leather armrests. Maybe I was growing, too, because I was managing to stay in my seat.

Maybe Noah was a good influence on me after all...

"Your previous convictions, not to mention your recreational pursuits," Judith added, her eyes flickering to me as she cleared her throat, "have a direct effect on our brand's name."

"Recreational pursuits?" I whispered under my breath. Turning to Noah, I raised a brow in question and he shook his head, looking just as puzzled as I was.

"The sex tape, Noah," another voice said from behind us. A millisecond later, the sound of a door closing firmly filled my ears.

Swinging around to see who had walked in, my mouth fell open when Tommy Moyet, Noah's best friend from high school, entered my peripheral vision.

"Apologies for my late arrival." Tommy walked over to the table and took a seat on Noah's right, never once glancing in my direction.

I didn't miss the cool way Tommy ignored my presence, but I also didn't miss the warmth and relief in Noah's eyes when Tommy entered the room. In fact, Noah visibly sagged in his chair.

"Traffic was hectic," Tommy continued to say with a dismissive flick of his wrist.

Shrugging off his crisp, gray suit jacket, Tommy discreetly fist-bumped Noah under the table before turning his attention back to the board.

Taking Noah's file of paperwork, Tommy flicked through

each page, looking mildly amused, before taking the board to town. "Ms. Rembrandt, do I need to remind you that Noah's previous convictions and private affairs have nothing to do with this meeting?"

Judith's face reddened, but she quickly recovered. "A black mark on your client is a black mark on our company."

"And yet your CEO was more than aware of my client's black marks when he signed him to the company less than two weeks after his release," Tommy shot back calmly. "In fact, he's made a pretty penny selling my client's life story to the media."

Uh-oh. Tommy hit a nerve with that comment.

Judith's face turned an unflattering shade of purple "Be that as it may, Mr. Messina should conduct himself in a professional manner at all times..."

"Did you watch the tape?" Tommy countered lazily.

I sat forward, completely emerged in watching this old lady take a verbal ass kicking.

"What video?" I whispered, nudging Noah. Deep down, I had a feeling I already knew, but I needed confirmation from him.

"Thorn." The look Noah gave me was one of fierce regret and I knew. I fucking knew.

"The elevator," I said, deadpan. The CCTV footage of Noah taking my virginity in the elevator of Kyle Carter's hotel. "You and me?"

Noah nodded slowly.

Groaning, I dropped my head in my hands and bit back the urge to howl.

Reese fucking Tanner...

Glancing around the room at her colleagues, Judith turned back to Tommy and nodded.

"I speak for all of us here when I say that yes, we all

watched the tape. We needed to see what sort of damage control was in order," she explained, red-faced. "It's our job!"

"Then you're all guilty of watching an unsolicited video of minors," Tommy shot back with a smirk. "Tut-tut, Mrs. Rembrandt."

Noah barked out a laugh and Judith cut him a look that said 'shut your damn mouth'.

"We...we...it..."

"You intentionally downloaded and watched illegally captured footage of a seventeen-year-old girl." Judith paled and Tommy grinned in victory. "Teagan," he said, addressing me for the first time.

"Yep?" I asked, mortified.

"These fine people have all freely admitted to watching unsolicited footage of you as a minor. Footage that was leaked without your consent or knowledge. What would you like to do?"

"I..." Oh shit, I wasn't prepared for this.

What did I want to do?

I wanted to go back in time and cut Reese Tanner a second asshole, but the past was unchangeable. The future however...

"I want Noah cleared of all responsibility regarding the fight in Cork," I announced. "Shut that shit down, close your case on my boyfriend, and I'll forget about what a bunch of perverts you all are."

"That's my girl," Noah chuckled. Shoving his seat back, he caught hold of my hand and half dragged me out of my seat. "See ya."

"Now wait just a damn minute," Judith spluttered, furi-ous. "We're not done here, Mr. Messina."

"Talk to my manager," Noah shot back, grinning. "We're out."

4

NOAH

Noah

"*N*oah. Get back here. I need to speak to you!"

Tommy's voice came from behind me, and reluctantly, I came to a halt in the middle of the empty corridor.

"Not now, T," I warned him, clenching my jaw.

This wasn't the time or the place for the conversation I knew Tommy wanted to speak to me about. Teagan, who was alongside me, looked up in confusion.

"What's wrong?" She asked, eyeing Tommy who was approaching us with a thunderous expression on his face.

"Nothing," I lied, reassuring her.

"Nothing?" Tommy snarled when he reached us. "Are you fucking with me?" Running a hand through his prematurely graying hair, Tommy laughed humorlessly. "One hour and you're jumping through hoops..."

"Not here," I snapped, inclining my head toward Teagan.

Clearly Tommy either didn't get my drift or didn't care,

because he continued to rant in my face like a fucking mad man.

"This isn't a game, Noah," Tommy sneered. "Picking fights outside bars? Walking out of the meeting like that?" Tommy shook his head in disgust. "This is your career, man, and when your ass is on the line, all of our asses are on the line."

"What the fuck did you expect me to do?" I snarled, losing my cool. "Let them rough her up?" I took a step toward him. "No one puts their hands on her!" My fists clenched. "Fucking no one."

"I'll tell you what I didn't expect," Tommy shot back. "I didn't expect you to be so stupid..."

And then she was there, by my side, defending me like a lioness.

"Don't you dare call him stupid," Teagan hissed. Stepping around me, she walked straight up to Tommy and pressed her finger against his chest. "Talk to him like that one more time and I'll fry your balls and feed them to you through a tube."

She was protecting me.

This tiny little woman, full of spunk and sass and heart. I'd never had that before. A teammate. An equal. Teagan made me feel like I was worth a helluva lot more than I actually was.

Jesus Christ...I think I fell in love with her all over again at that moment.

Holding my hand up to Tommy in warning, I took Teagan by the arm and half dragged her down the corridor and out of harm's way.

We rounded a corner and I sagged in relief when I spotted Lucky lounging on a bench in the foyer of the building.

"Go wait with Lucky," I told her. Releasing her hand, I nudged her over to my friend. "I won't be long."

Lucky, who had noticed us approaching, was already walking toward us.

"Blondie," he said with a grin. "Come take a walk with me."

His eyes flickered to mine and in that brief moment, I found a huge amount of relief.

With that fleeting glance, he reassured me that he had my back. I could trust him with Teagan.

Lucky wouldn't let me down.

"Noah, if you're in trouble because of me, I want to know about it," Teagan shot back heatedly. "If Tommy Moyet has a problem with me being here..."

"He doesn't," I interrupted. "It's just business, Thorn. My career. Nothing to do with you."

Teagan dropped her hands to her hips and puffed out a sharp breath. "I'm not dumb, Noah." She stared hard up at me, silently demanding an explanation.

I didn't give her one.

I didn't trust myself to speak.

Turning my back on her, I stalked back to where I'd left Tommy.

"I don't like this, Noah," Tommy said unapologetically when I reached him.

Turning his back to me, he shoved his hands in his pockets and looked out the floor length window. "I think she's a menace, a liability, and completely unworthy of you."

I stepped back, putting a few feet between us. It was either move or hit him, and as pissed as I was at Tommy, I didn't want to hurt him.

"I need you to *not* talk about her like that," I warned him, grasping at the last thread of my patience. "Ever again."

"It's how I feel, man," Tommy shot back indignantly, swinging around to face me. "That woman is about the worst fucking thing on this planet for you. She's going to take you down, Noah. One way or another." I opened my mouth to speak, but Tommy continued. "Your rental was trashed. You are being threatened. Hell, we are all being threatened, and you are dangling Teagan in front of JD like a bleeding lamb to a great white..."

"Careful, T." Running a hand through my hair, I pulled hard on the ends, urging myself to calm the hell down. "One more word against her and I'm going to lose my shit."

"You haven't thought this through," he said accusingly. "Bringing her over here?" He threw his hands up in the air. "Taking her on tour with us?"

"I've spent the last seven years thinking about nothing else," I snarled, chest heaving.

"And if she leaves you again?" He roared. "What are you going to do then? We both know she's a flight risk."

"She won't do that to me."

"And what if the guy she's been seeing comes looking for her?" Tommy spat. "What if her uncle calls her home? Have you thought about that? Have you thought about how crazy this is?"

Tommy ran a hand through his hair and groaned.

"You don't know her, Noah. She's a girl from high school who screwed you over real bad. She's a liability to us. We're your team. I was there when the shit hit the fan back in high school," he snapped. "I watched her ruin you. Repeatedly. I know what she represents to you."

"Do you want to keep your job?" I snarled, clenching my knuckles so tight that I felt them crack. "Because one more word about her and you're fired."

"Do you want to keep yours?" He shot back angrily.

"Because keep fucking around with her and you'll be out of one."

"Obviously not," I snarled. "You're fired."

"Are you serious?" Hurt was splayed all over Tommy's face. "Noah, we've been friends for ten years," he added in a pained voice. "You're putting some woman over our friendship?"

"Not some woman." Releasing my fists, I wiped my palms against my thighs. "*My* woman. And one hundred percent."

"Noah," Tommy protested, but I was done being patient.

Turning my back, I walked away from his sorry ass before I did something I would no doubt regret.

"You have training in an hour," he called out, finally getting my message. "Quincy and Beau are waiting for you at the gym on fifth – Noah! Are you hearing me?"

"Fuck your training," I seethed as I continued walking. "Fuck the disciplinary board. In fact, fuck you all."

"And your fight next weekend?" Tommy shouted angrily.

Heavy footprints came from behind me.

Seconds later Tommy's hand was on my shoulder. Swinging me around, he looked straight into my eyes. "Fuck that, too?"

"I'll be there on fight night – like always," I shot back, furious, roughly shaking his hand from my shoulder. "And I'll win – like always..."

"Noah, you need to train –"

"No." I held my hands up between us and took a step back. If Tommy was smart he would back the fuck up from me. "I need people to stop telling me what the fuck to do."

"So what?" He demanded. "You're not going to train anymore?"

"I'm taking two weeks off," I replied. "I'll be at the fight, but I need some time with her."

"This is *exactly* what I was afraid of," I heard him mutter under his breath.

"Seven years, Tommy!" I roared. Inhaling a deep, calming breath, I forced myself to calm down before adding, "She comes first. She will *always* come first."

Tommy was silent for a long moment.

"I'm sorry, okay?" He held out his hand to me. "I'm just worried to death, man. The whole JD thing has me all fucked up and now she's here..." He swallowed deeply. "It just feels like everything is coming full circle again – and not in a good way."

My former step brother's face infiltrated my mind and just like that, my bad mood turned murderous.

Knowing that he had been watching Teagan all this time made my blood run cold.

He found her.

In one of the quietest places on this planet, that rat bastard found her. Worse, he'd intruded in her life, touched her private things, been in her apartment.

My hands balled into fists of their own accord.

Rage seeped through my body.

I was under no illusions that I was in the middle of a war.

I also knew it was a war I had to win.

Because Teagan needed me.

All of me.

Intact and alive with blood in my veins and air in my lungs.

I had sold my soul to the devil and it just so happened that my personal devil came with an Irish accent and blonde hair.

"He's here, you know," Tommy whispered. "In Vegas.

Lewis spotted him yesterday. Walking down fifth like he didn't have a care in the world."

"Don't tell her," I squeezed out. This was exactly why taking Teagan on the road with me was my only option. I'd followed my heart and now my heart was in immediate fucking danger. "Whatever else happens, make damn sure Teagan doesn't know he's here."

"I'm more worried about you, Noah," Tommy countered heatedly. "You're my best friend. If anything happens..."

"Nothing is going to happen to anyone," I said, making a promise I wasn't sure I could keep. "It's a fucking scare tactic. JD's trying to psyche us out." Sighing, I added, "Let him follow us. At least we'll know where to find him."

"What are you going to do?"

I'm going to take his life, that's what I'm going to do. "The less you know the safer."

5

TEAGAN

"*That* was insane!" I exclaimed when Noah and I had finally made it through the throngs of fans that had been waiting outside the MFA headquarters building, all desperately vying to get an autograph or a photo taken with my boyfriend. I was quickly learning that Noah's world was a constant paparazzi filled party.

Noah smirked. "I know."

Maneuvering the Lexus convertible that had miraculously appeared at the back of the building, Noah drove hard and fast. The beast of a car ate up the miles and we were soon several blocks away.

"You're such a badass," I teased, twisting sideways to look at him. "Blowing off your boss like that." Clearing my throat, I added, *"Talk to my manager,"* in a deep voice. "Totally badass."

Noah threw his head back and laughed.

"She's not my boss, Thorn." Reaching across the console, Noah took my hand in his and raised it to his mouth. "You are," he purred before pressing a hot kiss to the back of my hand.

"You are so full of shit," I shot back, a little breathless, because let's face it, Noah Messina just called me his boss. "So, what did Tommy say to you?"

Noah's body tensed. "Nothing important."

"Are you sure?" I asked, but Noah didn't respond. Choosing to move on quickly, I asked, "So, where are we going?"

"Wherever you want, Thorn. My schedule is free for the next two weeks." Shrugging, Noah dropped his hand to his lap, keeping ahold of mine. "Actually, I could eat something." He tugged on my hand and I had no choice but to shimmy closer – not that I was complaining. "Are you hungry?"

"Starving," I replied. "I feel like I haven't eaten in days."

"We could check out this place in – " His phone rang, and he paused mid-sentence before letting out a heavy sigh.

"Who is it?" I asked, curious, as I watched him dig inside his pants pocket for his phone.

"Tommy," he replied rather dejectedly, before swiping the screen and putting the phone to his ear. "What?" was the first word Noah spoke. "If this is about earlier..."

I listened intently, trying and failing to hear what Tommy was saying to Noah down the line.

I suspected that whatever news Tommy had for Noah wasn't good because the sudden tension in his body was both obvious and unnerving.

Shifting closer to him, I leaned forward and pretended to adjust my sock, when in truth, I was just trying to eavesdrop.

Noah glanced back at me briefly and shook his head reprovingly.

Busted...

Sheepishly, I sat back and crossed my arms.

"Whoop-Dee-Fucking-Doo, I can make that back in three fights," Noah argued down the line, voice rising. "Just get it done, T."

With those final words, Noah tossed his phone down, unaffected when the expensive piece of technology clattered against the floor.

I managed to remain quiet for all of three seconds before asking, "What was that about?"

"He was calling about that damn video," Noah shot back, clearly fuming. "It's everywhere, Thorn. T said that it's on so many sites that it would take months to clear them all."

"Okay," I said calmly, wondering why the hell I wasn't freaking out right now. Noah was obviously thinking the same because when I caught him glancing at me, his face was set in a deep frown. "What are you thinking?"

"I'm wondering who the hell is sitting in my car right now," Noah shot back. Shaking his head, he ran a hand through his hair. "I was sort of expecting you to freak about ten minutes ago."

"What's the point?" I said. "Everyone in the Hub saw us having sex when it leaked seven years ago. What's another couple of million viewers?" Shrugging, I clasped my hands together. "We can't change it, and we can't make it go away."

"So what should we do?" Noah asked, clearly confused.

"We should download that sucker and have a good time with it."

Noah's jaw fell open. "You little perv."

"I happen to believe I looked damn good at seventeen," I shot back, not missing a beat. "And I want to see what all the fuss is about."

"You want to watch porn together?" He choked out, pulling at the collar of his shirt. "And you looked better than good at seventeen," he added. "You looked fucking ethereal." Smirking, he added, "You're like a fine wine, Thorn."

"Ugh. Please," I said, holding up my hand, stopping him from saying one of the cheesiest one liners of all time. "But yeah, why shouldn't we watch it?"

Noah's brows furrowed together. "Why watch it when we can just do the real thing?"

"Why not watch it while we're doing the real thing?" I offered smoothly.

His brows shot up. "Yeah, I'm sold," he said with a thick voice. "Download the damn video."

I watched him like a hawk as he shifted around on the seat, clearly uncomfortable, and pulled at the collar of his black shirt.

"By the way, I'm off the hook with the disciplinary board."

"You are?" I squealed in delight. "So what does this mean for your career?"

"Tommy said I'm on probation for three months," he replied, a little less tense. "But I'm free to fight."

"We should book into a motel somewhere." Pulling myself onto my knees, I leaned over and whispered into his ear. "So we can celebrate all day – with the video."

"Fuck yeah!" Twisting his neck from side to side, he pulled at his collar and let out a groan. "You're not screwing with me, are you, Thorn?" Turning his face, he looked at me with a puppy dog expression. "You're not going to shatter my dream and tell me you're joking?"

"Your dream?" I grimaced. "For all of five seconds."

"Five fantastic fucking seconds," he shot back with a smirk.

"You'll see," I replied.

There would be no seeing about it. I could barely suppress the urge to rip the man's clothes off.

I would be on my back the moment that man gave me the nod, but he didn't need to know that.

Chuckling under his breath, Noah reached forward and switched on the stereo.

Ironically, Selena Gomez's *Hands to Myself* blasted through the speakers.

Smiling to myself, I pulled my hair out of its makeshift bun and knotted my hands in my messy, blonde hair, wiggling my body suggestively, moving to the sexy beat of the song.

I was on a major high after blowing off Noah's bosses. I was feeling empowered and recklessly in love with the man beside me.

In all honesty, I couldn't believe how much I lucked out with this man. Being here with him now, after all the shit and the trouble?

Well, it was sort of mind blowing.

"Look at the trouble you're causing me," Noah groaned, glancing up at me before looking back at the road.

"I have no idea what you're talking about," I replied sweetly, feigning innocence.

"My dick, Thorn," Noah evaluated, adjusting the very noticeable bulge in his jeans. "I've pitched a fucking tent, baby."

"Oh my god," I laughed, flopping back down to a sitting position. "What are you, twelve?"

"Turned on, Thorn. I'm fucking turned on," he countered unapologetically, clamping one strong hand on my thigh. "You're the one shaking your ass in my face."

"Pull the car over and my ass could be yours right now," I teased, waggling my brows, forcing myself not to laugh as I nudged his arm with my elbow. "And everything else..." I added suggestively.

Glancing sideways at me, Noah bit down hard on his lip and growled.

"Keep laughing," he warned, smirking cockily. "You're the one who's not gonna be able to walk straight after I get you into bed."

A shiver of carnal promise jolted through me and my clit throbbed in anticipation.

I silently debated with myself for a few minutes, torn on whether or not to continue tormenting my boyfriend. I knew full well Noah wasn't joking around when he said I wouldn't be walking straight tonight.

The man was a freaking machine...

"Okay, let's play a game!" I blurted out, dragging my mind out of the gutter.

Noah cocked a brow. "What kind of game?"

"A 'getting to know each other better' game."

Reaching under my seat, I rummaged around in my purse, grinning when I retrieved my faithful iPod. "Let's play songs that remind us of each other."

Syncing it with the car stereo, I flicked through dozens of songs until...bingo!

Taylor Swift's *Out of the Woods* blasted from the car stereo and I blurted out, "Leave it on." Cradling my iPod to my chest, I smiled sweetly at him. "Please?"

I knew this wasn't Noah's choice of song, not by a long shot, but it was mine and I grinned in victory when his fingers paused over the on/off button before choosing to turn up the volume.

"You're a pain in my ass," he grumbled in defeat and reclaimed my hand, smoothing soft circles over my fingers with his thumb. "A fucking thorn in my side."

"It reminds me of you," I told him. "And that's the name of the game."

"Really?" He husked, confusion written all over his face. "This one?"

"Yes, really." It was the truth.

This song had always reminded me of us and I felt each word right down to my bones.

Kicking off my dollar-store flip-flops, I rested my bare feet against the dashboard, and closed my eyes.

"Of us," I whispered, reveling in Noah's touch – in the feel of his hand on mine.

Tipping my head back, I let myself enjoy the feel of the wind in my hair. I couldn't stop smiling. I didn't care how goofy I looked.

I felt... happy.

When the song was over he snatched my iPod from my hand.

"My turn," he announced, his attention flickering between the road and the little screen of my iPod before finally settling on a song.

The lyrics of Ron Pope's *In my Bones* filled my ears.

Immediately, tears filled my eyes.

"This one reminds me of you," Noah said quietly.

The haunting, melancholy melody enveloped us like a blanket of angst and painful memories, causing my heart to hammer against my ribcage.

A heavy pain settled over my chest, a pressure of sorts...a feeling of regret.

"This is a shitty game," I muttered when Noah offered me the iPod after the song had ended. "I don't want to play anymore."

"Come on, Teagan," he said with a smirk. "You wanted to play..."

"Let it go, Noah."

"Let what go?" he laughed humorlessly. He shook his head, clearly agitated. "You're the one throwing a hissy fit over a fucking song."

"Because you aimed that song at me like a loaded gun, Noah."

He knew this was about more than a song.

"And you shot me through the heart," I tossed out, red-faced. "Congratulations, you hit a bullseye. Mission accomplished."

"Thorn..."

"No," I snapped. Grabbing the stupid fucking piece of metal, I tossed it back in my purse before crossing my hands over my chest. "I'm not playing."

"*I'm not playing*," he mimicked my voice and laughed. "You're such a fucking baby."

"That hurt, Noah. I don't even think you realize how much, but it hurts."

I immediately felt like a girl, but I couldn't help it.

My emotions were all over the place.

It was like I was riding a freaking rollercoaster and I had no control over what happened next.

"I don't want to sound like a baby," I added. "But the way you're speaking to me right now... well, it makes me feel like you hate me a little more than you love me."

"I don't hate you," he was quick to say, tone gruff. "You know I love you, right?"

I opened my mouth to respond but Noah swerved the car into a nearby pullout and slammed on the brakes so hard all trains of thought faded out of my mind.

Killing the engine, he threw his car door open and got out.

Stalking around to my side of the car, he jerked my door open and pulled me roughly out of the car.

Slamming my back against the car, he towered over me, looking terrifyingly beautiful.

"Words, Thorn." Winding his fist in my hair, Noah tugged hard, causing my face to lift upwards. "They're just words from a song." His eyes were dark as coal, blazing with heat and fire, and scorching me. Drawing me closer. Literally closer. "If I wanted to hurt you, I wouldn't do it with a fucking song."

"But it did hurt," I whispered.

My body moved towards him, an automatic reaction to his heated gaze.

He was snaring me, one blink at a time.

I wanted him badly, and he knew it.

"Because I know you haven't forgiven me." My words were little more than a breathless pant. "And I'm scared you never will."

"I'm in love with you," he replied heatedly. Taking my hand in his, he pressed my palm against his chest. "Feel that?"

I nodded slowly, feeling his heart hammering against my hand.

"Only you do that to me, Thorn. Only you make my heart race like that," he told me, before ducking his head and claiming my lips.

His kiss took my breath away and every argument before that moment seemed inconsequential.

He cupped my neck with both of his hands, drawing me closer, and I kissed him back deeply, pouring everything I had into it.

"I wasn't expecting this," Noah told me when he finally broke the kiss. Rubbing my cheekbones with his thumbs, his eyes drifted over my face, settling on my eyes. "I wasn't expecting you to burst into my world and shake the foundations of everything I've ever known."

"Well, it's not like I was prepared for you either," I replied, heart racing, as I fell deeper into his brown eyes.

In this moment, I wanted to drown in those brown depths.

"See this through with me," he said quietly. Moving his hand to cup my chin, he tilted my face upward and sighed. "And I'll do better."

"I'm in, Noah," I replied, meaning every word as I wrapped my arms around his waist and hugged him tightly.

"Everything's gonna be okay, Thorn." Noah's arms came around me. "We'll get through this."

I felt his affection in his touch, but as much as I tried to push it from my mind, I was swallowed up by the fact that he didn't acknowledge my fears about him forgiving me.

The way Noah had aptly changed the subject assured me that I had been dead on the money when I said I thought he never would.

"Here," Noah said when we were back in the car. Flicking through the iPod, he settled on a song and cranked up the volume. "This one's for you."

Nickelback's *I'd Come for You* blasted through the stereo.

I couldn't stop the smile from spreading across my face as I laid my head on Noah's shoulder and reveled in the words of his love song.

6

NOAH

I wasn't entirely sure if Thorn had been serious or not about watching the video, but when I walked out of our ensuite bathroom and saw the laptop opened up on the bed, my dick was hard in an instant.

Wearing only a t-shirt, Teagan was sprawled across the bed on her stomach, with her feet in the air, and a frown on her face as she tapped furiously on the keyboard.

"Got it," she squealed excitedly. Looking up from the screen, she caught my eye and grinned. "Are you ready for this?"

"Go for it." I lowered myself onto the bed and readjusted the towel I had wrapped around my waist. I sure as hell wasn't about to pass up the opportunity to watch some porn with her.

Besides, I needed the distraction.

After my run in with Tommy earlier, I was feeling all worked up.

I didn't think two weeks off training to spend time with Teagan was too much to ask for.

I was under no illusions as to how little time I would be able to spend with her once the tour started.

It would be intense as hell traveling from state to state, sleeping in a different hotel room every night, and I needed to give Teagan as much of my attention as I could before it kicked off.

Knowing JD was lurking around the place wasn't exactly helping my mood either.

I knew the time would come when I would be put in a position where I would have to do some pretty fucking bad things to get that prick off my back permanently.

I had made peace with that.

On the flight home, I had come to terms with the fact that one of these days I was going to have to take him out.

But that day wasn't here yet.

Not when after seven long years, I finally had the girl.

Tonight I was focusing everything I had on my Thorn...

Teagan clicked play on the laptop and then quickly scrambled up the bed toward me. "I'm so nervous," she chuckled, tucking herself into my side.

"Stop fighting this. I know you feel it, too. This burning heat between us. This primal rawness..."

"Noah..."

"Oh my god," Teagan groaned, covering her eyes. "They didn't even bother to edit out our conversation."

I couldn't answer her.

My gaze was riveted to the screen where an eighteen-year-old version of myself was getting the seventeen-year-old version of Teagan onto her back.

"I was such a dick," I muttered in disgust as I watched myself strip her down and spread her open.

"You had some good moves back then," Teagan

commented dryly as she peeked through her fingers. "For a teenage boy. You whipped my bra off faster than I could."

I knew enough about women to know that replying was a trap. There was no right answer in this circumstance and I couldn't lie if I wanted to.

Teagan knew I had a past. I'd screwed around when I was younger, fucked more than my fair share of girls in high school.

Come to think about it, I'd lost my virginity at twelve to a girl twice my age around the back of an old warehouse after a fight.

And I'd done plenty before that.

Christ, I'd been taking bras off women long before Teagan had grown enough breasts to fill one, but admitting that would mean almost certain castration.

Kyle and Lee's youngest boys entered my mind then and disgust filled me.

Cash and Casey were only seven years old. I was only a couple of years older than them when I started fucking around with girls. But they had parents who loved them to teach them right from wrong. They had a mother to show them affection. They would never have to seek it in the way I had...

"You're a fast mover."

"I just know what I need. I've been craving you underneath me ever since you went head to head with me in that black thong and t-shirt..."

The moans coming from the laptop dragged me out of my thoughts.

Turning my attention back to the screen, I watched the younger version of myself bury my face in Teagan's virgin pussy.

She was thrusting herself into my mouth and I was lapping it up like a fucking horned up teenager.

And then my bare ass was on full display as I slid a condom on my junk like a goddamn pro.

"Are you sure you want this?"

"Uh-huh."

"Open your legs, Thorn. Wider..."

And then I was taking her. Right there on the floor of the elevator. Riding her hard like a goddamn animal.

Teagan was screaming bloody murder as she clawed at my back and dragged me down on her body.

"Mmmm...."

"Are you okay?"

"Uhhh...yessss.... don't...stop..."

My attention drifted from the screen to where Teagan was curled up beside me.

She was lying on her side with her cheek nuzzled into my chest, one thigh tossed over my legs, and she was rocking her hips against me.

I didn't think she realized she was doing it, but my dick certainly did.

The harder I fucked her in the video the more she rocked against me in real life. I could remember the smell of her that night; it was the same one as now – coconut scented shampoo and freedom.

I closed my eyes, breathing her in, reveling in her. Loving her more than she would ever know.

Her hand slipped beneath the towel that was covering me and the moment her fingers curled around my fully erect dick a hiss escaped my mouth.

My eyes flew open.

The feel of her flesh on mine fucked with every fiber of my being and set me on fire.

Jesus, I was burning for her.

Thrusting myself into her touch, I watched Teagan as she watched us on the laptop.

She never took her eyes off the screen and I never took mine off her face.

"You were a virgin. You were so tight, but I just thought... I didn't realize..."

Her hand moved faster, pulling hard...

"I was not a virgin, Noah. I was with my last boyfriend for three years. We had..."

Her thumb traced over the crown of my cock.

"Stop talking, Don't talk to me about other guys."

"Sex. He fucked me – a lot. Sorry to burst your little virgin bubble."

She rubbed against me, rocking her hips gently.

"Your blood is on my cock. And your thighs are smeared with it. So stop fucking lying about who's been inside you, Teagan, when it's perfectly clear the only person who has had the pleasure of fucking you is me."

The soft moan that escaped her lips drove me fucking wild with want.

"Go screw yourself, Noah..."

The bed dipped beside me.

"You already took care of that, Thorn!"

Teagan settled between my legs and lowered her face to take my dick in her mouth.

Cradling her cheek in my hand, I gently guided her, pushing myself deep inside her mouth then pulling back before she gagged. "I shouldn't have done that."

"Hmm?" Teagan hummed against my dick, head bobbing up and down, as she deep throated me.

"I shouldn't have taken you in that elevator," I groaned. My head fell back against the headboard when she cupped my balls. "You deserved better than a dirty fucking floor for your first time."

"You didn't know it was my first time," she whispered before taking me back in her mouth. Her blonde hair was like a pillowing blanket of white snow, splayed over my body. Looking down at her made my heart race so damn hard.

"But I knew it was *our* first time." Closing my eyes, I let out a sharp hiss when the head of my cock hit the back of her throat. "I should have...fuck." My hands were in her hair. "I should have done better with you." My thrusts were getting more urgent. "Been a better guy to you back then..."

Releasing my dick with a loud pop, Teagan leaned over my body and said, "We have twelve days until you officially start the tour." Kneeling back, she dragged my t-shirt that she was wearing over her head and dropped it down on the bed. "That's two hundred and eighty-eight hours of no interruptions."

My eyes roamed over her naked body, taking in every fucking inch of her beauty.

"We can lock ourselves away from the world," she continued to say as she pressed her hand against the bare skin of my chest and smiled down at me. "And spend every minute of those one hundred and twenty hours making it up to each other."

Grunting from the feel of her hand on my chest, I covered it with mine, and used my other arm to pull her down so that she was flush against me.

"You had me the moment you walked your sexy little ass out of your uncle's house and tossed that can of paint on my car and you know it." Stroking her cheekbone with my thumb, I exhaled a shaky breath. "I love you, Teagan

Connolly, pain in my ass, thorn in my side." Smirking, I added, "I love you hard."

"Why?" One small word from her lips that let me know Teagan wasn't as confident and uncaring as she let the world think she was. "Why me, Noah?" She added quietly.

"Because you never try to impress me, but you end up impressing me anyway," I told her honestly. "You're completely yourself whether we're alone, or in a room with fifty others. And you saw the good in me before anyone else realized there was any good to be found." I brushed her hair out of her eyes, tucking the long blonde strands behind her ears.

"You follow your heart," I continued to say. "You're vicious, spontaneous, and reckless. And you love with the whole of your heart, regardless of the consequences." Sighing, I added, "I think the question you should be asking is how could I *not* love you?"

"Wow," she whispered after a long pause. Slapping my chest, she sighed, "I think you just might have made me pregnant with those words."

"Shut up, you little fruitcake," I laughed.

Rolling her onto her back, I hovered over her, careful not to press my full weight down on her tiny frame. Teagan might be a loudmouth, but she was dainty...willowy... fragile.

I was constantly checking myself when it came to this little spitfire.

"You make me happy," I confessed, rubbing her nose with mine. "I've never had that before you."

Another truth.

This woman brought to the surface emotions inside of me that I'd long since buried.

She reminded me of a summer evening during childhood when the sun shone high in the sky and youth rolled out before you like a never-ending carpet of possibilities.

"You make me whole," she replied before lifting her face up and claiming my lips with hers.

"Damn, Thorn, you can't say shit like that to me," I groaned against her lips. "And expect me not to eat you up whole."

"Eat me up whole?" Teagan waggled her brows. "That sounds like it could be fun."

Rolling away from me, Teagan threw herself onto her back and grinned devilishly up at my face.

"Come on, Messina," she teased, folding her arms behind her head, her hazel eyes taunting me. "Ravish me! Go right ahead and eat me up whole."

My lip curled up as I studied her pretty face. I couldn't fucking help it.

Pulling myself onto my knees, I faked a sigh and tugged the sides of her panties downwards.

"The things I do for you," I muttered before lowering my mouth to rest between the apex of her thighs.

"Yeah, because it's such an ordeal for you, right?" Thorn shot back without missing a beat.

That's my girl...

The second my tongue touched her swollen clit Teagan's hands were in my hair, pulling on me like she was riding a goddamn horse.

"Oh my god," she mewled, thrusting her hips upward to my awaiting mouth. "Yes...fuck, Noah, please...hmm."

Her enthusiasm drove me on, pushing me.

The little puffs of air she exhaled were all the encouragement I needed.

Running my tongue lengthways up her slit, I slipped two fingers inside her tight pussy and used my tongue to press down hard on her clit, giving her that pressure she was crying out for.

"Yes..." she cried out, breathless. "God...baby..."

I stopped mid-stroke and sat back on my haunches.

The shit eating grin on my face was spreading from ear to ear as I watched my little Thorn writhe on the bed.

"Wha-why'd you stop?" Teagan cried out in frustration.

Clamoring to support herself, she rested her weight on trembling elbows and glared through her spread thighs.

"What the hell is so funny?" She demanded in a throaty tone of voice.

"You are," I told her, not trying to hide my amusement. "You called me baby."

"Yeah," she replied in confusion as she blinked rapidly. "So?"

Grabbing at my hair, she pushed my head back down.

"I thought you said I wasn't supposed to call you baby?" Trailing my finger down between her glistening lips, I dipped my tongue inside her, groaning when the sweet taste of her touched my tongue.

"Stop talking," she mewled, tugging on my hair, "and start eating."

"Yes, boss," I chuckled before doing just that.

7

TEAGAN

"*I* don't want you to die."

Dawn was breaking outside. The birds were singing. The sun was rising. And Noah and I were lying on our bed with the blankets crumpled up around us.

We had spent the last five days crammed up in this hotel suite, snacking on unhealthy food, watching crummy movies, and not bothering to get dressed.

Not having anyone interrupting us or demanding his attention was even better.

We had spent the night going over everything – and I mean every little detail – from our past and it was only now that I was getting to the core of Noah's issues.

"Nobody's dying, Noah," I assured him.

Stretching out my leg, I used my toes to rub his bare stomach.

He was lying crossways at the foot of the bed, looking stressed out.

His hair was a mess, ruffled from running his hands through it.

All he had on was a pair of black sweatpants.

The moment my foot touched his stomach, I felt the muscles bunch together and tighten.

Snaking a hand around my ankle, Noah caught hold of my foot and pressed it harder to his stomach.

"Famous last words, Thorn," he grumbled, caressing my ankle with his thumb.

"What do you mean?"

"The only people I have ever allowed myself to care about have died at the hands of the Dennis family." His voice was gruff and thick with emotion. "My mother. My father...well, the guy I thought was my father," he laughed humorlessly. "There's only one person left."

He stared pointedly at my face.

"I'm not leaving you," I promised, refusing to allow the fear to overthrow common sense.

"You saw what they did to my mother, Teagan. What they made me do?" Noah covered his face with his huge arm and sighed heavily. "They want to take you from me because you are the only thing I ever took for myself – you are the only living soul I ever took the risk of loving."

"I am *not* leaving you, Noah," I repeated slowly. "JD can kiss my ass. It's going to take a hell of a lot more than bullets, flowers, and stupid notes to take me away from you."

"If anything ever happened to you because of me," Noah squeezed out. "Well, they better have a cell strong enough to keep me locked in because I would burn the fucking world down."

"What if we set up a meeting with him and find out his demands?" Shrugging, I added, "Surely there's something we can offer him to make him go away."

I thought that was a just and rational suggestion, but

from Noah's reaction you'd swear I'd asked him to steal the hope diamond for me.

"Are you insane?" He roared.

Leaping off the bed, he began to pace the floor like a caged animal.

"No," I shot back, insulted. "I'm trying to think outside the box here." Rising up on my knees, I began to plot. "If it's money he's after then you have it. Hell, I can sell my half of the gym – it wouldn't be much, but I could get sixty grand for it."

"Jesus Christ, you really are fucking crazy." Laughing humorlessly, Noah ran a hand through his hair. "There's must be something funny in the water over in Ireland because the Teagan I remember wasn't so fucking gullible."

"I am *trying* to figure a way out of this for us."

"There is *no* way out of this for us," he roared into my face. "Your fucking blood is the *only* currency he's interested in!"

Hearing Noah lay it out there in black and white caused my stomach to twist.

"I was just trying to help, Noah," I mumbled, red-faced and trembling.

"You want to help?" He snarled, chest heaving. "Then stay alive. Stay out of harm's way and stay the fuck away from JD Dennis!"

"I wasn't going to go after him myself," I choked out, wrapping my arms around my body. "I just thought that..."

"Good, because he would *kill* you, Teagan. He would take your life the first chance he got," Noah hissed, as he ran a hand through his thick, black hair. "I will fight for you. I will protect you. Hell, I'd give my fucking life for you. But I will not –" His voice broke off as he stalked toward where I was kneeling.

Cupping the back of my neck with one hand, Noah dragged me forward, leaning down to press his forehead to mine.

"Just...just leave JD Dennis to me, okay?" He exhaled a shaky breath, and then roughly kissed my forehead. "Forget about him. I have everything under control."

"But..."

"No buts," Noah barked, knotting his fingers in my hair. "I don't want you worrying about that prick." He kissed my forehead again, softer this time. "I'll sort everything out."

"Fine," I said in retreat and Noah visibly sagged. "But would you at least teach me how to fight?"

"What?" Noah took a step from me, brows furrowed in confusion. "Why?"

"So I'll be able to defend myself," I replied honestly. "I want the peace of mind of knowing that I have at least some measure of protecting myself." Stepping closer to him, I reached up and cupped his cheek. "Teach me how to fight, Noah."

"Absolutely not," he said in a gruff tone.

"Noah..."

"No, Teagan," he warned. "I'm not pushing you around. Forget it. It's not happening." Shrugging his shoulders, he let out a sharp breath. "You don't need to raise your fists, Thorn. You've got my fists to do your dirty work."

"And when you're not with me?" I shot back defiantly.

"Then you'll have Lewis," Noah countered swiftly.

"And who the hell might Lewis be?" I demanded.

Smirking, Noah took my hand and dragged me through the suite towards the door.

"Lewis is head of security," Noah announced as he swung back the door. "And your new bodyguard."

My jaw fell open when my eyes took in the huge barrel

of a man standing outside our hotel room door. He was dressed in black from head to toe.

Huge was an understatement.

I'd never seen a man so big in my life.

I found myself studying his bald head and the huge scar that ran from his scalp to his jawline.

He was the definition of built like a brick shit house.

"Noah," Lewis acknowledged in a deep timbre voice. Turning his attention to me, he nodded curtly. "Miss Connolly."

"Just Teagan, please," I replied, offering him an awkward half wave.

Christ, he was enormous.

I had to crane my neck to look up at his face.

Heck, Noah was 6'4" and this guy was even taller.

Come to think about it, he vaguely resembled one of the doormen from a nightclub back home in Galway. Old Lorry, people used to call him – for obvious reasons.

"Teagan." Lewis nodded in confirmation before returning his attention to Noah. "Everything okay?"

"Everything's fine, Lewis," Noah assured him before closing the door.

"How long has he been here?" I demanded the moment the door was closed.

"Since we arrived."

"And you didn't think to tell me?"

"I'm sorry." Noah shrugged sheepishly. "I was preoccupied."

"With what?" I hissed. "And you need to work on your communication skills, buddy!"

"With you," Noah admitted shamelessly.

Taking a step toward me, he snaked his arm around my waist and pulled me flush against him.

"I finally got you home," he said gruffly, eyes locked on mine. "You're the only thing going on in my mind right now."

"Okay," I breathed, feeling my resolve melt into a puddle at my feet. "Good answer."

8

NOAH

"*I* was afraid of you."

We were sitting on the floor in the living area of the suite, with a half-eaten pepperoni pizza between us, and a deck of cards in our hands.

Teagan was kicking my ass playing rummy and just like the past two days, we were hashing up the past.

I couldn't hide the fact that I was fucking thrilled I had Teagan back on this side of the Atlantic.

Now all I had to do was keep her here.

Taking a sip from my beer bottle, I smirked. "You hid it well."

"I didn't have much of a choice, did I?" She studied her hand of cards. "Not when the ever so powerful Ellie was sniffing around waiting for me to let my guard down." Scrunching her nose up, Teagan tossed a card down on the pile before picking up another. "She tortured me, Noah."

"I know." Picking up her three of spades, I tossed my seven of clubs down on the pile. "I'm sorry she was such a nightmare."

"You don't have to do that," Teagan said, frowning. "You

don't need to apologize for them anymore. They're not your family anymore, Noah. They never really were."

"I guess old habits die hard."

"You hated me in the beginning," she admitted, not looking up from her hand. "And I hated that you hated me, so I decided I would hate you more than you could ever hate me."

"That's pretty fucked up, Thorn."

"I was insecure and friendless," she shot back. "I had just arrived in a new country and had made enemies with the hottest boy on my street – hell, in Boulder. What else was I supposed to do?"

"Back down."

Teagan smirked. "Not in my nature."

"No," I mused. "It's definitely not."

"Rummy. I win. Again." Placing her cards down in front of me, she grinned like the cat that got the cream. "Pick your poison, Messina."

"Fine," I grumbled before taking a swig of my beer. "What do you want to know?"

This was a stupid fucking game.

Teagan was a fucking card shark and I hadn't won a hand in seven games.

She was using this winning streak to pump information out of me – her prize for winning.

"I want to know about your mom."

My heart began to race.

My palms started to sweat.

"Teagan, I don't..." I broke off and ran a hand through my hair, forcing down the painful memories and tsunami of regrets. "I don't talk about her."

9

TEAGAN

*W*hen I asked Noah to tell me about his mother, I knew it could go one of two ways.

Really good or really bad.

I didn't want to upset him, that hadn't been my intention at all, but I wanted him to open up to me.

We were getting so close.

I wanted to know it all.

Crawling across the carpet to where he was sitting, I placed my hand on his muscular thigh.

"You can tell me anything," I assured him, unsure whether it was a good idea or not to ask Noah to bring up the ugliness of his childhood. "I'm good at keeping secrets."

Groaning, Noah grabbed the tub of ice-cream and spooned a large amount of chocolate chip into his mouth before stuffing the spoon back into the tub.

Flopping onto his back, he rested the tub on his bare stomach and sighed.

"She was always scared," he said quietly, not looking me in the eye. "And paranoid." He covered his face with one of his arms. "She didn't trust anyone. Not a goddamn soul. She thought the whole world was out to get her." Pausing, he roughly cleared his throat. "She...was a lot like me actually."

"Noah," I sighed heavily. "You're not like her."

"Aren't I?"

"No." Climbing on top of Noah, I straddled his hips. "You are beautiful." Taking his hand with mine, I peeled it away from his face. "You are *good*."

"She was, too," he choked out. "Before..."

"She was sick, Noah," I said, desperate to reassure him. "And she wasn't given the medical intervention she deserved.

"I know what Kyle and Lee think of her."

"I don't give a shit about what Kyle Carter thinks about her," I shot back heatedly. "She was a sick woman who got tangled up in something out of her control. She was your mom, and I, for one, am thankful she got stuck up in all that shit. Do you know why?"

I waited until he looked at me before continuing.

"Because she had you." I stroked his face and pressed a kiss to his brow. "You are my life and I'm so thankful you were born. I am so grateful to her for giving me Noah Messina."

"Teagan," he groaned, capturing my hand with his. "You're killing me here..."

"My dad's a raging alcoholic," I continued to say, forcing myself not to give into the desire of kissing the hell out of the man beneath me. "He as good as killed my mom and I've spent years being told not to love him. But you can't turn it off, Noah. They're our parents. The blood runs deep. So screw what everybody else thinks."

"Thorn..."

"So mourn your mom. And don't be ashamed to love her. No one has the right to judge you."

"You have a heart as big as the fucking moon," Noah said gruffly. "Do you know that?"

"You're the one with the big heart," I replied, meaning every word. "You volunteered your future to protect your mother. You risked your life in a burning car when you cut me out first. You buried my name that night, I know you did. You protected me from the Dennis family and the cops and the whole world."

Swallowing deeply, I placed my hand on his stubbly cheek. "You're fierce – like a lion – and you protect what's yours, regardless of how it affects you." Shivering, I added, "And you're doing it again. Still protecting me. Still keeping me safe. Guarding me like a lion."

"Don't be afraid of that piece of shit," he hissed angrily. "I won't let JD touch a hair on your head, Thorn. I fucking promise you that."

"I'm not afraid of him," I told him. "He doesn't have the ability to break me."

But you do.

10

TEAGAN

"So that's where you got the tattoo."

It was day nine of our hiatus and Noah had just finished giving me a detailed description of Lucky's makeshift tattoo parlor in prison.

I was still clutching my ribs like I was the one he had butchered and not Noah.

"You were lucky you didn't get septicemia," I told him as I lay on my stomach, watching Noah work out on the floor below.

All he had on were a pair of white fitted boxer shorts, and it was taking everything I had not to leap off the bed and grab his hard, tight ass.

"Trust me, Thorn," Noah said, breathless, as he continued to punish his body with brutal sit-ups. "Septicemia was the last thing I had to worry about in prison."

"Were you afraid there?" I asked, resting my chin in my hands.

"It wasn't so much fear as it was a sense of impending doom." Noah laid flat on his back for a moment before letting out a sigh and flipping onto his stomach.

Immediately, he started into a set of push-ups.

"Every night I closed my eyes not knowing if I was going to open them in the morning." He tucked his left arm behind his back and continued to do push-ups using only his right. "I'm a southpaw," he explained, panting slightly. "My right's a weakness in the cage. I need to change that."

"Max is left handed, too."

"Have you heard from him lately?"

"Not a word." Rolling onto my back, I folded my arms behind my head and sighed. "Last time we spoke, we got into a huge argument. I haven't heard from him since."

"Tell me about it."

"He's always hated my dad," I found myself explaining. "Long before my mother died. Patrick Connolly was never good enough for the good doctor's sister."

"I know that feeling." Noah grunted breathlessly. "Your uncle is a dick, Thorn," he added. "Seriously."

"He's just set in his ways," I replied. "The last time we spoke he told me that loving you was going to get me killed. He refused to make any effort to repair our relationship because, in his eyes, the moment you were released from prison I was going to fall into your arms and he would rather say goodbye to me then." Sighing, I added, "It was our worst fight. I've never heard him so mad."

Noah was silent.

"Of course, I told him he was wrong," I quickly reassured him.

Rolling back onto my stomach, I watched Noah as he continued to do push-ups.

"Say something," I whispered, noticing his darkened expression.

"He's right," Noah growled. "I've always been the worst kind of wrong for you."

Climbing to his feet, Noah stretched his huge arms over his head and I had to force myself not to drool at the sight of this beautiful man.

Reaching up over our bed, Noah caught a hold of one of the beams joining the four posts of the bed together and hoisted himself up.

"Hit me."

"What?" I settled on my knees, watching Noah pull himself up with his legs tucked behind him, ankles lock together.

"Hit me," he repeated, tone serious. "Every time I lower myself down, I want you to hit me in the stomach."

"And why on earth would I do that?"

"Tightens my core."

Lowering himself back down, he dangled in front of me until I gave in and lightly slapped his stomach.

"Harder."

I slapped him again, much harder this time.

Noah's response was a grunt of approval.

For the next fifteen minutes, Noah continued to do chin ups and I continued to slap him in silent harmony.

"I was late," I blurted out, breaking the contented silence between us.

Noah's brows furrowed but he didn't stop moving.

"When I got home to Ireland, I missed a period." Resting back on my knees, I felt my cheeks turning a deep shade of red.

I had no idea why I was talking about something that had happened so many years ago, only that I wanted him to know everything about me.

I wanted to fill him in on every single detail of my life from the moment we parted to the moment we reunited.

"Thought I was pregnant." Pulling at an invisible thread

on the bedspread, I looked up at his face and said, "Turned out that I wasn't, but I got one hell of a fright."

"Because you thought you were pregnant with my baby?" He froze midair, eyes locked on mine, giving nothing away. "Because you thought you had a convicted felon's seed growing inside you?"

"Because I was *eighteen* and *terrified*," I corrected him. "And you weren't with me."

"Fair enough." Dropping onto his feet, Noah cracked his neck from side to side before walking over to the window sill. "But I thought about you all the time."

I swallowed deeply. "You did?"

"I did." Pressing his hands against the sill, Noah stretched himself out. "Before I got up. After I went to bed. When I showered. During mealtimes." A popping noise filled the room and Noah groaned loudly. "I thought of nothing else." He twisted his neck from side to side. "Only you."

Sighing heavily, I rubbed the skin over my heart. "I missed you so much."

He turned his face to look at me. "How much?"

"Enough to lose my inhibitions when you finally came back for me and not take precautions," I admitted guiltily. "I should probably go about getting put on something," I offered lamely. We'd taken too many risks as it stood. "You know...for safety's sake."

Noah's eyes were blazing with sincerity and heat when he said, "I'm clean, Thorn."

Walking over to where I was kneeling, Noah tossed himself down on his back.

"We're given mandatory three-month blood tests because of the amount of blood we shed in the cage." He turned his head to look at me. "And I've never been with a woman bareback before you or since you."

"I'm not talking about preventing STDs." Turning onto my side, I cupped his cheek with my hand and smiled. "I meant preventing little Noah and Teagan's running around the place."

"What were you thinking of getting?"

"I don't know," I confessed, feeling stupid for being a twenty-five-year-old woman and clueless.

Aside from one regrettable night with Liam in which I knew for a fact we'd used a condom – I'd seen the evidence the following morning, tossed carelessly on his bedroom floor, not to mention the dreadful latex rash that had followed – Noah was the only man I'd ever been with.

Back when we were in high school, Noah had always taken care of it. He'd bought the condoms. He'd disposed of them afterward. He'd kept me safe. We'd only ever had one close call and even then, he'd protected me.

It was during Christmas break of senior year. I had snuck out of the house behind Max's back to be with him. We'd taken Noah's car up to our usual make-out spot on South Peak Road.

Things had gone a little far and before we'd known it, we were having sex right there on the mountain side in his Lexus.

The condom had broken and I remembered saying, in my orgasm induced frenzy, to keep going.

But Noah had immediately pulled out of me. Even though it must have killed him to do it, he stopped and told me that he wasn't going to risk my future by being selfish with me.

"I've never been on birth control. I've never had to..." My words trailed off as I pondered the notion. "Hope takes the contraceptive pill – for menstrual cramps - but it wrecks her cycle. And I really don't like the thought of putting a rod in my arm or having bimonthly injections."

"Then I'll take care of it," Noah offered after a long pause. Leaning closer, he brushed his lips against mine. "First thing tomorrow, I'll run out and grab a pack of condoms."

"And tonight?"

"I've already had you twice today." He smirked. "What's another night?"

"Okay," I teased. "Make sure you read the label when you're buying them tomorrow." I waggled my brows. "But don't forget to buy the..."

"Latex free ones," Noah filled in. "The blue box – not the green." Smirking, he added, "Yeah, I remember, Thorn."

"I was going to say don't forget to buy extra-large," I shot back, blushing, feeling both embarrassed and aroused that he remembered something so intimate about our past.

Noah frowned. "What color box are those?"

"I don't know." I shrugged. "Just read the label."

"If there's reading involved then you better come with me."

"Why so?"

"Because I can't read," he replied with a yawn. "I'm dumb, babe, you know that. All I'm good at is using my fists."

"No you're not," I all but roared. "Don't you dare call yourself dumb."

"Calm down," he chuckled. "This isn't a new thing. I've always been like this."

"Why didn't you tell me before?"

"I guess it never came up before."

"What about school?"

"In case it passed your attention, Thorn, I didn't do too good at school." Chuckling, he added, "I missed a lot of school. Hell, I didn't even go to mainstream school until I was seven, and even then we moved around so much I never really got a chance to settle down and get my teeth into it. I didn't have time to learn. I was too busy training to fight. I was fifteen before we settled down long enough for me to actually spend an entire year in one school, and by then I didn't care. I was hooked on the gym. I thought school was pointless, and I only went for a break from George and his shit. I was every teacher's worst nightmare."

"Noah, you're not stupid."

He shrugged. "Yeah, well, it doesn't matter now. I have the basics – and it's not like I'm gonna need books or anything in my career."

"I can help you," I offered.

"No thanks," he snorted.

"Noah, I'm serious." Kneeling on the bed in front of him, I pitched my plan. "I want to do this for you. You deserve better than this. You are one of the smartest men I know. You can do anything you put your mind to. Come on, I have faith in you. You're a badass."

"Fine," he grumbled. "Get the fucking kindle."

Noah read exceptionally slow.

He paused.

He fell over his words.

He threw the kindle down more times than he held it, but he didn't give up.

He kept going, and I found myself having to suppress the urge to jump on him every time he sounded out a word that he wasn't familiar with.

And that's how we spent the rest of our day; taking turns reading passages from Hope's raunchy novel.

11

NOAH

*M*y brother once told me, "Be careful, Noah. It's a very long drop kid, and there's no coming back up. I hope she's worth the fall."

Well, sitting in a bathtub with the woman I loved resting against my chest, I could safely say that Kyle Carter was right about three things.

First, the drop – more like plummet – was deep.

Deeper than what I'd been prepared for.

Second, there was no way back up.

I was sunk.

And thirdly, Teagan was worth the fall.

I'd never met an opponent in the ring as dangerous to me as the woman in my bathtub.

"What do you think is wrong with him?" Teagan asked. Yawning, she rested her head against my chest and trailed her fingers down my thighs. "Jordan, I mean."

"Who fucking cares." Shifting beneath her, I adjusted my erection from stabbing her in the back. "That piece of shit isn't good enough to breathe the same air as Hope."

"Noah," Teagan scolded, splashing my feet – which were

hanging out of either side of the tub. These oval shaped tubs were not built for men of my stature. "Don't be a dick."

"Is he or is he not the same guy who walked out the door and never looked back?" Wrapping my arm around her waist, I pulled her further up my body. "I don't care what his reasons are." Cupping one of her wet breasts in my hands, I tweaked her nipple, smirking when it hardened in my hand. "To me, Jordan Porter will always be that little prick who ran out on my niece."

"He's hardly little," she moaned, a little breathless. "He's like...six two."

"I could take him."

"Of course you could," she purred. "Big, bad fighter, you are."

"I knew we should have said something," I grumbled, moving my hand to cup her other breast. "Back when they got married?" I pinched Teagan's nipple and reveled in the moan that escaped her lips. "I knew it was a bad idea."

"It wasn't our place to tell," Teagan reminded me.

In fact, I was pretty sure she'd used those same words back then, too...

"...THIS IS A BAD IDEA, THORN," I GROWLED AS I SAT IN THE driver's seat of her Honda Civic outside the courthouse on fifth.

We weren't supposed to be hanging out together. Teagan was taking a huge-ass risk by being out in daylight with me.

So was I, but then again, I was used to breaking the rules when it came to her. I couldn't stay away from her.

"A really fucking bad idea."

"Noah," Teagan warned as she applied her lipstick in the rearview mirror. "She's my best friend."

"And her brother is my best friend," I shot back, unbuckling

my seat belt.

Reaching behind my seat, I grabbed a coat for Teagan to put on. It was freezing outside. It had been snowing heavily all morning and she had too much skin on display for this kind of weather.

"How long do you think he'll stay my best friend when he finds out I was in on this? We need to tell her parents."

"It's not our place to tell," Teagan told me before mushing her lips together and making a kissing sound. "And besides, this is a happy day!" She used her baby finger to wipe the edge of her pink lip. "Be happy for them."

"Yeah, they get married and what do I get? A one-way ticket to Kyle Carter's fist."

"You're being dramatic."

"And you are being really fucking innocent if you think that Kyle won't hold us responsible for this shit." Shaking my head, I readjusted the silvery-grey tie Teagan had bought me.

I looked like a fucking tool in a pink goddamn shirt and grey suit pants and I made a mental note to never allow my girlfriend to go clothes shopping for me again.

Color coordinating, she'd called it...

Like I gave a fuck about color coordinating.

From the moment I laid eyes on her in that tight as hell pink dress, my only thought had been how much time would it take me to get her out of it.

"What can I do to put you at ease?" Teagan purred. "Hmm?"

My mouth ran dry as I watched Teagan hoist her dress up around her waist and climb over the console.

"Well this is a pretty good start," I muttered when she straddled my lap. Immediately my hands moved to her hips. "God, you're such a tease..."

"How badly do you want me right now?" Staring into my eyes, Teagan cupped my neck with her hands. "A little?" She rolled her hips against me, pressing down hard on my growing dick. "Or a lot?"

"Fuck me," I groaned, clenching her bare waist roughly. Thrusting myself against her, I leaned forward and caught her lip between my teeth. "You have me wrapped around your little finger." I released her lip with a pop. "And you know it."

"Have I?" She batted her eyelids innocently. "I think it's the other way around..."

"Teagan," I deadpanned. "I am wearing a pink shirt which, may I add, seriously questions my masculinity, because you wanted me to match your dress."

She smirked and I continued to rant.

"I am sitting in a car with you about to be an accessory to a wedding that I know will get me a severe ass-kicking by at least four men because you wanted me to be your date."

"Noah," Teagan chuckled, but I cut her off as I continued to piss and moan.

"Not to mention the fact that I am rocking a serious case of blue balls because you know putting your pussy on my dick is a sure fire way of getting me to do whatever the hell you want me to do." I thrust my erection against her to drill the message home. "You know damn well you have me wrapped around your finger."

"I happen to think you look incredibly sexy in your shirt," Thorn purred. Dipping her head to my neck, she bit down hard on my flesh. "And I know you don't want to be here, but I promise to make it up to you later..."

"Except I know you won't." Stifling a growl, I leaned back and cocked a brow. "Since you gave me a very weird and very animated run down on your menstrual cramps this morning."

"And since when did a little blood scare you?"

"I..." Whatever I was going to say evaporated and my jaw fell open.

Was she serious?

Winking, Teagan opened the driver's door and climbed out.

"Come on, tough boy," she said, "Let's go watch my best friend sign her life away."

With that, Teagan disappeared from sight, leaving me stunned in her wake...

"THAT WAS ONE BORING WEDDING," I SAID GRUFFLY, DRAWING myself back to the present. "But I had an awesome time on the way back home."

"I remember," Teagan whispered softly.

My phone rang out then, breaking the moment.

"Goddammit to hell," I hissed, muttering several other curse words under my breath. "I'll be two minutes."

Teagan sat up and I quickly kissed her temple before climbing out of the tub to retrieve my phone.

"So you're alive?"

Those were the first words I heard when I answered my phone.

Closing the bathroom door, I padded over to the bed and sat down.

"Who wants to know?"

Lucky chuckled down the line. "How's the reunion coming along?"

My lips tipped up in a reluctant smile. "Did you want something, man?"

My reply only made Lucky laugh harder.

"You're busy, it's cool," he said good-naturedly. "I'm just calling to let you know that I've had Tommy blowing up my phone since the a.m. – Quincy and Beau, too."

"Yeah?" I ran my free hand through my hair and stifled a growl. "And what's up their asses?"

"Well," Lucky said cheerfully, "Since you haven't been taking any of their calls since Blondie arrived – or showed up to training – they've roped me into calling and brokering a truce." Pausing, he added, "Breakfast tomorrow sound good?"

"Fuck no, Lucky," I growled. "I told T I wanted some time off."

"I know," he placated. "And for what it's worth, I agree you need a break, but you know what the guys are like." Lucky sighed. "They're worried about the tour – afraid you're gonna bail on it."

"Like hell I am," I hissed, jaw clenched. Standing up, I began to pace the floor. "I'm taking that belt from Cole in December, man."

"Yeah you are," Lucky hooted and then added in a serious tone, "Just meet them for breakfast, man. Introduce them to your girl and be done with it."

"Fine," I muttered, reluctantly giving in. "But if it wasn't you asking me then I wouldn't be agreeing to this bullshit."

"Everything okay?" Teagan whispered, startling me, wrapping her arms around my stomach from behind, nuzzling her face against the bare skin of my back.

Catching Teagan's arm, I pulled her naked body against my chest. "Lucky, I'll talk to you later."

Dropping my phone on the bed, I slid my hands down to squeeze her ass. "I'm so fucking in love with you."

Teagan looked up at me with wide, lustful eyes as she curled her arms around my neck.

"I'm in love with you, too," she whispered.

Cupping my neck, she dragged my face down to hers and captured my mouth with her soft, swollen lips.

Hauling her into my arms, I kissed her deeply, putting into my kiss all the emotion I was feeling.

I groaned as her tongue swept over my lips and I opened up to take what she was giving me.

The vibration of her moan against my mouth sent shockwaves straight to my groin.

A tingling warmth spread through me and I took a step forward with Teagan in my arms and her lips on my mouth.

I felt the bed frame against my shins and gently lowered her onto the mattress before covering her wet, naked body with mine.

Resting my weight on one arm, I used the other to grab her thigh and wrap it around my waist. I settled between her thighs and thrust inside her in one swift movement.

With every thrust of my dick, Teagan squeezed me harder, sucked me in tighter. The pressure building inside of me was so fucking sweet it was almost painful.

Teagan's back was arched upward. She clenched her eyes shut as she jerked underneath me.

She was close.

So fucking close.

"I'm keeping you," I whispered against her lips. "I'm never gonna let you leave me again." Holding her face in place with my hand, I looked deep into her hazel eyes and whispered, "Give it up to me."

"Give...what...up?" She cried out, lustful eyes locked on mine, as she rocked her body against mine, tilting her hips upward, giving me more of her.

"Your soul." Claiming her lips, I plunged my tongue into her mouth and circled my hips, grinding my pelvis against her.

"I...can't give you what you already...already..." Teagan's

voice caught in her throat. It was muffled in her soft, guttural moans as her orgasm came to a head. "Own!"

Teagan shook violently beneath me, the walls of her cervix tightening so hard around my dick that I came hard inside her.

12

NOAH

"We really don't know that much about each other," Teagan puffed, jogging alongside me on the deserted sidewalk first thing on Friday morning. "I mean, we knew each other for a few months when we were kids."

Stopping to catch her breath under a streetlamp, she bent over and held her side.

Dawn was breaking, but the darkness still cloaked us in invisibility for a little while longer.

"We're practically strangers."

"We're not strangers, Thorn," I chuckled as I jogged on the spot, waiting for her to catch her breath. "And we definitely weren't strangers last night." Slapping her ass, I jogged backwards, watching her watching me. "Or this morning in the shower."

"Funny," she hissed out as she sprinted to catch up with me. "Noah, your legs are almost the entire length of my body." Rounding a corner, Teagan reached out and caught hold of my hoodie. "I can't keep up with you."

Taking pity on her red-cheeked face, I slowed my pace to a walk.

Wrapping my arm around her shoulder, I tucked her into my side.

"I thought you were supposed to be a gym instructor?"

"I thought you were supposed to be a human," she shot back, slapping my ribs with the back of her hand. "This is nice."

"Yeah." It was. Being with her like this reminded me of when we were kids.

God, I was fucking obsessed with her back then.

Putting myself in all types of shitty situations to be with her.

I guess some things never changed.

Her phone binged then, signaling a message, and Teagan bent down and removed it from her sock.

"No wonder you couldn't run," I commented dryly as I watched her unlock the screen and grin in amusement. "What's so funny?"

"Sean," she chuckled, tapping away happily on the screen. "You remember Sean, right? You met him at the club back in Ireland?"

"Yeah, I remember Sean." Remembering one important detail about his sexual preferences was the only reason I wasn't burning with jealousy right now.

"He wants a picture of you," she chuckled. "Come here." Tugging on my t-shirt, Teagan pulled me to a stop. Reaching up, she attempted to drape her arm over my shoulder as she held her phone out in front of us, snapping several pictures.

"Hey – what are you doing?" I hissed when Thorn grabbed the hem of my t-shirt, raising it up before taking several more pictures.

"What?" She shot back, tone innocent. "He wants to see the goods."

"Perv," I muttered under my breath. Her stomach grumbled loud enough for me to hear. "Are you hungry?"

"Starving," she confirmed, wrapping her skinny little arm around my waist. "I usually eat breakfast before exercising."

On the walk back to the hotel we were staying in, Teagan rambled on about the stupidest fucking shit and I hung on every word like the pussy-whipped idiot I was.

"And that's how you make meringue," she explained when we reached the entrance of our hotel. "But you can forget about it if it's a rainy day," she added, tone serious. "It's an old Irish superstition – oh, that and banging doors."

"Really?" I feigned interest as I held the door for her.

I didn't give a flying fuck about meringue.

In fact, I wasn't entirely sure what it even was or why slamming doors and bad weather had anything to do with cooking, but I liked Teagan's voice.

And hearing her talk gave me a weird sense of comfort so I encouraged the conversation. "That's amazing." *You little weirdo.* "Tell me more about that TV show you love so much." *I don't care what you say, just keep talking to me and one of these days I'm going to believe this isn't a dream.* "What was it again?"

Teagan's eyes lit up as we walked through the foyer of the hotel.

"The Walking Dead?" She offered, slipping her small hand into mine. "I have every episode saved on my planner, you know."

"That's the one." *Keep talking. Keep touching my arm. Don't leave me again.*

Grinning, Teagan gave me a series by series guide on all

aspects of The Walking Dead, leaving no character unturned.

Pulling my hood up, I kept my gaze cast downward as we made our way to the dining room, praying like hell none of the early risers in the hotel were MFA fans.

I was enjoying this time with her.

I didn't want extra interruptions from the outside world other than the ones waiting for us.

"Over there, Thorn," I said, pulling on her arm when she moved to sit at a table by the window. She looked up at me in confusion and I pointed toward the table where Lucky and they guys were sitting. "It's time to meet the team."

Teagan's eyes landed on the table and I felt her hand stiffen in mine.

"What's the problem?" I asked immediately, feeling like a dick for not mentioning meeting them for breakfast earlier.

"Nothing," she was quick to assure me. Smiling brightly, she said, "Let's eat."

13

TEAGAN

*D*uring breakfast, I was faced with the task of getting to know the men closest to my boyfriend. A backroom team that consisted of a group of five people – four of whom were professionally trained to deal with an athlete of Noah's caliber.

There was Quincy Jones, his coach.

Lewis McGowan, head of security, who I'd already had the *pleasure* of meeting.

Beau Brady, the physiotherapist/ nutritional advisor.

Tommy Moyet, head of PR.

And then there was Lucky...

I was actually really starting to warm to Lucky.

Since we'd met, the guy had been nothing but fun and charming. Lucky put me at ease, unlike the other four men sitting around the table.

I wasn't particularly fond of the four lettered swear word that starts with C and ends with T, but I had a feeling that Beau Brady was definitely a C U Next Tuesday.

Beau, I had quickly observed, was sly.

It wasn't an attack on his character by stating this.

It was merely a fact.

He had these beady blue eyes that took everything in. I'd met men like Beau before – Ciarán O Reilly anyone? – and I knew that I was going to have to watch my back with that one.

I could practically see the wheels of his brain moving as he watched me converse with Noah from across the table.

He was taking my measure.

In fact, I had a feeling he'd done that before ever meeting me in the flesh.

Quincy, on the other hand, was the opposite of sly.

He was a rude, obnoxious, loud-mouthed, old perv with a penchant for the female form.

In the time it had taken me to finish my cereal, I had observed no less than three circumstances where Quincy had overstepped the line with the teenage waitress serving us.

I also found myself biting my tongue every time he reminded us that he was the original Machine – which was every spare chance he got.

I wanted to scream, 'who the hell cares, old man? You're a washed-up fighter riding the coattails of my boyfriend's success train. Shut your bloody mouth'.

Lewis didn't speak a word throughout breakfast and after numerous attempts at trying to break the ice, I'd given up.

I didn't think Lewis was being intentionally cold towards me. I got the feeling that he was a closed off kind of guy who took his life seriously and job even more seriously.

He observed the room in that subtle way only men who'd spent years in the force did.

I felt oddly safe around him.

The worst of them all, and the president of the *I Hate Teagan* Fan-club, was Tommy Moyet.

Every time I made an attempt to speak to Tommy or make conversation with the other guys, he would either shoot me down or plain out ignore me like I wasn't sitting at the table.

I was under no illusions about what Tommy and the men thought of me.

His behavior at breakfast made it perfectly clear that he would tolerate me for Noah's sake, but he didn't trust me, and he liked me even less.

In Tommy Moyet's mind, I was enemy number one.

In my mind, Tommy was a grade-A dick.

The others followed suit and I got the distinct feeling that I had been transported back in time to senior year of high school.

Their disdain was both obvious and embarrassing and I knew Noah noticed it too because he kept trying to draw me into conversations with the men.

But the one thing I couldn't fault them on was their devotion to Noah.

They all loved him.

"...You might not care about your career anymore, but I do." Tommy's voice broke through my thoughts and I quickly turned my attention to where he was having a heated discussion with Noah.

I watched Noah's jaw tick as he leaned back in his chair, obviously waiting for Tommy to explain.

"The annual MFA benefit gala?" Tommy tossed his napkin on the table and let out a sigh. "It's tonight."

"I know," Noah muttered, scratching his head. "I'm not going."

"You're contractually bound to attend, Noah," Tommy

replied dryly. "So yes, you are. And I've had your tux dry-cleaned and delivered to your suite."

"Tux?" I turned and gaped at Noah. "I didn't even know you guys had balls."

"What?" Noah grinned widely. Ducking his face to my ear, he whispered, "What did you think was in your mouth this morning?"

"That's not what I meant." I flushed bright red.

I had aimed to slap his chest, but my traitorous hand decided to stay on the finely sculpted wall of muscle.

"I was talking about dances and...oh forget it." Seeing Noah's amused expression, I reached up and pinched his nipple. "You have a dirty mind."

"Learned from the best," Noah shot back with a smirk as he rubbed his pectoral. His focus was entirely on me and I felt everyone around us disappear.

"You're a little kinky, aren't you, Thorn?" He added. "Pinching nipples? If you want me to return the favor, you only have to ask."

"I'll remind you that I was wholesome and pure before you corrupted me with that..." I paused, racking my brain for a response. "Snake between your legs."

It was pathetic, but it was the best I could come up with. Noah confounded me. I couldn't think clearly when his face was mere inches from mine.

"I wish you had mentioned this ball thing earlier," I groaned. "I have nothing to wear."

Noah shrugged sheepishly. "I was kind of planning on blowing it off. But you heard Tommy. *I'm contractually bound to attend*." Noah pulled a face at his friend. "I fucking hate tuxedos."

Noah in a tux?

My eyes lit up in delight. "We are definitely going."

"It's going to be boring as hell," he warned me. "Full of inedible food and people who talk like they've swallowed dictionaries."

"And yet none of those people are the number one contender for the heavyweight title." Reaching over, I mussed his hair. "You are *Noah Messina*. You don't need to swallow any damn dictionary." Grinning, I added, "You can let your guns do the talking for you."

"Funny."

"Seriously though, I have nothing suitable for a ball."

"I had a dress sent up to your room for Teagan as well," Tommy announced, shocking the hell out of me. "I gathered Noah would be taking you as his date."

"You did?" My brows shot up in surprise. "Wow. Thanks, Tommy."

"It's white," he added in a petulant tone, like the color white would upset me. Shrugging, he added, "should fit you," before turning to speak to Quincy.

"Well, now I can't wait for tonight," Noah whispered into my ear, drawing me back to him.

"Oh yeah?"

"Yeah. It will be a preview," Noah teased, trailing his fingers over my shoulder bone. "Dancing with you in a white dress."

I threw my head back and laughed.

"What? You want to marry me now, is that it?"

I had expected Noah to get embarrassed.

I taunted him for that sole purpose.

I hadn't anticipated his response.

"I *will* marry you."

My heart stopped.

My jaw fell open.

Shaking my head, I looked up at his face and managed to squeeze out, "Noah Messina, are you proposing to me?"

"Teagan Connolly," Noah shot back with a knowing smirk. "When I do propose to you," he rubbed my bottom lip with his thumb and sighed in contentment, "you won't have to ask me to confirm it."

14

NOAH

*S*itting around a round breakfast table with the five men I spent twenty-four-seven with, I felt a huge amount of shame creep through me.

I had partially guessed that Tommy and Teagan's first official meeting would be an uncomfortable event, but I hadn't banked on Quincy and Beau being such pricks.

They weren't just ignoring Thorn.

They were flat out freezing her out.

Lewis, my heavy, wasn't talking to her either, but I knew from personal experience that it wasn't an attack on Teagan.

The guy barely spoke to *me* and I was paying him a fucking fortune to stand around and look ugly.

Thorn was putting on a brave face, pretending she didn't notice, and throwing herself into an animated conversation with Lucky.

"So, *Tygan,*" Beau suddenly piped up from across the table. "What do you plan to do all day when us guys are working? A tour bus full of men isn't exactly the right place for a woman."

I opened my mouth to tell Beau to watch his fucking tongue, but Teagan was already answering his question.

"Well, *Boo*," she replied, purposely mispronouncing his name the way he did hers, and I mentally high fived her.

My girl had some serious steel in her spine.

"Once Noah cuts me one of those pretty gold cards, I plan to spend most of my time shopping." Batting her eyelids dramatically, she flicked her long blonde braid off her shoulder and smiled sweetly. "And perhaps I'll redecorate the tour bus."

Beau, obviously not getting Teagan's sense of humor, looked horrified as he gaped across the table at her.

Lucky looked like he was about to piss his pants.

"You like hot pink, right Noah?" Clapping her hands together, she squealed. "Oh, how I love to shop."

Tommy leaned back in his chair and sneered, "Do you think you're funny?"

"Careful, T," I warned him. Dropping my hand on Teagan's thigh, I glared across the table at my friend. "Be very fucking careful."

"I think she's funny," Lucky offered up, unperturbed by the tension as he smiled warmly at Teagan like a proud teacher would his star pupil.

"It's okay, Noah," Teagan whispered. Covering my hand with hers, she squeezed gently before clearing her throat. "I think I'm being prematurely judged is what I think."

Turning her full attention on Tommy, she picked up her fork and stabbed a piece of bacon.

Pointing it at him aimlessly, she added, "Thanks for the dress, but you don't know me, Tommy." Shoving the piece of bacon into her mouth, Teagan washed it back with some orange juice. "You didn't know me back in high school and you don't know me now." Shoving her chair back, Teagan stood up with her chin jutting out proudly. "I'm not the girl you remember." She turned her gaze on Beau and then Quincy. "And I'm not the girl you were told about."

With that, Teagan swung around and walked away from the table with her head held high and her dignity intact.

Giving Lewis the nod to go after Teagan, I turned my attention to my so-called staff.

If I wasn't so fucking angry with Beau and Tommy, I would have been beaming with pride for the way Teagan had conducted herself, but anger was the dominant emotion coursing through me at this present moment in time.

Dropping my fork and knife down with a clatter, I shoved my chair back and stood.

"This is your first, your last, and your only fucking warning," I snarled, red-faced as I glowered at each and every person at the table. "When you speak to her, you do it with the same amount of respect as you would if you were speaking to me. You got that?"

"Sit your ass down, boy," Quincy snapped impatiently. "We've got fight tactics to discuss for tomorrow night."

"Knock the other guy out. Make it bloody. Win the fight," I shot back, glaring at Quincy. "There. Fight tactics covered."

Inclining my head toward Lucky, the only one I could tolerate at this moment, I nodded stiffly before turning around and walking out of the dining room.

15

TEAGAN

*T*here were three things I learned about myself during dinner tonight that I hadn't known before.

The first thing I discovered was that I happened to be quite partial to oysters. I would never have guessed it, but those slimy little fuckers were actually pretty tasty.

The second was the fact that I was capable of controlling my mouth when in company. Shocking, I know, but I discovered that side to me when I managed to endure a painfully long, one-sided conversation with Noah's boss, Nick Leversteen, on the side effects of erectile dysfunction during middle age.

And the third thing I realized was that I was willing to do whatever it took to hold onto the man sitting beside me.

As crazy and pathetic as it sounded, there was a desperation inside my heart that was urging me to hold onto Noah Messina for dear life.

Before tonight, I'd never had to acknowledge that feeling.

But it was there; a longing so intense I could hardly breathe through it.

It didn't help that Noah looked almost godlike as he lounged beside me, chatting with several people around our table. His arm was slung over the back of my chair.

The jacket of his tuxedo had long since been discarded. And the top two buttons of his white dress shirt were open, revealing a slither of chest hair and ink.

His black bowtie was undone and hanging on either side of his neck.

He trailed his fingers over the bare skin of my shoulder as he spoke to the man beside him, pulling me closer to him and further away from my sanity. I was losing myself to this man. I knew it. I couldn't stop it and I didn't want to.

A slender waiter, dressed all in black with his hair combed back, approached me with a champagne bottle in his hand.

"More champagne, Miss?"

"Yes. Thank you."

This was crazy...

Last Friday night I'd been holed up in my flat in Cork City, drowning my sorrows, and this Friday I was bumping arms with some of the most influential athletes in sports today, not to mention several actors I'd seen in blockbuster movies.

Shaking my head, I looked around, taking in the fancy decor of the ballroom.

Everything looked so...expensive.

To the outside world, I guessed I fit in with my full-length, white, Grecian-style dress, but inside I felt like a fish out of water.

The band playing on the opposite side of the ballroom was amazing. They were sweet, and soft, and played the crowd into their pocket with classic ballad covers.

The female lead singer had the most haunting, melancholic voice I'd ever heard, and I found myself hanging on every word she sang.

Noah was openly affectionate with me during dinner, and dutifully ignored the countless lustful stares and come hither looks he received from numerous women.

Having Noah claim me in a room full of his colleagues was like having all my Christmases come at once. Being his woman, after all this time, meant more to me than he would ever know.

If the rest of the tour went as well as tonight had, I could see a pretty great future on our horizon...

"So, this is the pretty little lady who tamed The Machine." The little old man on Noah's left, the one he had been talking to, smiled warmly at me.

Extending my hand across Noah, I smiled and said, "It's nice to meet you. I'm Teagan. Teagan Connolly."

"The pleasure is all mine, dear," the old man replied, shaking my outstretched hand. "My name is Travallion Leversteen, although most people around here call me Trav."

For a frail little man, Trav's handshake was surprisingly firm, and I quickly found myself drawn into conversation with him.

I quickly learned that Trav was the founder of the MFA, and Noah's boss Nick's father. Although he retired several years back, Mr. Leversteen Sr. liked to keep a firm eye on his legacy.

From our brief conversation, I discovered that the old man was an honest, no bullshit conversationalist.

I conversed happily with Trav Leversteen for most of the evening and Noah moved between chatting to the couple opposite us to other random people who were all vying for his attention.

We seemed to be in a place where we were comfortable enough to let the other spread their wings, and in sync with each other to join in when needed.

Trust, I realized, was the emotion I was feeling, and I smiled to myself.

We were finally starting to trust one another...

"Do you want to dance?" Noah asked, breaking me out of my daydream.

"Hmm?" Dragging my attention away from the band, I looked at my boyfriend.

Boyfriend...

Turning his chair toward mine, Noah clamped his hands on the sides of my chair and pulled me between his legs effortlessly. He leaned forward and his broad chest stretched the fabric of his white shirt. His narrow waist looked edible in the finely cut waistcoat sewn to him.

"I asked you if you wanted to dance with me," he repeated, lowering his face to mine, giving me his undivided attention.

His warm, alcohol scented breath fanned my face and I shivered.

I knew I was tipsy and teetering on the edge of full-fledged drunkness. The way the room spun around me and my body felt weightless assured me of that.

Noah had drunk twice as much as I had, but he was more buzzed than drunk.

In my defense, I wasn't used to having so much free alcohol at my disposal like Noah obviously was.

Tucking one of my curls behind my ear, Noah grazed my chin with his thumb. "You've been watching the dance floor all night."

His lips were so close to mine that I wanted to say, 'no, I

want to have mad, passionate sex right here, right now,' but I refrained – barely – managing to nod weakly instead.

Noah stared hard at me for a moment, his brown eyes searing me. "Yeah," he said gruffly before clearing his throat. "You need to stop looking at me like that, Thorn."

Raising my glass, I took a large gulp of my champagne, desperate to cool the burning inside of me. Wiping my mouth with the back of my hand, I tossed the remainder of my drink back and exhaled shakily.

My voice was throaty and needy – just like my body – when I said, "Like what?"

Noah's Adam's apple bobbed in his throat, his dark eyes turned an even darker shade of brown. "Like you want me to strip you bare and fuck you raw."

He reached an arm around me and grabbed a bottle of beer from the table before placing it to his lips.

I wasn't sure what to do or how to react. I wasn't going to deny what I desperately wanted to happen. So I remained silent, waiting for Noah to make the next move.

Standing abruptly, Noah reached for my hand, next move decided.

The band began to play a piano version of Elvis Presley's '*Can't Help Falling in Love*' as he took me by the arm and led me onto the dance floor.

"I never thought this was how our lives would turn out," I whispered, holding onto him as he guided me around the floor.

Noah chuckled. Taking my left hand, he cradled it to his chest. "It's different from the quarry, that's for sure."

His other hand was splayed against my lower back and I wanted to ask him where a street fighter learned to dance as well as he did, but I was afraid that I wouldn't like the answer, so I refrained.

This night was too perfect to screw up with past issues and old scores.

We were living in the now and I never wanted the night to end.

"I can do this for you now, Teagan," he announced with quiet affirmation and for the first time in what felt like a very long time, he sounded like the seventeen-year-old boy I fell in love with. "I couldn't give you shit before," he continued to say as he danced me around the floor. "But I can give you the world now."

"I don't want the world, Noah." Stretching up on my tiptoes, I pressed a kiss to his stubbly jaw.

If he never fought another fight for the rest of his life, or if he won a million more title belts, he was enough for me.

Releasing a deep breath, I lowered myself back down and rested my cheek against his chest. "I only want you."

"You've always had me." Noah dropped his chin to rest on my head and it was such a gentle, tender act that my heart raced in my chest. "We'll turn this around, Thorn," he whispered.

His heart was slamming against my cheek.

I was affecting him as much as he was me.

It was a comforting thought.

"We'll make it work," he continued to say. "I'll work harder to make this work with you than anything else." He pressed a kiss to my brow. "You'll be my first priority." He spun me out of his arms before pulling me back to his chest. "I won't ever stop trying to make our relationship work." His hand dropped to my waist. "I rushed in with you when we were in school." Spinning me out again, he pulled me back effortlessly, gliding us around the floor like a pro. "I fell head first but I have zero regrets."

My body was shaking, I was literally trembling all over, and I couldn't seem to control it.

"You were worth it all," he told me. "The pain. The prison time. The wait." Tightening his hand on my waist, Noah buried his face in my neck as we swayed to the music. "I wouldn't change a minute of it, because in *this* chapter of our lives, I get to keep you."

I found myself drowning in Noah's words and whispers of promise.

Clenching my eyes shut, I gave myself up to all he was and all he would be – because it would be enough.

He held me so close, touching my heart with his words, burning my skin with his touch, imprinting on me a lifetime of unspoken promises and goals.

Maybe it was the alcohol we'd both consumed too much of, or maybe it was the atmosphere around us, but there was something special about tonight.

I felt it and I knew Noah did, too.

It was like we were home.

After a lifetime of fighting tooth and nail for everything I had, it was comforting to be in the arms of the other half of me. The strong half. The man I could let my guard down around and trust he would keep me safe because I *knew* he would.

"I don't want tomorrow night to come around," I confessed. "Everything is going to change the moment we step out of this bubble and onto that tour."

"No, it won't."

"But it will."

"Teagan, I'm not changing."

"And I'm not either," I argued softly. "But it doesn't mean the world won't."

Noah's so-called team entered my mind and I blanched, clutching onto him for dear life.

"The universe hates us, Noah. It always has."

"I'm not going to let anyone separate us again, Thorn," Noah said in a husky tone. "Whatever it takes to keep us together, I will do it." Kissing my brow, he pulled me tighter. "You're mine. The only thing I got right in my lifetime of wrongs."

He trailed the back of his hand over the fabric of my white dress.

"One of these days I'm going to put a baby in your belly." He gently pressed my head back against his chest. "And I'll shave your legs when your belly's so big you can't reach your feet."

I held onto him a little tighter, drowning in his words and tender promises for the future.

"I'll do the night feeds," he continued to purr into my ear. "And I'll change the sheets."

Clamping his hand on my hip, Noah swung me away before pulling me back to him.

"I'm not a blow in, Thorn, and I'm not your father or your uncle." He pressed a quick kiss to my lips. "I won't put my career before you and I won't drown my feelings in a bottle."

He took my hand and sealed his hold over my heart.

I would never get over him. For the rest of my days on this earth, I would be devoted to Noah Messina.

"I'm going to buy you the biggest fucking house in Boulder and fill it up with babies."

Reaching up, I pressed my lips to his neck and released a deep breath.

"And I will never be your mother," I vowed, looking deep into his eyes. "I will never use your love for me as a weapon.

I will never put you into a position like the one you've spent your life fighting to get out of. "

He touched his forehead to mine and smiled. "I know."

"God..." Emotions crept through my heart, spilling out of my mouth. "I'm upset that I missed seven years of this." My happiness was being up-scuttled by the regrets of my past. "I should have stayed with you. I should have listened to you..."

"I was always going down, Thorn," Noah replied, comforting me. Tipping my chin upward with his hand, he looked deep into my eyes. "If you had stayed, it wouldn't have changed the fact that I had to go to jail."

"You mean everything to me." Shivering, I bit down hard on my lip. "I don't know if it's safe to feel this way or not, but I can't pretend anymore. I can't."

The heat between us was burning me.

The love in my heart was too much.

I felt like I would explode and every touch, kiss, and smile from Noah drew me closer to that moment. To this pivotal point in time.

The lights flickered above us.

The music filled my ears.

Emotions so deep coursed through my bloodstream, and I was fairly certain that Noah's hands on my body were all that were keeping my feet on the floor.

"I'm giving you everything I have this time," I promised him. Every single piece. I wanted to expose the ugliest parts of my soul because I knew he was the one person who would accept those parts.

Noah had stopped dancing.

He was staring down at me like I was a huge crossword puzzle.

He cupped my face in his hands and blew my mind with his words. "Let's do it."

"Do what?"

"Get married."

"What – like right now?"

"Why not? We're in Vegas. We're all the family each other has. What's stopping us?"

My heart was hammering so hard I thought it would burst through my chest as the music continued to blare around us.

"Okay, I think you've had far too much to drink."

"I love you. Drunk or sober. I want to marry you. Drunk or Sober." Noah grabbed my arm and pulled me flush against his chest. "Come on, Thorn. Make an honest man out of me."

"You're crazy," I exclaimed, wiping a bead of sweat from my brow. "You're completely insane."

"I know," he shot back, grinning. "But it's like I told you before; the crazy in me needs the crazy in you."

"I..." I took a step back from Noah and held my hands up in the air. "I can't... I don't..."

What was he asking me here?

"Are you serious?" I implored him with my eyes – I fucking begged him to be serious. My heart was screaming 'get into his arms, bitch' but I was so stumped I couldn't move. "You want to marry me?"

"Don't fight me on this," Noah shot back, prowling toward me. "Settle down with me."

His eyes were dark as coal, blazing with heat and fire, scorching me.

Snaking an arm around my waist, he pulled me back into his embrace. "Let me keep you."

"Okay," I breathed, nodding vigorously. "Okay, let's do it."

"Yeah?"

"Yeah."

Noah's lip turned up ever so slightly.

It was like he could hear my subconscious screaming 'kiss me' because he ducked his head toward mine and claimed my lips with a kiss that scorched me.

I felt so safe in his arms. Like his were the only lips mine were supposed to touch.

And I did.

I kissed him back hard, desperately.

Clinging to his broad shoulders, inhaling the smell of him.

My hand drifted upward, my fingers knotting in the hair at the nape of his neck.

Uncle Max was going to kill me.

Hope was going to flip when she found out that I got married behind her back, and yet nothing was going to change my mind.

I was going to marry Noah Messina.

"Teagan Messina," I whispered, breaking the kiss. "Mrs. Teagan Messina."

Noah laughed. "It has a ring to it." Taking my hand in his, he smiled down at me. "Are you nervous?"

I shook my head and allowed Noah to lead me off the dance floor. "Not about you..."

Out of the corner of my eye, I spotted someone familiar at the edge of the dance floor. "Hang on," I muttered, turning around to get a better look. "I think I saw someone I know."

"No you didn't." Noah's hand tightened on mine as he pulled me closer to the exit. "Let's just go."

"Noah, hold on, will you?" I pulled hard on my hand and Noah reluctantly released me.

I searched the room for the person I was sure I had

recognized, and when I found her, my temper flared the same color as her hair.

Reese Tanner...

"That bitch," I hissed seconds before launching myself across the dance floor.

A pair of strong arms clamped around my waist, pulling me back.

"She's not worth it," Noah whispered in my ear. "Come on. Just walk away."

"You're not surprised she's here." Swinging around, I shoved against Noah's chest and stepped back from him, giving myself some breathing space. "Why aren't you surprised to see her, Noah?" I repeated, furious.

"Because she's a fucking whore, that's why!" Running a hand through his hair, Noah let out an impatient growl. "Thorn, that woman has spread her legs to pretty much every fighter in the MFA. Last month she was hooking up with Horacio Vaughn. This month it's the heavyweight champ Anthony Cole. Next month it'll be some other poor bastard."

"And you?"

Noah's eyes darkened. "Don't go there, Teagan."

Guilt churned inside of me. "I'm sorry."

"Moral of the story, she's not worth it," he continued in a gruff tone. "Let's just go."

"Not worth it?" I shook my head. I couldn't let it go. "That woman took advantage of you, Noah!" She did more than just take advantage of him. She'd drugged him and forced herself on him, setting in motion seven long years apart for us. "I can't walk away...I have to say something."

16

NOAH

"*T*eagan, don't!"

I didn't know why I was wasting my breath. She'd never listened to a damn word I said before so why would she start now?

Letting out an exasperated sigh, I chased after my girl-friend who was hunting down the *one* woman on the face of this earth that I wished would drop off it.

Yeah, I'd known there was a chance Reese would be here tonight. There was always a chance she'd show up at these fucking things, which is why I *always* avoided them like the plague.

I couldn't stop Reese from fucking her way through every name card on the MFA, but I sure as hell could avoid her. Teagan, however, had different ideas...

"Reese fucking Tanner," Thorn sneered, barging her way through the crowd to where Reese was sitting. "I've got a crow to pluck with you!"

Reese, who was sitting on the lap of Anthony Cole, looking like the devil incarnate dressed in a blood red dress, looked a little frightened as Teagan approached. Her eyes momentarily widened in shock before she quickly snapped the shutters down and glowered back at Teagan.

"Walk away, bitch," Reese warned, curling her arm around Cole's neck.

"Oh, I plan to," Teagan shot back. "When I've scratched your poisonous eyes out of your plastic face." With that, Teagan snaked a hand out and grabbed Reese by the hair.

Dragging her off Cole's lap by the hair, Teagan managed to knock Reese to the floor before climbing on top of her.

A part of me wanted to jump in and pull Thorn to safety, but I refrained from doing so. She could handle herself. My girl was putting a beating on Reese and pride was swelling inside me.

Cole moved towards the women who were brawling it out on the floor and I took a step toward him and shook my head.

"Touch her and you won't make that fight in December," I warned him.

Anthony Cole didn't have shit on me and he knew it.

This was the last year he'd be sporting that shiny belt because I was coming for him.

"I bet you thought you were so clever!" Teagan hissed as she scratched and tore at Reese's face. "Doing that to him. And the text message you sent me?" A scream ripped through her throat as she grabbed Reese on either side of her head and slammed her skull against the floor. "Clever."

"You're crazy," Reese snarled, catching Teagan on the cheek with her nails.

Teagan fell back and Reese managed to climb to her feet.

Reese's face was marked with scratches and blood. Her hair was in complete disarray and her red dress was torn at the arm. "I'm going to sue you for this!" She hissed, clutching her cheek in her hand.

"Haven't you heard, bitch?" Teagan shot back viciously. "I'm certifiable." Scrambling to her feet, Teagan hacked up a huge ball of phlegm and spat it into Reese's face. "Try and sue me. I fucking dare you."

"Get her away from me," Reese screamed, rushing over to Cole. Throwing her arms around him, she sobbed into his chest. "She should be in a mental institution!"

"And you should be in prison," Teagan shot back, seething. "Being someone's bitch-wife."

Out of the corner of my eye, I spotted a line of security heading for us, headed by Nick.

"Shit," I groaned, wrapping my arm around Teagan's middle. "We need to go, Thorn."

"You better watch yourself with that one," Teagan hissed at Cole as I hauled her away. "She's like a rampant bout of herpes. You'll never get rid of her."

Teagan fought against my hold every step of the way as I carted her out of that ballroom.

"Let me go!" She screamed, hissing and flailing her arms and legs. "I wasn't finished with her. I wanted my pound of flesh and that bitch hasn't nearly suffered enough for what she's done to us, Noah."

"It's over, Thorn," I snapped, struggling to keep hold of her. She was like a fucking octopus in my arms. I'd never seen a woman squirm like her. "Let's just go before we both get arrested."

"I had her," she hissed.

"I know, baby," I soothed when we reached the sidewalk outside. "You got her good."

"I'm so mad."

"With me?"

"Yes with you," she hissed. "You should have let me kill her."

"And let you get arrested?" I cocked a brow. "Oh yeah, cause that's what a good boyfriend would do."

"This is all your fault." Shaking off my arms, Teagan stalked off in a huff. "Don't talk to me again."

"Of course it is. Everything usually is." Running a hand through my hair in exasperation, I called out, "Come on, Thorn. Where are you going?"

"Fuck off," she hissed as she walked a little faster.

"God fucking dammit to hell," I muttered as I chased her crazy ass down the strip. "You're a crazy woman," I growled when I caught up with her. Clamping my hand around her arm, I pulled her back into my embrace.

Surprisingly, this time she came without a fight. Wrapping my arms around her, I pulled her in for a hug.

"Thanks for not letting me get arrested," she mumbled, burying her face against my chest.

"No problem."

"And I'm sorry for telling you to fuck off."

"Again, no problem."

"I'm a pain in your ass, aren't I?"

"A huge one."

"But you love me anyway."

"That's right." I smirked, knowing she needed to hear me say it. "I'm in love with your crazy ass."

"So..." She looked up at me and smiled sheepishly. "Do you still love me enough to want to marry me?"

"Yeah, Thorn." For my sins. "I do."

17

NOAH

*A*s I stood in front of an obese version of Elvis with an over the top hairpiece and Teagan by my side, I couldn't stop myself from shaking my head.

This was without a doubt the tackiest, craziest, most insane thing I'd ever done but I swear it felt right all the way down in my bones.

I didn't give a shit if Elvis or the Pope officiated this.

All I cared about was getting her signature on that marriage certificate.

The newlyweds whose wedding Teagan and I had just witnessed were sitting behind us, snapping away like crazy on their cellphones.

They'd wrangled us into their impulsive nuptials and we were now returning the favor.

If I hadn't drunk so much, I would have known better than to allow cameras in here, but I was buzzed and excited and desperately in love with the woman whose hand was in mine.

The woman I had committed crimes to keep.

She was putting her life in my hands, giving me her word and pledging me half of her soul.

"I knew a boy when I was seventeen," Teagan announced when it was her turn to wing a speech together.

Swaying slightly, she turned her body to face mine and smiled so bright my heart squeezed in my chest.

"And that boy taught me a lot about myself."

Swallowing deeply, she exhaled a shaky breath.

"That boy taught me how to live in the moment. He taught me how to go after what I wanted. He taught me that it was okay to lean on someone else – that it was okay to admit when I was wrong."

Her voice caught in her throat then, and she quickly looked away and took a few deep breaths before continuing.

"That boy turned out to be more of a man than all the others and he cemented himself inside the deepest parts of my heart without me even noticing."

"Thorn..." I managed to croak out.

My voice was thick with emotion.

My legs were shaking like fucking crazy.

I was bursting with pride, standing here, hearing these words coming out of her mouth.

"You're my soldier, Noah Messina," Teagan whispered, smiling. "You always have been. And I want you to know that you can build your foundation of trust on my love for you because there's nothing more real and permanent than what I feel in my heart for you."

Officiating Elvis cleared his throat. "And you?" Waggling his bushy brows, he said, "You got anything you'd like to say to this pretty little lady?"

"Yeah," I muttered.

Pulling at the collar of my shirt, I forced myself to calm the fuck down and just tell her how I felt.

Without the slightest idea of what I would say, I decided to take a page from Teagan's book and wing it.

"Teagan, choosing you wasn't something I had the privilege of doing..." Pausing, I looked down into her hazel eyes and sighed. "Because there was no choice. You forced your way into my life and you blew it up. You were reckless and wild and crazy beautiful and I fell completely in love with you. There was no choice. You've always been the realest thing I've ever had..." My throat tightened and I had to take a minute to calm myself before continuing.

"I will take care of you," I promised. "I will be faithful to you. I will lay my life down to keep you alive. Whatever you need, I will be the one to make it happen."

Squeezing her hand in mine, I added, "I love you, Teagan. I don't know what else to tell you other than I'm in and I won't ever be out."

"I'm in, too," Teagan sobbed. Wrapping her hand around my neck, she pulled my face down to hers. "God Noah, I'm *so* in." Pressing her alcohol flavored lips to mine, she moaned softly. "And I always will be."

"Do you have rings?" Elvis asked, breaking the moment between us.

Sighing heavily, I pressed my forehead to hers.

I hadn't thought about anything.

"Sorry, Thorn," I muttered, feeling stupid.

"It's fine, just keep going. We don't need rings," Teagan told the officiator. Turning her attention back to me, she grinned and whispered. "I have an even better idea."

18

TEAGAN

"You're all mine now, Thorn," Noah said, claiming my mouth with his and I knew I would never care about another thing for as long as I lived, just as long as he kept kissing me.

I had done it.

I had married Noah Messina, and what was even more miraculous was that he had married me – of his own free will.

This man was absolutely lethal to me.

His smile alone seemed to have the power to control my mood – to elevate me.

And now he was my husband.

God...

With devotion in his eyes and sex on his mind, Noah broke our kiss and grinned down at me. "So what was your better idea?" Rubbing my nose with his, he sighed in contentment. "You said you had a better idea than wedding bands."

"I don't want a ring on your finger that you have to take

off every time you fight. I want something permanent." Smiling, I pressed one more kiss against his lips. "I want a tattoo."

Noah threw his head back and laughed. "Coming from the girl who once told me I needed to buy a coloring book and stop drawing on myself."

"What can I say?" Titling my head to one side, I grinned. "A girl can always change her mind."

SEVERAL HOURS, AND SEVERAL BARS LATER, NOAH STAGGERED out of the hotel elevator with me in his arms.

"Stop laughing," he grunted, as he struggled to put one foot in front of the other. "You're putting me off balance."

"Oh yeah," I choked out. "I'm the one putting you off balance." I couldn't stop laughing as he tried and failed miserably to swipe the door with the key fob. "It has nothing to do with the alcohol you consumed."

"You're a bad influence on me, wife," he slurred, finally managing to open the door of our suite. Misjudging his steps, my usually balanced husband – *husband* – staggered over his feet, resulting in us landing in a heap just inside the doorway of our suite.

"Oh my god," I cackled through fits of laughter. "I can't breathe." Everything was spinning. The walls. My head. My words. And I'd never been happier. "You're so funny."

"Told you I'd do it," Noah slurred from somewhere underneath me. "Told you I'd carry my wife over the thrush hold..."

"Thrush hold?" My laughter turned into screams of hysteria. "Oh...oh...I can't even..." Struggling to calm myself, I managed to choke out, "It's called a *threshold*."

"You'll be laughing," Noah shot back, managing to roll me onto my back. "When I violate your threshold tonight."

"You couldn't violate a carrier bag in your condition," I teased. Not that I was in much better condition. "I can't feel my tongue." Sticking my tongue out, I touched it with my fingers. "...eriously...oah...I...ant...eel...i...ongue..."

"I'm...in love with you," he slurred, dropping his head onto my chest.

"I'm in love with you, too...oh!" Pushing against Noah's shoulders, I tried to dislodge myself from under his body. "Let me up. I need to pee!"

"Stay." Clamping his hands on my hips, Noah nuzzled his nose against the fabric of my dress covering my stomach. "*Copulate*."

"Really?" I sighed happily. "You remember that?"

"I remember *everything*," he chuckled as he struggled to climb to his feet.

When he finally managed to stand up, he reminded me of the leaning tower of Pisa.

Reaching down, he grabbed my arm and pulled me to my feet.

Struggling to maintain my own balance, I padded after Noah who was staggering into the bedroom and attempting to strip his clothes off on the way.

"What are you doing?" I giggled, following after him.

"Getting ready to violate that threshold."

19

NOAH

*M*y phone was blowing the hell up.

For the last forty minutes, a constant stream of vibrating and fucking beeping noises had been drilling through my brain.

I wanted to make it stop, but I couldn't get off the goddamn bed.

My hands were shackled to the bedpost and the only person who knew where the keys to release me were just so happened to be passed out beside me with her ass in the air.

"Noah," Teagan moaned, twisting in the sheets. "Make the noise stop."

"I can't." Pulling on the handcuffs that had me bound like a bitch, I let out a heavy sigh. "Didn't think I'd be back in cuffs so soon."

The hammering on the door began out of nowhere followed by some more beeping.

"Noah...please!" She wailed. Dragging a pillow out from underneath her head, Teagan cradled it to her stomach. "I'm dying here." Whimpering, she curled up in a tiny ball. "My head is trying to leave my body. It's so bad."

"I told you to stop after the second bottle of Jack." I specifically remember telling her that right before she tied me to the bed. That was right after I violated her threshold for the third time.

Jesus, drunken sex with Teagan was fucking unbelievable.

I needed to get her oiled up more often.

"You told Drunk Teagan to stop," Teagan moaned. Opening one mascara smeared eye, she peeked up at me and held a finger in the air. "Drunk Teagan didn't give Hungover Teagan the message."

Sitting up ever so slowly, Teagan held her arms out at her sides, as if she was genuinely afraid she would topple over. Her hair was the definition of a crow's nest and I swear to god she never looked more beautiful.

"Noah," she whispered, eyes locked on the black ink circling her ring finger. "Did we?" Turning her face to me, she blinked rapidly. "Jesus Christ, we did!"

Getting married on a whim in Vegas may have been my idea, but tattoos instead of bands on our ring fingers? Well, that was all Teagan.

Hangover forgotten, Teagan scrambled onto her knees and crawled up my body. "Oh my god," she breathed. Grabbing a hold of my left hand – that was still cuffed to the bedpost – Teagan examined my freshly inked ring finger. "We're married!"

Grabbing my chin with her hand, Teagan lunged forward and planted a kiss on my lips. "You actually married me!"

"At what point in time last night did I give you the impression I had cold feet?"

"You didn't," Teagan replied sheepishly. "I just..." Shaking her head, she let out a laugh. "I just...God, Noah. I'm your wife. Your freaking wife!" She flopped back onto the bed beside me and giggled. "I still blush when buying tampons at the pharmacy and now I'm someone's wife."

"My wife," I corrected. "Not someone's. Mine."

"Wife." Teagan bit down on her lip and breathed. "Noah Messina is my husband."

"Damn fucking straight."

"You managed to tie me down, save me from prison, and tramp stamp me all in one night?" Letting out a whistle, Teagan patted my thigh. "Your powers of persuasion are beyond impressive."

"Noah, you better open the fucking door now, boy!"

Quincy's voice filled my ears and I groaned.

"Do you have any idea of what time it is?"

"Do you think you could kill him for me?" Teagan asked. "Or throat punch him to shut him up?"

"Baby, unless you untie me, I can't do a damn thing," I told her with a smirk.

"I can't...I sort of made the keys fly." Teagan nodded toward the window where it was barely bright out. Shrugging, she smiled sheepishly. "Um, yeah...Sorry?"

"Sorry?" I laughed and pulled on my shackles. "You will be when I get out of these." Shaking my head, I asked, "Where did you get those anyway?"

"You don't remember?" Teagan grinned. "They were a wedding gift from Bill and Betty."

"Bill and Betty?" My brow furrowed in confusion. "The couple that got married before us?"

"Yup." Teagan cocked a finely curved eyebrow and smirked. "And I might have been drunk, but from what that Betty woman told me, I think it's safe to say that ole Bill was in for a treat last night...."

"I can hear you guys!" Tommy's voice filled the room this

time as the merciless banging continued on the door. "Open the door right this second or I'll have Lewis kick it down!"

"What's the fucking emergency, asshole?" I roared, losing my patience. Teagan flinched and covered her ears and I mouthed sorry before calling out, "It's too damn early for banging down hotel doors."

20

TEAGAN

"*I*'ll get it," I told Noah. I didn't particularly want to open the door and let Tommy and Quincy inside of our little bubble, but the fuckers wouldn't stop banging and my poor head couldn't take much more.

Climbing off the bed, I covered Noah's waist with a sheet before rummaging around the carnage on the floor in search of a shirt.

Finding one, I slipped it over my head before padding through the suite to the door.

"How are the newlyweds?" Tommy sneered when I threw back the door, glaring at me like I was a poisonous insect.

I opened my mouth to answer him, but Quincy shoved past me, storming through our hotel suite like a hurricane. With one last look of disgust, Tommy stalked past me.

Lewis, who was standing outside in the hallway, nodded politely to me. "Good evening, Teagan," he acknowledged before turning his back on me, his guarding resumed.

Good evening?

Shaking my head in confusion, I closed the door and

wandered back into the bedroom where it was going down like Donkey Kong.

"Are you fucking crazy?" Quincy was roaring. "You're all over the goddamn internet. Getting hitched in Vegas? Real classy."

When he reached the bed, Quincy flung his iPad at Noah.

The device bounced off Noah's rock hard abs before landing on the carpet alongside the bed.

"That cost me a thousand bucks, guys," Tommy groaned, diving for the device.

Noah shrugged nonchalantly from where he was still shackled. "I didn't tell him to throw it."

"I thought you had more than one brain cell in that head of yours, boy!" Quincy continued to roar. "No prenup. No goddamn nothing."

"You think you can storm in here like you own the place and throw things at him?"

Noah must have some serious self-control, I thought to myself, because right now I was burning mad.

Bending down, I grabbed the first thing that caught my eyes – which just so happened to be one of my heels from last night.

Standing up with the silver heel in my hand, I swung my arm back and let it fly.

I couldn't begin to describe the satisfaction I felt when my heel clocked Quincy on the back of his head.

"You crazy fucking bitch," Noah's coach snarled, swinging around to glare at me. "What the hell is wrong with you?"

"You want to keep this going?" I demanded. "Fine." Reaching down, I grabbed my other heel. "I can go all day." I aimed my shoe at his head. "Call me crazy again. I dare you."

"Noah," Quincy hissed. "Call your girl off before I do something I regret."

"Wife." With a strength that I knew he possessed but still surprised me, Noah yanked one hand roughly, shattering the cuff before doing the same with the other.

So much for needing keys...

Noah then proceeded to climb off the bed and walk across the room as naked as the day he was born, without a blush on his cheeks.

"Wife," Noah said when he reached my side. "Call off *my wife*." Pressing a kiss to the top of my head, Noah stepped around me and pulled open one of the dresser drawers.

"The media are all over this," Tommy said before quickly averting his eyes from the sight of my naked husband in all his morning glory.

"Getting married in Elvis's Chapel?" Quincy piped up, tone laced with disgust. "Classy."

"Did you have a reason for bursting into our room this early?" Taking out a pair of black shorts, Noah quickly stepped into them and pulled them up to rest on his perfectly proportioned, narrow hips. "Or couldn't you wait to offer your congratulations?"

"Considering it's past eight in the evening and you're supposed to be at the arena fighting in forty-five goddamn minutes, then yeah," Quincy hissed, chest heaving. "I'd say I have a pretty good reason for bursting in on you."

Grabbing Tommy's hand, Noah muttered a string of swearwords when he checked the time on his watch. "Jesus Christ."

Holding the back of his head with his hands, Noah inhaled a deep breath. "Fuck," he finally whispered, eyes locked on mine. "How long were we asleep?"

"I don't know." I was so drunk when I fell into bed this

morning that up until now I'd thought it was still Friday. "It couldn't have been more than..."

"It doesn't matter!" Quincy growled, interrupting me. "What the hell are you waiting for? Let's go!"

Checking his watch, Tommy cursed under his breath. "If we're lucky we'll make it."

"Go," I urged when Noah's worried eyes landed on my face. "Hurry up," I added, shoving him toward the bedroom door.

"What about you?" Noah asked as he slipped on his pants and then his shoes. "I don't want you here on your own."

"I'm not alone. Lewis is outside." Pushing him toward the door, I reached up on my tiptoes and pressed a kiss to his cheek. "Go fight. I'll clean up and follow after you guys with Lewis."

21

NOAH

I didn't want to leave Teagan on her own less than twenty-four hours after we got married, but if I didn't make that fight in time, Nick would have my balls nailed to his office wall.

Tommy and Quincy were on one side of me, urging me toward the door, Teagan was on the other, and I did something completely out of character.

Leaving this room went against my gut instinct.

I couldn't explain why I felt this way – only that I had a niggling feeling in the pit of my stomach. That feeling was screaming *Don't go. Don't leave her. You'll regret it.*

"As soon as I grab a shower, I'll be there," Teagan continued to reassure me, smiling up at me through mascara-crusted eyelashes, looking more beautiful than any other woman I'd ever laid my eyes on.

She cupped my stubbly cheek with her small hand.

"Noah, go," she added, noticing my hesitation. "I'll be fine with Lewis."

"She's right, Noah," Tommy interjected. "You trust Lewis." Opening the door, he pushed me out before following after me. "You hand-picked the guy. He's perfectly capable of manning the fort while you're gone."

But I didn't want to be gone.

I didn't want to do anything except spend every second of the day with Teagan.

What was I doing?

"Tell me everything's okay," I said to Tommy when we were sitting in the back of a cab on the way to the arena.

"Everything's okay," he replied quickly.

Throwing my head back, I sighed heavily. "I feel...riled up." I had no idea why I felt so out of sorts but it didn't bode well with me.

"I never would've guessed," Tommy replied dryly. Shrugging, he added, "It's probably the alcohol still in your bloodstream."

"You know you're not supposed to drink that crap before a fight," Quincy growled, offering up his two cents worth.

"Yeah," I replied, not believing for one minute that alcohol was the root of my worries.

What a fucking horrifying feeling it was; to have everything you ever wanted and know that at any moment in time it could be snatched away from you?

That's how I felt about Teagan.

Unluckily for Roy Wicks, that feeling followed me all the way into the cage.

22

TEAGAN

*T*ommy wasn't lying when he said the media were all over mine and Noah's hasty nuptials.

By the time I had showered and made myself somewhat decent, Lewis and I had spent twenty minutes trying to get from the foyer of the hotel to the car.

Paparazzi over here were insane.

I'd never seen the likes of it.

Noah was obviously prime meat to them and because I was his former flame and current squeeze, their words not mine, I was now hot property.

I'd had at least a dozen cameras shoved in my face already.

Even now, as I sat in the back of the fanciest car I'd ever been in, waiting for Lewis to escort me in to watch Noah's fight, paparazzi continued to snap furiously outside the limo. I didn't know why they were bothering when the windows were tinted, but whatever.

The moment the car door opened, flashing cameras and the sounds of screaming infiltrated my senses, both blinding and deafening me.

Whoa...

"This is crazy," I whispered to myself as Lewis opened my door and gestured to me.

Climbing unsteadily to my feet, I studied the crazed mob surrounding me. Startled, and quite frankly, overwhelmed by the media, I wrapped my arms around myself in dismay as I studied the hordes of people blocking the sidewalk to the arena entrance.

"*Mrs. Messina!*"

"*That's her, the one in the pictures!*"

"*Can we get a comment?*"

"*Who is she?*"

"*The girl from the video.*"

Oh yes.

The delightful video of me losing my virginity.

The CCTV footage of Noah and I getting it on in the elevator of the Henderson Hotel was still doing the rounds on the net.

"*That's her. That's his wife.*"

Teagan Connolly, unintentional porn star...

"*Her?*" I could hear the disbelief oozing from their words. "*But she's so plain.*"

"*I know, right?*"

Super.

As if I didn't have enough issues.

"*He could have any woman and he picks* her?"

"*He probably knocked her up.*"

Cameras and microphones were thrust toward me as Lewis led me through the crowds.

Keeping my head down, I kept close to Lewis, feeling completely out of my comfort zone, not to mention under-dressed in jeans, flip-flops and a gray tank top...

When we eventually got inside, Lewis and I were

escorted to our seats by several security guards. I was shuffling into my seat in the third row, with Lewis close on my heels, just as Noah's entrance song, Roy Jones' *Can't be Touched,* blasted through the arena.

I sagged in relief.

For a while I'd been worried I wouldn't make it on time.

The screaming around us went through the roof. Everyone was on their feet cheering for my husband – everyone's clear favorite.

"Ladies and gentlemen, for your pleasure, for one night only, we have a knockout fight," the announcer called excitedly. "That's right, folks. MFA veteran and three-time former heavyweight champion, Roy the wringerrrrr Wicks. And going against him tonight, a crowd favorite, it's your very own bad boy from the wrong side of the tracks. Noah the Machine Messsinaaaaa!"

When he entered the cage, Noah bounced lightly on his feet; a challenge for a man who was 6'4" in height and 245 pounds of pure muscle.

Ignoring his opposition who was already in the cage and trying to taunt him, Noah rolled his shoulders and twisted his neck from side to side, loosening up.

I'd never thought much about the arena's MFA fights took place in when I watched them on the television, but being here in the flesh was intense. The place smelled of sweat and blood and bleach.

The cage, the metal bars, the scent of sweat mixed with tobacco and alcohol was poignant. The blood thirsty screams of the crowd were kind of arousing in a screwed up way.

When the match official called both men to the center of the ring to touch gloves, the screaming and cheering went through the roof.

The bell rang and Noah curled his lip up and smirked.

And then he attacked.

Noah looked so fricking hot, I could hardly contain myself as I screamed out his name like a lunatic, cheering him on all the way.

His opponent reminded me of a ninja. He was all high kicks and fancy foot patterns.

But Roy Wicks was old and it showed.

He was no match for my guy.

Blocking Roy's aggressive uppercuts effortlessly, Noah embarked on an impressive onslaught of shots, and he did all this while dancing around the mat like it was second nature to him. Fortunately for Noah, I knew that it was true. This was what he'd been brought into the world to do, and my man was the best.

"He's doing well tonight."

Tommy's voice came out of nowhere, surprising the hell out of me. Maneuvering through the row, he settled down on the empty seat to my right.

Startled by Tommy's appearance, I sank down on my seat and smiled. "He's incredible."

When he didn't say anything else, I refocused my attention on the cage. My heart soared in my chest when I saw that Noah had managed to get Wicks on the mat, where he had him locked in a submission maneuver.

"I know what you're trying to do," Tommy whispered in my ear.

My blood ran cold in my veins.

"And what's that?" I replied, not taking my eyes off my husband.

"Quit acting, Teagan," Tommy sneered, moving closer to me. "You didn't want a damn thing to do with Noah when he was down on his luck, and low and behold, the minute he gets back up on his feet, you're back, sniffing around like the proverbial penny."

"You're wrong about me," I said shakily. "I'm not that kind of woman."

"Every woman is that kind of woman." Tommy laughed harshly. "I give it a month. You'll be draped in his money like every other gold-digger." His voice turned colder. "Clever move, by the way, not having him draw up a prenup. You move fast, Teagan."

"I love him," I snapped. Turning to face Tommy, I looked into his eyes and said, "You might not want to believe that, but it's true." Scraping together all my courage, I added, "And I'm not going anywhere. So you might as well get used to me being around the place."

"Is that so?" Tommy raised a brow. "Well, I want you to know that I'm going to make it my life's mission to expose you for what you truly are."

"Aaaaannnnd your winner, ladies and gentleman. Noah the machine Messsinnnnaaaa!" the announcer called out, freeing me from Tommy's nerve racking glare.

On shaking legs, I stood and cheered for my husband, forcing a smile.

Inside, I was terrified.

23

To: Hope Carter
Subject: RE-READ MY SURNAME!
From: Teagan Messina
Don't freak out on me.... but I got MARRIED! Yes, you read that right. I am officially a married woman now. And before you say that I've made a huge mistake or that I've rushed into things, just remember how supportive I was when you wanted to marry Jordan *the dick*.
PS: I love you. I miss you. I need you to come see me <3

To: Teagan Messina
Subject: WTF????
From: Hope Carter
Did you smoke something? What the heck am I reading here? You got married? When? Where? Details, Teagan. I need details asap!
Also, please refrain from calling my husband a dick.

Though he is a huge one, you know how stabby I get when people talk crap about him.

PS: We probably shouldn't refer to him as my husband either – not when he acts like the complete opposite.

Also, now that you're married to Noah, does that make you my *aunt*?

Ugh. Creepy...

And I miss you too, weirdo.

To: Hope Carter
Subject: I've always been your agony aunt. Now it's on paper! J
From: Teagan Messina

OMFG. I didn't think about it like that. I married my best friend's *uncle*. But yeah, I guess it kind of does make me your aunt now...at least by marriage. And if we ever take the plunge and have kids...they'll be *cousins*!

Weird...

To: Teagan Messina
Subject: Has *Uncle Dearest* knocked you up already???
From: Hope Carter

Be careful, Teegs. The men in my family are known to breed like rabbits.

My grandfather seems to have an army of sons littered across Colorado and my dad's never knocked out less than two at a time – three in the case of Cam, Colt and Lo. Breeding multiples could be a hereditary thing you know...

. . .

To: Hope Carter
Subject: My uterus is empty!
From: Teagan Messina
No, he hasn't *knocked me up yet*, and don't even think about
it. You know how superstitious I am. You could jinx me
with that kind of talk.
Ugh... Now I'm all freaked out.
Thanks a lot Hope!!!!

To: Teagan Messina
Subject: Don't be silly and wrap that willy!
From: Hope Carter
Anytime, precious.
Now, go and guard that uterus with the best contraceptive
money can buy. You're going to need it – just ask my poor
mother. J
PS: How's the guy? Is he still with you guys?

To: Hope Carter
Subject: Guy? What guys?
From: Teagan Messina
Guy???? Spill your beans, lanky!!!!

To: Hope Carter
Subject: Holy Shiiizle
From: Teagan Messina
Do you mean LUCKY??? He's good. He's very hot, and very
single...

To: Teagan Messina
Subject: Forget it...

From: Hope Carter
How do you do that? How do you turn an innocent question into something...not???

"What's so funny?"

Noah's voice drifted through my ears, dragging me back to the here and now – which just so happened to be a tour bus on the interstate between Las Vegas and Phoenix.

"Hope," I chuckled, before locking my phone and slipping it back into my pocket. "She has an uncanny ability of terrifying me to my core." Shuddering, I filled Noah in on Hope's emails about multiples and breeding like rabbits.

"No wonder she's a writer," Noah said in an amused tone when I had finished my tale. Shaking his head, he ran a hand through his hair and smirked. "The girl has some imagination."

"True," I agreed. "Do we have much further to go?"

Noah looked out the window, and then down at his watch. "Another hour or so."

"Great." *Not.* I was feeling stiff and uncomfortable after three hours of constant driving. "Another hour in this... heat." I gestured toward the window of the bus.

There wasn't a blade of grass in our peripheral.

Sweet Jesus, I couldn't breathe.

Back home in Ireland, the month of April usually consisted of a touch of sunshine and the odd shower of rain.

Over here, it was like a freaking desert.

Pulling at the collar of his shirt with his hand, Noah twisted his head from side to side before reaching up above our heads and switching on the air-con. "Better?"

After a moment, a steady flow of cold air blew into my face and I nodded in relief.

Noah wrapped his arm around my shoulders and I snuggled back into his embrace, preferring to melt rather than move an inch away from him.

"I like this," I mused, stroking my cheek against the cotton of his shirt. "Just being here. With you."

"Good," Noah said in his deep, gruff voice. Tightening his arm around me, he leaned over and kissed the top of my head. "Because I like having you here."

Out of the corner of my eye, I noticed Beau walking toward us and I quickly averted my eyes, not bothering to look at him or attempt to make eye contact.

We'd been on tour for a little under three weeks now, and I'd learned pretty quickly not to bother trying to talk to any of Noah's team. With the exception of Lucky, none of them gave me the time of day.

They just loved to run to Noah whenever I did something inappropriate. Like last weekend in Vegas, when I threatened to cut the busboy's shaft off for touching my butt, or the weekend before when I drank a teeny-tiny bit too much after Noah's victory over Roy Wicks and had decided it was a good idea to break into Tommy's hotel room and teepee the hell out of it. Honest to god, it was like I had three evil step-sisters waiting in the wings to throw shit on my path and up-scuttle me at any given time.

The poor choices I had made when I was seventeen were still hanging over my head and blackening everyone's opinion of me.

Beau stopped at our seat to talk to Noah about something or other. I turned my face toward the window, pulled my phone out of my pocket and busied myself with answering some long overdue emails.

I was trying this new thing where I didn't allow Beau or any of the guys to draw me into arguments.

Every time they were close to me, I found myself mentally reciting the age old saying *'not my monkey, not my circus'* over and over again in my head.

It marginally helped with my rage over how they treated me and the way they spoke down to me when Noah wasn't around. Well, I still wanted to throat punch both of them, but so far I was managing to restrain my natural instincts.

I was under no illusions as to what these men thought of me, or the threat they posed to my marriage – Tommy had said as much.

Forcing myself to refocus on my phone, I stared down at the screen and quickly swiped through the junk mail cramming up my mailbox.

I was in the process of deleting a newsletter from a gym I'd subscribed to back home when my eyes landed on an email listed below from harteyboy3829@cssgym.ien.

Immediately I knew who the email was from. It was the same address he'd had since secondary school.

My thumb hovered over the screen for a long moment while I contemplated reading it or not.

What good would come out of it?

Liam had hurt me beyond repair.

There was no going back for me – no friendship to repair.

No nothing...

Clicking the delete button, I erased Liam's email before letting out a bittersweet sigh and curling into my husband's chest.

"You good, Thorn?" Noah asked when Beau was gone.

Keeping quiet wasn't my thing. I'd never been known as

a person who minced her words, but Noah looked so...happy.

I didn't want to ruin it by complaining about his staff. After all, they were like family to Noah and had been with him since his release from prison.

Who was I to come in and screw that up?

The girl who ran out on him when things got tough?

Nodding against his chest, I whispered, "I'm good, Noah."

"Do you want to do some reading?"

My head shot up in surprise. "Do you?"

Noah shrugged. "I've been thinking about Hope's story that we were reading..."

"*Love Recaptured*?" I squealed, clapping excitedly. "It's her best work yet."

"Yeah." Noah smirked. "Get your Kindle out. I want to know what happens."

Blinking rapidly, I repressed the urge to swoon. "So you fight, you work out, you're hot, *and* you like the same books as I do?" Fanning myself dramatically, I grinned like an idiot.

"What can I say?" He shot back with a cocky smirk. "I'm perfect."

24

I couldn't feel my ass.

Never mind being asleep, I was fairly certain my butt cheeks were flat out dead.

Sitting on an upturned crate in the corner of a down-trodden gym for the past eight hours wasn't exactly my idea of fun times, but Noah was on fire tonight.

I'd never seen a man do so many chin ups in my life.

I'd stopped counting at eighty-seven – I'd had to because if I had to watch Quincy punch Noah in the gut one more time during a chin up I was going to kick some ass of my own.

It was a masochistic training regime; taking a beating while working every muscle in his body to the max – but it worked for Noah.

He seemed to thrive on the pain and intensity.

We had arrived in Dallas just before noon this morning, and just like he'd always done in every new place we'd stayed since we arrived in the states, Noah went straight to the gym to check out his latest facilities.

It didn't matter what city we were in, Noah always

sought out the gyms populated by lower middle class to work out in.

It was obvious that he preferred being around people similar to those he'd grown up with. Fancy equipment and shiny boxing rings weren't my husband's thing.

He was a backstreet fighter, he made no apologies for who he was and how he was raised, and his fans loved him more for it.

And me being the pathetic, career-less woman I was, tagged along with him.

It was now a quarter after eight in the evening and I was bloody starving.

The fans that had been in the gym earlier had graciously dispersed an hour or two ago, giving Noah some time to focus on his training for his upcoming fight tomorrow night.

The only ones left now were Noah, Quincy, Tommy, Beau, Lewis, and three other men whose names I didn't know – or care to learn.

I'd met so many new people lately that I'd quickly given up trying to remember names. The only ones I kept count of were the ones who were continuously present.

As usual, I sat alone in the corner, and as usual, no one spoke to me. I was dutifully ignored by every member of Noah's team.

At least they were consistent in their treatment of me.

Lucky was out running 'errands'. I knew what kind of errands Lucky was running and they involved the illegal kind.

He was hunting around every lowdown bar and strip joint in town for JD and his men.

He did the same thing every time we arrived in a new place, and to be fair to Lucky, he was very thorough because none of us had gotten so much as a whiff of JD or his gang of goons since Ireland.

The guys thought I didn't know about their little *routine*, but I was blonde, not stupid.

"Teagan?"

Lifting my head, I noticed Beau walking toward me and I think I withered a little inside.

Oh god, this was all I needed...

It was a real pity Beau was such an asshole.

His good looks and pretty blue eyes were overshadowed by that horrible personality of his.

"Yes?" I forced myself to say when Beau was standing in front of me, clad in his standard gym attire that consisted of shorts and a wife beater.

"You're distracting him," Beau said coldly, arms crossed over his chest. "Quincy wants you out of here while he's training."

What was new? "Quincy never wants me anywhere Noah is," I replied in a weary tone.

Yeah, being unwanted was a joy to behold...

Inhaling a calming breath, I placed the paperback that I had been reading down on my lap before answering him.

"Look, Beau." I was trying real hard to stay out of these assholes' way. "I'm not bothering anyone. I'm sitting in the corner." Picking up my book, I waved it in front of my face. "*Reading.*"

"Don't get comfortable, Teagan," Beau hissed in a low tone before slowly backing away. "Your time here is temporary."

"Yeah, yeah," I shot back, smothering my hurt with sarcasm, as I waved him off with my hand. "I'm nothing but a whore draped in Noah's money." Refocusing on my paperback, I pretended that I didn't care that nobody liked me, and in all honesty, I'd endured worse bullies in my life. Beau and the guys were a litter of kittens in comparison to Ellie Dennis and Reese Tanner.

Ugh, the mere thought of Reese's name caused every nerve in my body to stand on end.

One of these days I was going to cut that bitch.

It was a silent vow I had made to myself when I discovered she had raped my husband – one that I re-pledged when I discovered she would inevitably show up on this tour at some stage.

Unable to push the *she-bitch* from my mind, I tucked my book into my purse and stormed through the gym in the direction of Noah. I had too much anger burning inside of me, and Beau's taunts and threats only antagonized me further. "Will she be there tomorrow night?" I demanded when I reached my husband.

Stopping the punching bag he had been pummeling from swaying, Noah wiped a fine layer of sweat from his brow with his forearm. "Will who be where tomorrow night?" He was breathing hard and was dripping in sweat.

"That bitch Reese Tanner," I all but snarled. Anger burned inside of me. "Do you know when we'll see her again?" Noah had a fight tomorrow night. Those fights were always followed by after parties. I needed to know if I was going to run into her again. I wanted to be prepared...

"I couldn't care less about that woman, Thorn," Noah told me in a breathless tone. "And neither should you."

"She's going to get her comeuppance for what she did to you." I rested my hip against the huge training bag, and mentally patted Noah on the back for being able to make this two-hundred-pound bag bend like his bitch.

"I've been known to throw a mean right hook, you know,"

I added, making a conscious effort not to drool over my husband. He wasn't making it easy though.

Bobbing back and forth on his bare feet, Noah looked inhumanly beautiful. Clad only in a pair of black shorts, his muscles were on full display, not to mention his sinfully sexy tattoos.

On Noah's back was a huge crucifix with wings sprouting out of each side. The wolf on his left calf had been there for as long as I'd known him. His arms were covered in swirls and loops.

My eyes wandered over his stomach to the Celtic scribe on his hip bone and then to the red rose on his side with a jagged lone thorn sticking out.

Letting out a grunt that sounded like a mixture of impatience and lust, Noah hooked his hands under my arms and lifted me out of the way.

"Stem the homicidal notions, Thorn." Pressing a quick kiss to my forehead, he fell back into stance, fists up. "She's not worth the hassle."

"No," I countered evenly. "But you are."

"Am I?" He muttered under his breath. "Could've fooled me."

Ouch...

I would *not* cry.

I refused to give any of these bastards the satisfaction of knowing they were getting to me.

I could handle their jeers and their hate, but I couldn't handle that from Noah.

He hadn't thrown shit at me for a while and I'd honestly hoped that we were over that part...

"I'm here," I offered, loathing myself for my weakness. "I'm with you." Folding my arms across my self protectively, I forced back a cold shiver. "I've given up my whole life to follow you."

So let me back in...

Stopping the punching bag once more, Noah turned and faced me. "I'm sorry, Thorn." He was slightly breathless. Sweat trickled from his brow as his eyes roamed over my body. "I shouldn't have said that," he added before falling back into a furious pattern of uppercuts and body blows.

"No," I whispered in defeat before turning away and heading back to my crate. "You shouldn't."

Out of the corner of my eye I spotted Lucky had returned from his errands and was prowling toward me with a pair of boxing gloves.

I sagged in visible relief.

Lucky was fast becoming my best friend around here.

His eyes met mine and he smirked. "Ready for round two, Blondie?"

I forced a smile and crooked a finger toward him. "I was born ready."

25

NOAH

*M*y wife was too damn sexy for her own good.

Teagan looked fucking gorgeous as she bounced around on the gym mats, fists primed in front of her face – like a spunky little kitten – poised and ready to pounce on Lucky.

My former cellmate who was enabling this sparring session, was grinning at Teagan fondly – too fondly.

In fact, he was too fucking close to her altogether.

He needed to back up and quickly.

This playacting friendship those two had quickly struck up was riling me up.

I was beyond agitated and I didn't like it.

Not one fucking bit.

"Concentrate Messina," Quincy snapped, drawing me back to the task at hand.

Shaking my head, I dropped back and began jabbing the speed bag furiously. I couldn't concentrate worth a damn when she was here, and when she wasn't, my concentration levels were even worse.

I was a fuck up.

Sabotaging my goddamn marriage with cheap jabs and pathetic fucking grudges.

Goddammit, I wanted to kick my own ass for being such a dick to her...

I'd been trying so hard to put it all behind me, and hell, I'd been doing a good job.

"Good. Good. Good. Atta boy. Now...Release!"

I did.

Putting every ounce of strength I had in my body into my left fist, I slammed it against the bag, enjoying the feel of pressure in my muscles as the bag jolted back and forth violently.

"Good, now switch," Quincy ordered, breaking through my thoughts, and immediately my foot pattern changed.

I fell into stance, jabbing with my left, a sensation that was fucking alien to me.

Jabbing viciously, I worked myself up until my last ounce of energy released in the form of a right hook.

"God fucking dammit, Messina," Q snarled, tossing a bottle of water at me. "You couldn't beat on a pussy with that right hook."

"You don't beat on a pussy, Q," I shot back, stopping the bag with my hands. "You worship a pussy." Reaching down, I picked up the water bottle and took a deep swig. "You make that pussy yours."

Moving over to the heavy bag, I fell into stance, throwing punch after punch, enjoying the pain rippling through my body with every blow.

"You fuck pussy." Slamming my fist against the bag, I turned my head toward Quincy and smirked. "If you're fighting a pussy then you're doing something very wrong."

"You're a smart ass, ain't you?" Quincy shot back, red faced. "Think you're the only one who's been at the top of the food chain?" Snarling, he turned his attention to the bag. "I was the king of this world long before you were a twinkle in your daddy's eye, Messina," he growled, slamming his fist into the bag. "Remember that."

I watched as Quincy stalked out of the gym, followed by Pepe, Fornez, and Kabrich, three suits from one of my main sponsors.

My attention quickly landed on Thorn and Lucky play-acting around.

Immediately, I was incensed with this visceral urge to mark my territory.

Jesus Christ.

My feet were moving toward her before my brain could catch up.

"That wife of yours is like a miniature ninja," Lucky chuckled as he dodged Teagan's flawing fists.

"Can you give us..." I let my words trail off as Lucky nodded, quickly getting my drift.

"Okay, time out Blondie," he called out to Teagan. Holding his hands up, he slowly backed away from us. "I need a smoke."

"Can we talk?" I asked, turning my attention on Thorn when Lucky was out of earshot.

I needed to fix this, somehow.

I just wasn't sure how.

"Nope," Thorn huffed. "I'm busy."

"Doing what?" I shot back, amused. "Looks like you've lost your sparring partner."

"Keep on walking, King Dick," she countered, face red. "I've had enough verbal sparring for one day."

"I'll let you hit me," I offered, feeling like the king of dicks for hurting her.

"Fine," Teagan growled, turning to face me. "I'll spar with you if you promise not to go easy on me."

Cocking a brow, I smirked. "I don't hit girls, *baby*."

"Let's go, Messina," she growled, holding her fists up all fucking wrong as she danced around the mat. "Hit me with your best shot."

I stood with my hands on my hips and a shit eating grin on my face as I watched my little Thorn stalk me, pouncing at me like a playful kitten and then skipping a few feet out of my reach, concentration etched on her pretty face.

"Careful," I teased, blocking one of her jabs with the palm of my hand. "You don't want to break a nail."

Teagan's face reddened in frustration and I let her pound me.

"I'm going to K.O your ass," she hissed, throwing her fists wildly toward my midsection.

I considered it foreplay for later when I would return the favor and pound into her.

Stepping closer, Teagan faltered when I reached out and clenched her hip with one hand.

Hooking my foot under hers, I toppled her with one clean sweep.

She hit the mat with a thud, with me landing on top of her.

"If you were a gentleman, you'd let me beat you," she groaned, eyes closed, as she lay on her back on the mat.

"I thought you said I wasn't supposed to take it easy on you?"

Straddling Teagan's hips, I pinned her arms above her head and smiled. "And whatever gave you the impression that I was a gentleman?"

Her sweat glistened chest was rising and falling quickly, causing me all sorts of problems.

Lowering my face to hers, I pulled her swollen bottom lip into my mouth and sucked.

"You...ake...e...so...ad," she growled, struggling to speak. "The...orst... kind of...oad...age."

Chuckling, I released her lip and claimed the soft skin on her neck that was covering her hammering pulse. "Road rage?" I teased. "We're in a gym, Thorn."

"And now you're laughing at me and making me even madder," she moaned. "Perfect. Thanks for that, asshole."

"I'm sorry," I confessed guiltily.

Teagan tensed beneath me.

Pressing a soft kiss to her skin, I tucked my face into her neck and sighed. "About earlier...about everything."

"Don't do it again, Noah," she whispered. Sighing heavily, she wrapped her glove covered hands around my neck. "I'm tired of having my past thrown in my face."

A sudden shadow fell over us, followed by the sound of someone clearing their throat.

"Are you going to get some actual training done today, Noah?" Tommy asked, annoyance evident in his tone, as he glared down at us. "Don't make me ban her from the gym – because I will."

"I bet you'd love that," Teagan muttered under her breath, eyes narrowed on Tommy.

Slapping her hands against my chest, Teagan pushed against me and said, "I'm going back to the hotel. I'll see you after training."

Reluctantly, I rolled off Teagan and let her up. I remained on the mats, watching until she had stalked out of the gym, followed closely by Lewis.

"Was that necessary?" I asked, climbing to my feet.

"She's screwing with your form, Noah," Tommy shot back, unapologetically. "You've been missing training sessions. The ones you show up to, you're constantly distracted. You have a fight tomorrow, man."

Shaking his head, he added, "If you don't start getting your head in the game, Conroy is going to hand your ass to you."

"The only person who's gonna get his ass handed to him is you if you don't start being nicer to her." I had enough problems without having to worry about this crap.

He was convinced she would be the prime ingredient in my downfall.

Either way, I wasn't giving her up again.

I loved her harder than I knew what to do with it.

"Everything and everyone she knows is on the other side of the Atlantic Ocean and you need to start being a little more welcoming."

"I am being nice to her," Tommy shot back with a glare. "Nicer than she deserves after all the shit she's pulled on you."

"Be. *Nicer*," I warned him. "I mean it. Teagan is my wife. I won't have you disrespect her."

"We'll see how long that lasts," Tommy muttered under his breath.

"Don't make me choose," I snarled before turning my back on my best friend. "You won't win."

26

NOAH

"There is something very wrong with you," Lucky drawled as he leaned his back against the bar, whiskey tumbler in his hand. "Seriously. You're an asshole."

He didn't have to tell me what I already knew.

"I fucked up earlier," I admitted, knowing full well what Lucky was talking about. My stupid fucking comment to Teagan in the gym. He'd heard it and he was letting me know that he wasn't impressed.

"So you did," Lucky mused, pressing a bottle to his lips. "So you continue to."

Ordering two glasses of whiskey from the bartender, Lucky pushed one toward me.

"Keep fucking up and you'll be sleeping on your own." Picking up his tumbler, he tossed the amber liquid down his throat before setting the glass back down. "Permanently."

"I'm *trying*," I said in a warning tone not to push me.

"Then *try* harder," he shot back just as vehemently. "That's your woman, asshole. In the flesh." With that, Lucky walked off muttering something about needing a smoke, leaving me alone at the bar.

Sinking down on one of the stools, I tossed my drink back and ordered another one.

I wasn't supposed to be drinking, I was on a strict regime, but the more whiskey I poured down my throat, the more tension drained from my body.

Lucky was right.

I was an asshole.

I needed to make it up to Teagan – make her happy.

I could do that with sex.

Hell, I made her happy every fucking night with my dick, but I needed to give her more.

She deserved more from me...

"No prizes for why you're drinking the night before a fight?" Tommy's voice filled my ears and I bit back a groan. "Woman troubles?"

He was all I fucking needed right now.

"Careful T," I warned in a low tone. "I'm feeling really unstable right now." Picking up another glass, I tossed it back and flagged down the bartender to bring me another. "One word against my wife and I'm going to lose my shit."

Taking a seat on the stool beside me, Tommy continued to goad me. "You're slacking in the gym, Noah. You're distracted and your form is weakening. Gaps are opening in your defenses. We've all noticed."

Standing up, I knocked back another drink. "Shut the fuck up, T." Stepping around my bar stool, I walked over to my oldest friend and said, "Let's not pretend this intervention has anything to do with my form."

He didn't even try to deny the fact that this conversation had nothing to do with my fighting and everything to do with my marriage.

Holding onto my temper by the skin of my teeth, I

leaned into Tommy's face and said, "If you can't respect my wife then you have no business working for me."

"Noah..."

I was done.

Turning around, I stalked out of the bar and headed straight for the elevators.

Slamming my hand down on the keypad, I stepped inside and continued up to the top floor of the hotel.

I spent a good five minutes standing outside our suite, calming myself down before going inside.

Lewis, head of security, was outside standing guard, and right about now he was the only one doing what he was fucking paid to do.

When I found my wife, she was sitting cross-legged in the middle of our bed with her acoustic guitar resting on her lap. With her eyes closed, Teagan strummed her fingers against the strings as she sang her own version of Banks' *Beggin for Thread.*

Her throaty tone set alight every nerve in my body.

The words wrapped around my heart like ivy.

I could listen to her sing for the rest of my life and never grow tired.

"I forget I'm not there anymore," I blurted out when Thorn had finished her song.

Her eyes sprang open in surprise. "God Noah," she breathed, sagging against her guitar. "You almost gave me a heart attack."

"I meant in prison or in a ring – that was a beautiful song by the way," I continued to say as I approached her. "Thorn, the way I was brought up... I'm used to being hard. Being on guard. Being... cruel." Sinking down on the edge of the bed, I sighed heavily. "But with you, everything's different."

Frowning, Teagan set her guitar down on the bed before

crawling over to where I was sitting. "Noah, what's going on?"

"Throwing the past in your face earlier." I dropped my head in shame. "It was shitty of me." My shoulders sagged. "I don't know why I did it."

"Oh, that?" Teagan waved her hand in the air like it was nothing. "No biggie." Waggling her perfectly shaped eyebrows, Teagan fell onto her back and patted the mattress beside her, winking suggestively. "If you're feeling bad about it, I know several ways you can make it up to me."

"Be serious," I shot back, feeling too guilty to joke around. "You were upset."

She shrugged. "And now I'm over it." Biting down on her bottom lip, she purred, "Last chance, *Machine!*"

"You're so lovable." Tossing myself onto my back, I laid down beside my wife and turned my face to hers. "Do you know that? I never had a fighting chance with you, did I?"

"Noah, it's okay." Reaching down, Teagan took my hand in hers, entwining our fingers. "I'm not leaving again."

I'd been a dick and she was reassuring me, understanding me.

Christ, this woman never ceased to amaze me.

"Let's go out."

"What?" Excitement sparkled in her hazel eyes. "Where would we go?"

"Wherever you want," I shot back with a smirk, desperate to please her. "Just the two of us."

Spending time alone together was something I knew we both desperately needed.

"Okay," Teagan squealed, leaping onto her knees in a move that would have made a ninja envious. "The latest *Jurassic Park* movie is out. We could go see it?"

I nodded. "Sounds good."

"Okay then." Pressing a quick kiss to my lips, she leapt off the bed like a woman on a mission. Racing over to her purse that was resting on the back of a chair, Teagan dug inside it and retrieved her phone.

"Let's see." She scrolled through her phone for a few minutes before saying, "There's a showing at nine at the theater three blocks from here?"

Teagan's phone suddenly began to ring in her hands. Frowning, she swiped her finger across the screen and placed it to her ear. "Hope. What's up? Hope? Hello?"

"What's up?" I asked, sitting up.

Teagan shook her head in confusion. "She must have called me by accident...omigod!" Slamming her phone against her chest, Teagan ran over to where I was sitting and turned on her loudspeaker.

Immediately the sound of Jordan and Hope's voices filled the room.

"You had this amazing family," Jordan was saying. *"And you had my dad, Hope. Mine. I never got shit from him, but all of you guys did. Derek chose your family over my mom – over me."*

My gaze immediately went to Teagan, whose eyes were bulging so much they looked like they were about to pop out of their sockets.

"I'm not your father, Hope!" Jordan continued to say. *"That perfect love? You won't get that from me because I can't give you* normal. *And you deserve normal."*

This wasn't right.

Listening in on their private conversation.

"Maybe we should hang –"

"Shh!" Teagan interrupted, clamping her hand over my mouth.

"You're afraid to give me more," Hope shot back in a furious

tone of voice. *"You're a coward, Jordan Porter. Tell me the truth. Dammit, be honest with me for once in your life."*

"You want honesty? Fine. I'm not the person you think I am," Jordan roared. *"Don't push for more, Hope. You don't want to know the truth."*

"I do!" Hope screamed back at him. *"Tell me. Give me a goddamn explanation for why you left?"*

"You'll never look at me the same way again..."

"Tell me!" She screamed louder. *"Give me something. Dammit to hell, Jordan, stop hiding behind your built up walls and tell me!"*

"You want to know?"

"Yes!"

"You really want to know?"

"Yes, Jordan. Dammit, I want to know..."

"Fine," he roared, voice breaking. *"I was..."*

"Okay," I interrupted, ending the call.

"No!" Teagan screamed, throwing her hands up in sheer dismay. "*Why*?" She asked in a pained tone. "Why would you do that to me?" She looked truly distraught. "He was about to tell her something!"

"Exactly," I shot back. "He was about to tell *Hope* something – not us."

"I can't believe you ruined that for me," she muttered sullenly.

"Believe it or not, I happen to have morals, Thorn," I chuckled. "And those morals include being against eavesdropping on people's private conversations."

"Well I don't." She glared at me. "This is the worst kind of cliffhanger."

27

NOAH

*M*ortification wasn't the reaction I'd been hoping for when I handed my wife the bridal set I'd bought her from *Tiffany's,* but that's what I got.

Maybe I should have chosen a more private location to give her the gift. A gym full of sweaty men wasn't exactly romantic.

I was fucking clueless...

"You can exchange them for something else if you don't like them," I said as I watched Teagan study the diamond engagement ring and matching wedding band. "I know you said you wanted something more permanent, but every man should buy his wife a ring." Or at least that's what I'd thought.

Going off Teagan's reaction, I'd got it wrong. *Very* wrong.

"Noah," she whispered, cheeks reddening. "It's too much." Swallowing deeply, she looked up at me. "These must have cost you a fortune."

One hundred and thirty grand, but I wasn't about to tell her that.

"You're worth it," I said instead. "And a hell of a lot more besides." She needed to know that our wedding might have happened on a whim, but our marriage was something I'd been planning for a long time.

There was only one woman for me, the only person I'd ever commit myself to for a lifetime, and she needed to know that woman was her.

"They're perfect," she whispered, cheeks stained pink. With shaking hands, I watched Teagan slide both rings onto her ring finger.

"So am I forgiven?" I dared to broach the subject. "For hanging up on the call?"

"I suppose you are." Teagan cocked a brow, clearly deep in thought. "If you promise to never tease me about the dinosaur thing ever again."

"THANKS FOR THIS," TEAGAN SAID. SHE HAD TAKEN A SEAT IN THE back row of the theater and I had handed her the bucket of popcorn she'd demanded. "It means a lot," she continued to say with her mouth full of popcorn.

"It's fine, Thorn." Guilt swarmed inside me as I took my seat beside my wife.

She shouldn't have to thank me for taking her to the goddamn movies.

It was something I should be doing on a regular basis.

Reaching my arm around her slim shoulders, I pulled her close.

"I've heard good things about this one," she said, snuggling into my side.

Teagan continued to ramble on throughout the entire movie and my mind continued to torment me with images of her with that prick...

"I need to leave," Teagan blurted out toward the end of the movie, startling the shit out of me.

"Why? What's up?" I turned to look at her and was fucking horrified to see tears streaming down her face. "Jesus, Teagan, are you okay?"

"I-I can't..." Blubbering, she wiped her nose with a tissue I hadn't realized she'd been holding and shuddered. "They killed him, Noah."

"Yeah..." Confused, I looked back at the screen to see if I was missing something.

Nope, I wasn't.

"Thorn, he was the bad guy, baby."

"It's just so sad," she sobbed into the tissue. "I didn't want him to die."

I racked my brain. "The guy just killed millions of innocents?" Was she kidding? "You didn't want him to die?"

"Don't make me feel bad for it," she wailed, jerking out of her seat...

SMOTHERING MY LAUGHTER, I DRAGGED MY THOUGHTS BACK to the present and nodded. "Consider it done."

"Whatcha got there, man?" Tommy said when he came to stand beside me, eyes locked on Teagan's hand.

"Nothing," Teagan was quick to reply.

Frowning in confusion, I watched as she tucked her hands behind her back.

Letting out a whistle, Tommy reached out and grabbed Teagan's hand. "You better win your next three fights if you want to break even after buying *that*."

"I didn't ask him to buy it," Teagan hissed, looking up at Tommy like she'd done something illegal.

"What?" Shaking my head, I looked down at my wife. "He knows that, Thorn," I said slowly. "Right, T?"

"Right, man," Tommy agreed. "It suits you, Teagan," he offered before wandering off in the direction of the punching bags.

"Why are you so embarrassed?" I asked her once Tommy was out of earshot. "Is it because of the price? Because Tommy was only screwing around about winning three fights, Thorn. I can easily afford it."

Teagan's face flushed bright red. "It's just... I'm not used to this," she confessed, biting down on her plump lower lip. "The last present I got from a man was –" She frowned for a moment before looking up at me. "Well, from *you*. Back when we were in high school."

An abnormal amount of guilt shot through me then.

Guilt for being gone all those years.

Guilt for not being there for her...

"Well, get used to it," I said, tone gruff and thick with emotion. "Because this is only the start of what's to come."

28

TEAGAN

"What are you doing down there?"

Lucky's voice sounded from above me and I groaned internally.

Busted...

Looking up from my perch, I smiled sheepishly. "Hey."

"Hey back." Lucky's blue eyes searched mine, clearly looking for an answer to my unusual dining preferences. "Care to explain why you're sitting in a bathroom stall eating your lunch?"

"Only if you care to explain why you're peeking over said bathroom stall to ask me," I shot back with a smirk, tucking my dog-eared paperback back into my bag.

"I was worried about you," Lucky replied without a hint of embarrassment. "Haven't seen you around all day."

"That's because I've been hiding." Standing up, I tucked my half-eaten sandwich back into my bag before opening the stall door and stepping out.

"From who?"

Falling into step beside me, Lucky followed me back into Noah's dressing room.

"The three hounds of the Baskerville," I offered, not caring that Lewis was standing at the door of the dressing room, dutifully guarding me from *nothing*.

"Ah," Lucky said knowingly. "The delightful trio that consists of Beau, Tommy, and Q."

Nodding, I tossed my bag down on the wooden bench, and sank down beside it. "They're such a bunch of assholes, Luck," I whispered, finding myself confiding in my husband's former cellmate who had come to sit beside me. "Tommy is still judging me based on my seventeen-year-old self." Dropping my head in my hands, I stifled a groan. "And Quincy and Beau are hating on me because Tommy told them a bunch of ugly stories about me." I inhaled a shaky breath before looking up at him. "I'm not that girl from high school who goes around breaking guitars off her boyfriend's head or destroys his car with paint anymore..."

"Wait?" Lucky interrupted, holding his hand up. "You broke a guitar off Noah's head?" When I nodded, Lucky burst out laughing. "Badass, Teegs. Bad-fucking-ass."

Shame crept through me at the memory.

"I did worse than that," I admitted. "A lot worse."

Lucky was quiet for a long moment before he said, "People change, Teagan."

"Yeah, they do." And I wished like hell everybody else would realize that, too. "I don't care though," I added, lying through my teeth. "I don't need anyone's approval to feel validated."

I didn't but it would be nice.

It wasn't easy not fitting in everywhere I went.

"I'm here for Noah," I reaffirmed. *Not his money...*

The memory of Tommy's expression when Noah had given me a credit card the other day was still imprinted in my mind. I didn't care about his cash. I didn't care about anything except Noah.

Why couldn't they get that?

"The guys can think what they like."

"Hurts though," Lucky replied carefully. "Being the odd one out."

"No," I shot back. "I'd have to care about them for it to hurt, and I don't."

"Whatever you say, blondie," he chuckled. "But for what it's worth, I find you thoroughly amusing."

"Thanks..." I cocked a brow and studied the grin on his face. "I think?"

"It's a compliment," he reassured me with a wink. "Keep doing you, Teagan. Be yourself and eventually everything will fall into place for you."

"It's just so exhausting," I admitted, my voice barely more than a whisper. "Constantly having to watch my back around them... and I miss home." But I knew I would miss Noah more if I weren't here. "Forget I said that." I shook my head. "I'm just being dumb."

"It's not dumb," Lucky countered quickly. "It's human nature." Shrugging, he added, "I'd miss home, too, if my roommate looked like yours." He let out a whistle and pulled at the collar of his shirt dramatically. "I ain't never seen a woman like her before."

"As much as I think you'd be good for her," and weirdly enough, I *did* think Lucky would be good for Hope, "she's taken," I told him. "Hope has been in love with Jordan since the day she was born."

"Who?" Lucky cocked a brow. "The flinching guy?"

"The *what* guy?"

"That guy who was with her in the hotel?" Lucky informed me. "Well, he flinches. A lot."

"How do you even know these things?"

"God gave us two ears, two eyes and one mouth for a reason, blondie." I rolled my eyes which caused Lucky to laugh. "You don't agree?"

"Lucky, all I know is that I don't fit in here." That was the understatement of the century. One month on tour and it was safe to say that I was most definitely the cat amongst the pigeons – or in my case, the pigeon amongst the cats.

"That makes two of us."

Lucky's response caused me to turn and frown at him.

"What?" He chuckled. "Do you honestly think they want his former cellmate on tour with them?" Lucky cocked a brow and grinned. "Teegs, you may be the scarlet woman, but I'm Noah's white-trash homeboy."

"White-trash homeboy?" That brought a smile to my lips. "You do realize that from now on, every time I look at you, the words of The Offspring's *Pretty Fly for a White Guy* will be playing in my head?"

"Do you wanna know a secret?" Lucky teased, his blue eyes dancing with mischief.

"Always," I shot back, shifting closer so Lewis didn't overhear us.

"Okay, but you can't tell anyone," he added, tone suddenly serious.

"I won't."

Cupping his hands around his mouth, Lucky leaned toward my ear and whispered, "I had that CD when I was a kid."

"You dick." Shaking my head, I poked him in the side with my elbow. "I thought you were going to actually tell me something real."

"It was a real CD," he shot back innocently. "A good one, too."

"Something real about *your life*, Luck," I grumbled.

"There's really not much to tell," Lucky said after a pause. "I was just your stereotypical good-guy. I did *good* things for people. I got *good* grades." He stared straight ahead as he spoke, jaw clenched. "And then bad came into my life. And *bad* took all the *good* away."

I didn't know what to say.

Noah had told me what had happened to Lucky's girl-friend, but I didn't want to bring it up until Lucky told me personally. He was hurting. I could see the pain in his eyes. The unresolved anger and silent rage.

My god, Lucky was hurting so bad inside...

So in typical Teagan fashion, I said the first thing that came to mind in my bid to cheer him up. "I'm allergic to latex."

"You're allergic to latex," Lucky deadpanned.

"Yep." I nodded.

"How does that even *happen*?"

"Oh, it happens," I replied solemnly. "And it's no joke." With that, I began to animatedly recall the first time I real-ized my aversion to the proteins inside latex rubber...

NOAH AND *I* HAD BEEN SLEEPING IN MY ROOM AND *I'D* WOKEN UP *fifteen minutes ago, feeling like someone had doused my vagina in gasoline and set me on fire.*

"Jesus Christ, it burns!" I howled as I stood in the bathtub in the upstairs bathroom of Uncle Max's house with the shower nozzle directed towards my thighs. "What did you do to me?"

"Nothing, I swear!" Noah shot back in a hushed voice, pleading his innocence as he drew back the shower curtain. "Keep your voice down," he added. "Your uncle is right down the hall."

Noah wasn't supposed to be in my house – let alone in my

bathroom with me naked, but I didn't care about that right now. All I cared about in this moment was the fact that my vagina was killing me.

"Oh shit," Noah choked out when his eyes locked on my inner thighs. "Thorn..."

"I'm on fire," I wept, keeping a continual, steady flow of ice cold water on my...area. "Noah, make it stop. Please..."

Running a hand through his hair in despair, Noah leapt into the tub in his boxer shorts.

Dropping to his knees at my feet, he began to blow – and not in a sexy way. "God, baby, your skin is blistering!"

"Why is this happening to me?" I cried out, grimacing in agony.

"I don't know," Noah shrieked back. "I've never...I don't..."

The bathroom door slammed inward so hard that it knocked against the opposite wall, and in walked my uncle.

"Oh my god," I screamed out, grabbing at the shower curtain. "Get out!"

"Jesus," Noah grunted, quickly climbing to his feet to shield my body from view. Lamely, he said, "This isn't what it looks like, Dr. Jones."

"She's allergic to latex," Uncle Max announced in a livid tone as he picked up a towel from the hamper and tossed it at Noah before throwing another at me. "And I gather from the area she's having a reaction in, it's from a condom."

"Oh my god," I repeated, dying on my feet of mortification.

"I didn't know," Noah shot back, horrified. He turned to look at me. "I didn't know, Thorn."

"I'm going downstairs to get some antihistamines for my niece," Max said in a deathly cold tone of voice before turning his back on us. "If I find you still here when I get back, I'll have you arrested for trespassing..."

·   ·   ·

"I DON'T KNOW WHAT'S MORE DISTURBING ABOUT THIS picture," Lucky chuckled when I finished giving him a rundown. "Noah trying to blow on you, your uncle walking in on you two, or the fact that you just told me all of that in vivid detail?"

I grinned. "I tend to be over-divulging when I'm around people I trust."

He raised a brow. "And you trust me?"

"Is there a reason I shouldn't?" I countered with a smirk.

Lucky shrugged. "The rap sheet from my old correctional officer would drum up several reasons not to."

"Look at me." I raised my left hand in his face. "I'm married to Noah Messina. Do you think I care what some stupid rap sheet says?"

29

TEAGAN

*I*f someone was to ask me to describe my feelings for Quincy Jones, then I would have to tell them this:

I hated my husband's coach with every fiber of my being. I loathed him worse than I did the dark, and I wished him a lifetime of uncontrollable bowel movements.

Unfortunately for me, hating the man didn't make him disappear.

Being nice to him didn't help my cause either.

So instead I tried to ignore him.

I ignored his cruel comments and I forced myself to hold my tongue when all I wanted to do was go batshit crazy on his dumb ass.

Like earlier tonight for instance, when Noah knocked Demetri Malloy out in the first round.

Instead of actually being happy for his protégé, Quincy had chewed Noah up for not giving the crowd a better fight.

And then, when we'd arrived at the casino styled nightclub to celebrate Noah's victory, Quincy had hissed the words, "Sit down, look pretty, and keep that smart mouth of yours shut," in my ear before dragging my husband off to mingle, leaving me all alone with Dick One and Three.

Sipping on my glass of chardonnay, I pretended Tommy and Beau's stares and dirty looks weren't affecting me, when in truth, they were making me feel all of two feet tall.

I knew what they said about me behind my back – and to my face.

I knew they wanted me off this tour.

The only thing I wasn't sure of was the lengths they were prepared to go to in order to make that happen...

"Do you have a drinking problem?" Beau asked as he studied my almost completely drained glass.

"That would be her father," Tommy offered up.

"Did you know that alcoholism is an inherited gene?" Beau taunted. "A genetic defection – a mutation of sorts that is passed down." Shrugging, he added, "Maybe you should get yourself tested."

"Maybe you two should get yourselves a hobby," I shot back, forcing my features to remain impassive, even though I was breaking inside. "That way you wouldn't have so much time on your hands to worry about my family genetics."

Standing up with as much dignity as I could muster, I placed my glass down on the table and walked away from them before I caved and showed them how much their words had hurt.

Slipping through the crowd, I didn't stop walking until I was inside the ladies' bathroom, with a stall door barricading me from the rest of the world.

Lowering the lid of the toilet, I sank down and dropped my head in my hands.

Even though I was mentally ordering myself not to cry, traitorous tears continued to fill my eyes.

I wasn't sure if I could take much more of this.

I loved Noah. I did. But those guys were making my life miserable.

I was lonely and I desperately wanted to go home.

But I couldn't bail on him.

Not twice.

That's why I kept my mouth shut when the guys threw jibes at me.

That's why I pretended I didn't care.

That's why I was currently sitting on a grime infested toilet lid and weeping into my hands.

———

WHEN I FINALLY MANAGED TO COMPOSE MYSELF, I LET MYSELF out of the toilet cubicle and walked back through the bar to our booth.

Ignoring Beau and Tommy, who were still sitting around the table, I lowered myself onto my seat and stared straight ahead, refusing to make eye contact with the men who were determined to make my life a living hell.

I spotted Noah over by the bar and decided to focus my whole attention on him.

Stonewashed denim jeans hung low on his hips.

A crisp white shirt melded to his chest like a second skin, emphasizing his bulging muscles and deep, sun kissed tan.

His black hair was wet, ruffled, and as per usual, standing on the top of his head in that sexy, natural way.

A beer bottle hung loosely from his right hand as he leaned against the bar, deep in conversation with Lucky.

Rolling his shoulders, Noah twisted his head from side to side as he spoke to the man beside him, obviously loosening up from his fight earlier on tonight.

My mouth ran dry as I coveted him from my perch.

It didn't pass my attention that every female in the bar was gawking at my husband.

Knowing that all those women wanted him and he was going to bed with me tonight was one hell of an ego boost.

Every once and a while he took a sip from the bottle and when he did, my eyes immediately went to his throat.

Watching his Adam's apple bob as he swallowed caused the muscles deep in my groin to tighten and flex.

Lucky said something then – something funny –and Noah threw his head back and laughed.

It was a rare sight and I felt oddly jealous that I wasn't the one making him laugh.

Guilt churned inside me as I studied his handsome profile.

How could I even contemplate leaving him again?

As if he felt my gaze on him, Noah turned around.

His eyes roamed across the bar as if he was seeking me out, and when he found me, his gaze was so intense, his brown eyes penetrating me, owning me with a single glance.

He was choosing me with his eyes, claiming me with his smile, and owning me by just breathing.

It was at that moment I realized something; it didn't matter how much we hurt each other or how badly we fought, I was his beta and he was mine.

Our love was permanent and unfaltering.

It was so strange how Noah had forced his way into my world at seventeen and, just like that, my internal arrow had switched.

Without my permission, my heart had directed itself toward Noah Messina.

My soul had unanimously claimed his soul as its mate, and wherever he would go from that point on I was sure to follow, regardless of common sense, heedless of the consequences.

Turning his back on his friend, Noah prowled toward me and my toes curled in nervous anticipation. The way he bit down on his bottom lip caused my skin to tingle all over.

"Thorn," he acknowledged in a deep, gruff tone when he reached me.

His dark eyes flickered with heat, just like his infamous temper, except it wasn't anger I saw in his eyes tonight.

It was concern.

Snapping out of my lust induced trance, I forced a smile. "Noah," I replied, a little breathless.

His eyes were locked on my face and I couldn't look away.

Sitting down beside me, so close that I had to twist around to face him, Noah leaned into my ear and whispered, "You good, Thorn?"

His voice held a tint of uncertainty, though he hid it well.

"I'm good, Noah," I replied, not taking my eyes off him. "You?"

He took a swig from his bottle before settling it down in front of him. "Tired," he admitted gruffly. Leaning back in the seat, Noah turned his body to face me, giving me his full attention. "I could sleep for a year and it wouldn't be enough." He studied my face with dark, perceptive eyes. "What's wrong?"

Everything. "Nothing," I lied, forcing a smile. Twiddling my thumbs, I struggled to find something to say that wasn't going to ruin this rare moment of peace between us. "I'm in."

His dark brown eyes softened. "I know, Thorn. Me, too."

Hearing Noah say he was 'in' was more important than hearing the words 'I love you'. Being 'in' meant everything – he'd told me as much all those years ago. You could love someone but being in love with them was so much deeper – so much more.

Stateless' *Bloodstream* was blasting from a nearby speaker and I swear I felt the words of the song right down in my bones. It was as if the lyrics had been written to describe how I felt for this man. The love I felt for Noah... it was so overwhelmingly consuming.

Shifting closer to me, Noah drew me against him, encircling me in a haven of safety. "I'm so fucking nuts for you," he whispered in my ear and I had to bite back a moan.

His alcohol scented breath was fanning my cheek and when I felt his thumb brush over my bare thigh, my eyelids fluttered shut of their own accord. "My little Thorn."

Biting down hard on my lip, I sagged against him, wanting nothing more than to disappear inside my husband and never resurface. It was soft, tender, intimate moments like this that made all the guys' cruel comments and nastiness so worth it.

"I'm drunk," he added in a slightly slurred voice. "But I mean it, Thorn. I love you... I love you so fucking much."

"I believe you," I replied quickly in a pained tone as I clenched my eyes shut and inhaled the smell of his cologne and soap. I struggled to stay in my seat; the urge to climb onto Noah's lap and bury myself in his arms was almost too strong to resist. "I love you, too."

"When this tour's over and done with, I'm going to take you home," he continued to say. "Back to Ireland. Hell, I'll even face your uncle with you if that's what you want." Dipping his face to the curve of my neck, he nuzzled my skin with his nose. "Whatever it takes to make you happy and keep you happy." He pressed a kiss to my collarbone. "I'll do it."

The things he could make me do, the way he could alter my way of thinking.

He had so much power over me. I was weakened in his presence and built up in his absence.

Desperation mixed with raw emotion swirled through my veins, bounding me eternally to him.

He was my forever.

"I just want you, Noah," I choked out, drowning in my feelings for him. "You're my *home* and you're my *family*. All I want is a happy life with *you*."

We were running from danger and I was playing with fire by simply being with this man.

He was treacherous to my body, dangerous to my soul, and irresistible to my heart.

I couldn't contain my feelings. I was bursting at the seams with love for this man.

Passion was overriding my common sense – my sense of shame.

Everything evaporated around me and all I was left with was Noah.

"Noah Messina." I caressed his face with my hand, tracing over every line and curve that I'd already memorized by heart.

Noah closed his eyes as I touched him. "You have no idea what that does to me," he confessed, leaning into my touch, nuzzling the palm of my hand with his grizzly jaw. "Your touch." He exhaled a sharp breath. "Feeling you feeling me..."

My heart was going wild in my chest, hammering and fluttering against my ribcage. Every nerve in my body was alive with electricity as I trailed my fingers over the faint scar line above his left eyebrow, then the slight bump on the bridge of his nose that had been broken more than once before moving lower to stroke my thumb across his whiskered chin.

He was so beautiful.

Inside and out.

"Teagan Messina," Noah whispered tenderly, opening his eyes to look at me. A small smile broke out across his face. "I never had a fighting chance against you, had I?"

"I told you I could take you," I teased before leaning in and claiming his lips with mine.

Noah growled against my mouth.

His arms came around my waist.

Seconds later, he was pulling me onto his lap and taking control of the kiss. *Taking control of my heart...*

Digging his hands into my hair, Noah pulled my face toward his.

Dropping his face to touch mine, he stared so intently into my eyes that I almost couldn't handle the raw emotion of it all.

"You saved my life," he rasped, nails digging deeper into my scalp. I welcomed his touch. I savored the raw, rough feel of his touch. "From a life of crime." He kissed me hard before pulling back to look into my eyes. "From a future of being alone."

Sighing heavily, I trailed my fingers through his hair as both adoration and desperation coursed through me. "Noah, you never needed saving. You just needed to wake up."

"I'm awake now," he whispered, thrusting himself upward.

"Yeah?" I breathed, feeling his erection pressed against me.

His hands tightened on my waist. "Yeah."

30

NOAH

I couldn't keep my hands off Teagan all the way back to our hotel room.

Staggering out of the elevator with my wife wrapped around me, I kissed her frantically, hardly able to hold back. I wanted her so badly.

Her lips were on mine, our tongues dueling viciously; scorching me, burning me to within an inch of my life.

The alcohol in my veins, mixed with the adoration in my heart for this woman, was driving me out of my goddamn mind.

The moment we were inside our room with the door closed behind us, I was on her.

"I love you," she cried out when her back slammed against the door, with my body covering hers.

"I love you, too," I growled against her lips as I ripped at her little red dress, desperate to be buried inside. "So damn much."

Dropping my hands to her thighs, I dragged the tiny slip of a dress she had on over her head, exposing her bare breasts. "You're beautiful," I whispered as I palmed her small, perky breasts in my hands and ground my hips against her.

It didn't matter what color dress she wore, or whether she had fancy lingerie on or not.

My wife was a walking, breathing temptation to me.

One I could never resist.

"I want you inside me so bad," she begged, tightening her legs around my hips, thrusting her pelvis against me. "Now."

Slipping my hand inside the plain white cotton panties she had on, my breath hitched in my throat when I felt her slick heat.

"Christ, Thorn," I grunted, as my fingers slid inside her without effort. "You're soaking, baby."

"Yes...harder..." Moaning loudly, Teagan threw her head back as she rolled her hips against my touch and instantly, I knew what she needed. "Noah..."

Pulling my fingers out of her, I dropped my hands to cup her ass and walked her over to the bed before tossing her down on her back.

Ripping her panties from her body, I spread her eagle on the bed before dropping to my knees between her legs. Dipping my face to the apex of her thighs, I swiped my tongue down the length of her slit, reveling in the taste of her.

"Noah," she cried out. Entwining her fingers in my hair, Teagan pulled and yanked on my hair as I thumbed her clit with my hand and worshiped her pussy with my mouth.

"I could eat you all night," I growled, loving the sounds and mewling noises that came from her mouth. Christ, she was fucking heaven on my tongue. This woman... she had me.

All of me.

"Noah," she cried out again – louder this time.

Her fingers tightened in my hair. Her pussy clenched around me.

"I know," I purred, doubling my efforts to get her off.

I fucked her with my mouth, hard and rough, enjoying the control she was giving me, the pleasurable sounds from her throat.

She was close.

Fuck, she was almost there.

"I'm going to..."

I flicked her clit hard and she came apart around me, jerking violently beneath me.

31

TEAGAN

"*H*appy birthday to you. Happy birthday to you," I sang down the phone. "Happy birthday best buddy. Happy birthday to you..."

"Thanks," Hope replied sadly. "It's not the same without you here, though."

"I know." Hope and I had celebrated our last eight birthdays together. Being on opposite sides of the Atlantic Ocean for her twenty-sixth one felt all wrong. "Did you get my present?"

"The backup hard drive. Yeah. It was really thoughtful, babe."

"Don't say I'm not looking out for you," I teased, feeling elated at the sound of my best friend's voice.

"So how's married life on the road?"

I glanced across the table at Lewis, who was sitting opposite me, and then down at my plate. "It's..." *Lonely. Isolating. Nothing like what I thought it would be.* "Different."

I looked around at my surroundings, and then down at myself. I was sitting in the restaurant of the latest swanky hotel we were staying at. Noah was working out at the gym down the street and as usual, I was alone. It wasn't exactly the vision I'd anticipated when I'd left Ireland with Noah two months ago. "It's...yeah. It's definitely different."

"Good different?" Hope asked, letting her voice trail off.

I could hear the concern in her voice.

"It's good when I'm with Noah," I filled in brightly. *But those moments were far and few between...*

"And how often is that?" Hope countered observantly.

"He's a busy man," I replied defensively.

Because of his crazy work schedule, I hardly spent any time with Noah. In the ten weeks that we'd been on the road, I'd discovered that the life of a MFA fighter's wife was a lonely one.

When we were together at night, everything felt right for a little while. It was the only time we were completely alone... but then we woke up, and it was back to training and traveling...

"He has like a bazillion interviews every day and endorsement commitments to uphold." Not to mention his inhumanly intense training regime. "Did you know he's the face of Huzzah for Men?" I didn't, or at least I hadn't until last month. "They're like the biggest sports clothing company this side of the hemisphere."

"I did know, actually," Hope replied. "But I'm more concerned about you."

"I love him, Hope," I told her, biting my knuckle. Loving Noah made me weak. It made me pathetic and I loathed the woman I was turning into. "And it's only been a couple of months. Things will calm down after the tour."

I was clinging to that little spark of hope.

Praying like hell that one day soon we would be able to settle into a home – a permanent one.

"Are they still being jerks to you?" She asked, and I felt my cheeks turn pink.

I couldn't talk about it, not with Lewis sitting across from me, but I wanted to.

I wanted to piss and moan and howl to my best friend about the bullies that were making my life hell.

"Same as always," I replied, hoping that would be enough for Hope.

"And what about JD?" She asked. "Any more delightful bullets on pillows?"

"Hardly." I mentally sagged in relief. "We haven't gotten as much as a whiff from JD the Troll." *And long may it last.* "It's been blissfully quiet on the JD frontier."

"Thank god," Hope said with a sigh of relief. "I'm worried about you, Teegs."

"I'm safe," I assured her, feeling a stinging sensation in my eyes. "But I'm missing my best friend like crazy."

This was only the second phone call we'd had since I left Ireland in March.

We texted and emailed each other but it wasn't the same.

I missed her.

Hell, I missed Uncle Max, even though he was a stubborn jackass.

I missed Sean.

The people I'd spent the last seven years of my life with were gone.

I was surrounded by strangers who hated me, and a man most women would cut my eyes out to have.

"Ditto," she chuckled, though it sounded more like a broken sob. "We don't talk enough anymore."

"So," I said, daring to breach the topic. "How's Jordan? Is

he being nice to you?" I knew he was still in Ireland. She'd said as much in her last *super-vague* email.

"He's not like I remember," she finally replied after a long pause. "He's changed, Teagan. He's not my Jordan. Not anymore."

"Change is good," I offered. Lifting up one half of my sandwich, I bit down. "You know the saying," I mumbled between mouthfuls. "A change is better than a rest."

"No, Teegs," Hope argued sadly. "He's a grown up now. Like a real man. He's not my Jordy. He's Annabelle's fiancé."

"He's *your* husband," I corrected, speaking for the first time about the biggest secret I'd ever kept for my best friend.

Hell, the biggest secret I'd ever kept, period.

The secret that had floored me all those years ago....

I WAS LOITERING AROUND IN THE BACK STAIRWELL OF THE Henderson Hotel where I was waiting for my boyfriend – who wasn't supposed to be my boyfriend – to come out of the gym.

Hope, who had given me a ride because Uncle Max had my driving privileges revoked, was keeping me company.

I hadn't seen Noah since the whole allergic reaction to the condom incident the day before yesterday, and I was worried. Actually, I was more than just worried. I was pretty damn mortified. It wasn't every day a girl broke out in a blistering rash after having sex with her boyfriend. It also wasn't everyday that said girl's legal guardian walked in on the scene...

"If I tell you something, do you promise not to tell a soul?" Hope asked, drawing me out of my reverie.

"The jury's still out about whether or not Noah has a soul, so can I tell him?" I joked. Noticing Hope's expression, I turned and gave my best friend my full attention. "Hope, you can tell me anything."

Hope turned to face me and grinned. Her crystal clear skin looked flawless, her blue eyes danced with mischief, and I was immediately green with envy. Hope was gorgeous – blatant, eye-catching gorgeous – and it was hard to be around her without feeling slightly inferior – or in my case, majorly. "I'm getting married!"

My jaw fell open. "You're getting what now?"

"Married!" She grinned, revealing a set of pearly white teeth. "Tomorrow. It's all arranged, and I want you to be my witness."

"You cannot be serious?" I deadpanned.

Hope scrunched her nose up and frowned. "I don't need advice or a lecture, Teegs."

"I'm not. I'm not..." Jesus, this was too much to take in at ten o'clock in the morning. "So, let me get this straight," I muttered, more to myself than to Hope. "You're getting married tomorrow?"

Hope nodded earnestly

"To Jordan?"

"Yes," Hope chuckled, "to Jordan. Who else?"

"Oh my god." I wanted to scream, are you crazy, but I didn't. I couldn't. I was freaking speechless...

"I know this sounds sudden and rushed," Hope continued to say, interrupting my panicked thoughts. "But it's really not. I've been planning this day my entire life...shit – the guys." Grabbing onto my shoulders, Hope turned me toward the glass doorway before hissing in my ear, "Not a word of this in front of my brothers."

The moment my Noah walked through the double doors with Colt and Cam at his side, the air expelled from my lungs in a heady gasp.

His eyes locked on my face and I could see his surprise at seeing me here.

"Alright boys," Hope announced as she stepped toward her

brothers and wrapped her arms around their shoulders. "Let's leave the lovebirds to it."

Surprisingly, Colt and Cam didn't toss out any smart comments or illicit innuendo – well, Cam winked dramatically at Noah as they walked past, but that was all.

Remaining perfectly still, I forced myself to breathe, all while my heart thundered in my chest as I waited for Noah to claim the space between us.

"Thorn," Noah said gruffly when he reached me. Dropping his gym bag on the ground at my feet, he cupped my neck with his hands, eyes locked on my face. "You good, Thorn?"

I knew what he was asking me.

Was my vagina okay?

Suppressing the urge to close my eyes and shiver at the feel of the heat emanating from his body, I whispered, "I'm good, Noah."

"Let's get out of here," he growled, his breath fanning my neck. This time I did shiver. It was an unstoppable reaction.

Shaking my head, I sagged forward slightly, finding my balance against my boyfriend's huge frame. "You're treacherous, Noah Messina."

"I'm life," he shot back with a smirk before wrapping his muscular arm around my shoulders. "Let's go..."

EVEN WHEN IT ALL WENT TO SHIT BETWEEN HOPE AND Jordan, she had continued to wear her wedding band on her pinky finger.

Right up until the last time I saw her, Hope had been wearing that ring.

I was dying to ask her more about Jordan, but I managed to refrain – barely. I begrudgingly had to admit that Noah was right. It wasn't *morally ethical* to eavesdrop on people's conversations.

Whatever...

"He's yours, Hope," I noted before taking another bite of my sandwich. "Remind him of that."

"Like you reminded Noah?" Hope teased.

"Exactly."

I was three bites into my prawn sandwich when something happened inside of me.

Something strange.

"Oh my god," I heaved, gagging.

"Teagan?" Hope's concerned voice came through the line. "Are you okay?"

"Hope. I have to go!" Tossing my phone down, I clamped my mouth shut, and froze in my seat, un-breathing, as a huge wave of nausea washed through me.

Lewis, who up until this moment had been dutifully ignoring me, cocked a brow. "Are you well, Teagan?"

Was I?

I didn't think so.

Swallowing the piece of fish in my mouth, I inhaled a slow breath, but that only made the queasiness worse. "I..."

Ugh, speaking was a really bad idea...

Dropping the remaining piece of my sandwich onto my plate, I covered my mouth with my hand and sprang out of my seat.

A bead of sweat trickled down my forehead as I desperately rushed towards the restroom, all while fighting back the overpowering urge to throw up.

I could hear Lewis calling my name from somewhere behind me, but I didn't dare stop or attempt to answer him.

I didn't have to look back to know that he was following me.

The man shadowed me everywhere, and I guessed Noah paid him a pretty penny to do so.

I had no idea why my body had decided to turn on me like a traitorous bitch, but right now I couldn't think too much about it.

I was a woman on a mission and that mission was finding an outlet for my regurgitated prawn sandwich and fast.

Barreling my way through the holy grail of a door with the symbol of woman on it, I sprinted into a cubicle and dropped to my knees just as the contents of my stomach decided to make a dramatic exit from my mouth.

32

NOAH

*W*atching Teagan suffer through four days of food poisoning was fucking torture. Knowing there wasn't a damn thing I could do to make her feel better made it even worse.

Even now, as I swam lengths in the hotel pool with Lucky, all I wanted to do was turn around and run back upstairs to check on her.

I was fully aware that these things had to run their course, but it didn't make it any easier.

"How's Blondie today?" Lucky asked me when I stopped to catch my breath beside him. "Still sick?"

"It's fucking awful, man," I growled, thinking of my wife thrown over the toilet in pain. I didn't like feeling helpless. It was a feeling that sure as shit didn't sit well with me. "She's so small, you know?" Shaking my head, I removed my swimming cap and tossed it away. "I swear she's lost ten pounds since Sunday."

I climbed out of the pool and waited for Lucky to join me before heading over to the hot tub. "She's just about keeping water and crackers down now."

"She'll be okay, man," he assured me, climbing into the hot tub. "Remember that time I got food poisoning after eating that hotdog?" He shuddered. "It was two damn weeks until I could put one foot in front of the other."

"That was prison food, man," I countered gruffly. "I'm surprised either of us made it out of that hole in one piece given the shit they fed us."

"Isn't that the truth," Lucky agreed solemnly. "By the way, I might need to go away for a few weeks next month."

"Really?" I turned and looked at him. "Where?"

"It's...Hayley's anniversary is coming up." Lucky rubbed his face with his hand and sighed. "It'll be my first one out of prison."

"Sure, man," I choked out, not knowing what else to say. "Take as long as you need."

Here I was complaining about Teagan having food poisoning when Lucky's girl was six feet under.

I was an insensitive asshole.

33

TEAGAN

"So...good," I mumbled around my burger as I tucked into the delicious meat and seasoning, groaning in delight when the mayonnaise hit my tongue, sending a riveting attack of flavors through me.

By the time I had reached the hotel restaurant, I discovered they had already finished serving dinner, so I headed to the front bar instead.

Not bothering to scope out the menu, I'd chosen a burger and fries. Not the healthiest of options, but after almost nine days of crackers and water, I needed some greasy comfort food.

I didn't ask Noah if he wanted to join me for dinner. I knew what the answer would be after last time – a predominant *no*.

According to Beau, I was the devil on my husband's shoulder when it came to his diet.

According to the rest of his team – with the exception of Lucky – I was just the plain devil.

One stinking room service order of junk food in Phoenix

and I wasn't to be trusted with my husband's nutritional requirements anymore.

It wasn't like I didn't know what I was doing.

I'd trained as a fitness instructor in college, I'd co-owned and managed my own gym and I was in damn good shape myself.

The food thing was just one more black mark to add to a long list of the invisible *Teagan isn't good enough for Noah* checklist that everyone seemed to have.

"Sounds it," Lucky, who had decided to join me, replied dryly, drawing me out of my reverie. "Don't forget to chew, Blondie," he added with a smirk before taking a sip from his beer bottle.

"Lucky, have you ever heard the phrase: *sarcasm is the lowest form of wit*?" I shot back, reaching for a fry. "And if wit was shit you'd be constipated." Grinning, I poked out my tongue and waggled my brows at him.

"I... did you just compare my personality to a bowel movement?" he asked, blinking.

"Well, do you ever stop to think about the words you're planning to say before you actually say them?"

"Okay, I'm pretty fucking confused with this conversation right about now," he shot back with a wolfish grin.

Folding my arms, I leaned back in my seat in delight. "Good, I aim to please."

"You know," he teased, leaning across the table toward me. "If your goal is to please me with that mouth of yours then maybe you could lower your aim and apply a little suction." Shrugging his shoulders, he added, "Just saying."

"Ugh," I fake gagged and tossed a fry at him. "Suck on that, convict."

"You know I'm only yanking your chain, Teegs," Lucky

chuckled, taking my comment on the chin like a real trooper. "You know I'd never look at you like that."

"Yeah, yeah," I shot back, rolling my eyes.

Lucky was a strange guy.

For all his darkness and secretive behavior, he had a really great personality.

He sort of reminded me of the older brother I never had…

"Glad to see you back to yourself," he added in a genuine tone. "Noah was worried."

"I know," I replied dryly as I devoured my meal. Noah had been like an attention deprived puppy dog all last week. I had food poisoning. I wasn't dying, but you'd have sworn I had been the way he behaved.

Even though I'd told him not to, he'd skipped most of his training sessions, choosing to remain in a vomit aroma scented hotel room with me instead.

"So why the quick exit from the gym earlier?" Tearing off little pieces of bread, Lucky tossed them aside absentmindedly, all while he looked straight at me, steel blue eyes locked on mine. "The guys giving you shit again?"

"You could say that." Grabbing my beer bottle, I put it to my lips and swallowed deeply. "Or you could say I've reached my quota of dickheads for one day." Of course, I was the one who'd paid for Noah's tardiness. First thing this morning, when I walked into the gym, I'd gotten an earful from Quincy on how my sick ass was wrecking everything and if Noah didn't win the fight tonight it was on me.

Setting my bottle back down, I clasped my hands together and forced myself to block all thoughts of Quincy Jones from my mind.

"Do you think I could duck him if I tried?" I asked instead, inclining my head toward Lewis, who was standing at the bar several feet away from us, discreetly doing his job. I cocked a brow and studied Lewis's ginormous build before taking another bite of my burger. "He's strong, I'll give him that. But I'm faster."

"Nah." Picking up a coaster, Lucky began to pick away at the edges. "He'd enjoy the chase."

"You know, I'm really going to miss you when you're gone," I admitted, feeling a pang of lonesomeness at the thought of Lucky not being here for a while. "Do you really have to leave tonight?"

"You'll survive, Blondie," he shot back tenderly. "And yes." Checking his watch, he let out a sigh. "My flight's booked and paid for."

Needing to go home to Colorado for a few weeks to sort some stuff out was all the information Lucky had given me when he told me he was leaving earlier, but I had a feeling it had to do with Hayley.

"You're still in love with her, aren't you?" I blurted out tactlessly.

Lucky didn't reply, but the way his jaw strained as he stared through me was answer enough.

It hurt my heart to think that Lucky was still trapped in the past, loving a woman who had been dead for over a decade, knowing that any future love of his would have to compete with a ghost...

"I'm sorry," I whispered guiltily.

"Forget it," he said after a moment, voice strained. He cleared his throat before adding, "Are you going to order dessert?"

"Is the sky blue?" I shot back with a smirk. "Of course I'm going to order dessert..." My words trailed off the second my eyes landed on Noah, who was walking toward our table. He had a beer bottle in one hand and a hotel fob in the other.

"Jesus," I breathed, appreciating my husband's appearance as he prowled toward me, freshly showered and dressed in blue jeans and a tight white t-shirt.

Noah's voice trickled down my spine like an ice cube when he reached us. "You good, Thorn?"

Lowering my beer bottle to rest on my lip, I looked up at him through hooded lashes. "I'm good, Noah." I studied his beautiful face and the sexy stubble sprinkled over his jawline. "How was the gym?"

"Okay!" Lucky announced, interrupting us

Reluctantly, I tore my eyes away from Noah. "What?"

"As much as I'd love to stay and watch you two eyeball fuck each other," Lucky stared pointedly at me first and then Noah, "I have places to be."

"You're leaving tonight?" Noah's tone was full of surprise.

"Yep. There's a flight to Denver with my name on it," Lucky shot back, clapping my husband on the shoulder. "I'll see you guys in Vegas at the end of the summer," Lucky added before he slipped silently away, leaving me alone with my husband.

Taking the seat opposite me that Lucky had vacated, Noah picked up the half torn beer mat and twisted it around between his fingers. He stared hard at me for a long moment. "How are you feeling?" His brows furrowed in concern as he eyes trailed over my body. "You look...smaller."

"Relax." I pointed to my half-eaten burger and laughed. "A few more of these and I'll be back to my pre-poisoned self." Picking up a fry, I dipped it in mayo before stuffing it into my mouth. "You need to stop worrying about everything," I added, touched by his concern.

"You got a dress for the after party tonight?"

"No," I groaned, suddenly remembering that Noah had

an appearance at some highflier club after his fight tonight. Shaking my head, I took another swig from my bottle. "Count me out."

"Why?" Noah's visible muscles bunched beneath his shirt. "Are you still sick?"

"No." *God...* "I'm just tired, Noah." Aside from being sick last week, I was still suffering the repercussions of not getting to bed until five every morning for the past few months. "I'm not made like you guys."

Noah sat forward, placed his bottle down and rested his elbows on the table, clasping them loosely together. His broad chest stretched the fabric of his t-shirt. "Teagan, I know these parties aren't exactly your thing..." Cracking his knuckles, he let his words sink in for a moment before continuing. "But you're my wife. Your place is with me." The tone of voice he used this time left no room for protest. "I want you there with me."

I fought the urge to get snotty with his macho attitude, choosing to go down the road of tact instead. "To be honest, I'd be happier just staying in the suite tonight." I shrugged, uncomfortable. "I'm dizzy and tired and all I want is my bed."

In truth, I felt emotionally drained and physically exhausted.

It wasn't easy being on the road with all these men.

Noah leaned back in his chair, considering me with a caged expression.

Nervously, I took another sip of my drink.

"This isn't my world," I found myself explaining. Wiping my mouth with the back of my hand, I forced myself to look at him. "Mine is filled with green grass, yoga pants, and braless Saturday nights in. And besides, they're coming to see you, Noah. Not me."

That, I was sure of.

Most appearances Noah did were filled with overly zealous women.

It sickened me.

"You *are* me. So if I'm there, you're there, too."

I rolled my eyes. "You know what I mean."

"No, Thorn, I don't." His tanned, muscular hand reached across the table. Taking my hand in his, Noah stroked my knuckles with his rough, calloused fingers. "We're a team."

"All those women that go to those functions want to fuck you, Noah," I muttered in a petulant tone. "It's a fact... a gross, sickening fact. One I don't care to be subjected to every fucking night of the week."

"Are you getting pissy with me?" He asked, amused.

"I'm stating facts," I shot back, red-faced.

I was getting angry.

Why was I getting angry?

"Let's be very clear about some facts," he said, his tone suddenly void of all humor. "There will be no fucking of any kind unless it's *me* fucking *you*."

"I don't want to go," I muttered, appalled and, if I were being honest, a little turned on. "I'm not going."

"And you think I do?" He shook his head and growled under his breath. "I hate those things as much as you do, Thorn, but I'm contracted to attend. And you're not staying on your own."

"Don't even start thinking you're going to tell me what to do, Noah," I warned him right back. Okay, I was feeling irrationally angry. "Everything has been quiet on the JD front. No death threats. No rose covered beds or bullets. I'm sure one night alone won't kill me. I'll be safe as houses."

"Safe as houses," he snorted. "You have some weird ass

sayings, Thorn. You're not safe. Fucking demented, yes, but safe you are not."

"Did you come over here with the sole purpose of pissing me off and bullying me into doing what you want?" I shot back. "Because it's working. The pissing me off part, that is. The bullying, not so much."

"Actually, I came over to apologize."

I gaped. "To me?"

"Yes, to you." Reclaiming my hand with his, Noah continued to stroke my knuckles absentmindedly. "I should be doing more stuff with you," he added cautiously as he looked at my face with a puzzled expression etched on his. "I've been spending too much time training, Thorn, and not enough time with you. I'll fix it."

Okay, now I *was* going to cry.

What the hell was going on with me?

"Are you crying?" Noah asked, horrified.

"No," I snapped, wiping my eyes with the back of my hand. "I'm not!"

"Okay..." Standing up slowly, Noah extended his arms above his head and stretched. "I'm going to run up to the room and grab a shower before we have to leave." Concern was etched on his face when he added, "You sure you're okay?"

"Yes. I'm sure." Grabbing a fist full of fries, I stuffed them into my mouth before gesturing toward my half empty plate. "I'll be up when I'm done."

34

TEAGAN

I was rounding the corner of the foyer, feeling bloated and extremely satisfied, when the sound of my name being spoken caused me to halt mid-stride and Lewis to bulldoze into the back of me.

"Shh," I whispered, steadying myself with Lewis's outstretched arm.

Creeping over to the wall, I pressed my back against the concrete, and urged Lewis to do the same.

Reluctantly, he followed suit and stood with his back to the wall beside me.

"I want her off this tour!"

That was Quincy.

Holding my breath, I glanced sideways at Lewis.

The look on his face told me he'd realized who was talking, too.

The red stain of his cheeks told me he was embarrassed.

Suddenly it wasn't queasiness filling my body.

It was rage.

"She's distracting him. Three months of her trailing around and he's down in rank. He barely won his last fight against Dupree in points. If he doesn't win tonight, he drops down in rank to third. The woman needs to go."

"She's a problem for him alright." Beau piped up. "Quincy's right, T. Noah's form is all wrong. He's tense as hell. He's not giving the tour his full attention or commitment anymore. For Christ's sake, he's missed an entire week of training because of her."

"If we even suggest Teagan going home, it will cause mutiny." Tommy sounded like he was trying to placate the other men, but I knew he was enjoying them hating me. "And Noah? Well, he married her, didn't he? He's not gonna just send her away, now is he?"

"He might just do that," Beau piped up, voice suddenly smug. "When he sees what I've got planned tonight, Noah might just put her on a plane and send her packing..."

"What the hell's more important?" Quincy demanded, cutting Beau off. "Chauffeuring his fuck buddy around the country or winning the goddamn title? Because I've got to tell you, Tommy, I didn't sign up to coach no goddamn loser."

Pushing myself off the wall, I made to lunge around the corner but Lewis quickly dragged me backward by the back of my shirt.

"Don't," he grunted into my ear as he half dragged me in the opposite direction toward the elevators. "Do not prove them right."

"That bastard just called Noah a loser," I hissed in a low tone. "And me his fuck buddy!"

No one was going to talk about Noah like that.

Not while I had a breath in my body.

Lewis shoved me into a waiting elevator and slammed his hand on the keypad.

"What do you think confronting them would have

achieved back there?" He asked calmly when the doors closed.

"It would have made me feel better," I said hoarsely, rubbing my arm where he'd grabbed me.

"And Noah?" He countered coolly. "Did you stop to think how it could affect him – having his wife and coach going at each other?"

The elevator doors opened and we were walking.

"Your husband is twenty-one months into a heavyweight title quest," Lewis continued to say as he ushered me down the hallway toward my hotel room door. "A fall out in the camp at this late stage in the game will not bode well for him."

"But I didn't do anything to those guys –" my voice cracked and I quickly snapped my mouth shut, refusing to show any emotion.

Lewis was as bad as the others.

Lewis was with me all day every day. He knew how the guys treated me when Noah wasn't looking and he stood back and did nothing.

Using a key fob, Lewis unlocked the door of mine and Noah's suite and held it open for me. "It doesn't matter what you did or didn't do," he told me in a regretful tone. "You're a liability to Noah – a distraction – which makes you a nuisance to those of us whose livelihoods depend on keeping him safe and in fighting form."

"Is that what I am?" My eyes were watering. Traitorous fucking tear ducts again. "A nuisance?"

Lewis's gray eyes softened but the words he spoke hurt worse than his previous. "Noah's enemies have only one way of tormenting him. *You.* Noah's opponents have one way of distracting him. Also *you.* I would be a liar if I said it wouldn't be easier for all of us if you had never resurfaced."

35

NOAH

I knew there was something wrong the second Teagan came barreling into our bedroom. The moment she'd noticed me sitting on the bed, tying my laces, she'd rushed into the adjoining bathroom and locked the door.

Twenty minutes had passed since she barricaded herself in the bathroom, and I was running out of patience. – and time.

"Come on, babe!" Banging my fist for what felt like the hundredth time on the door, I rested my forehead against the wood. My phone was blowing up in my pocket, I knew I was running late to get to the fight, but wild horses couldn't drag me out of this room. Not while she was there. "Let me in."

""I just n-need a goddamn m-minute, Noah!" I heard her scream from behind the door. "Please."

"You've had twenty of those," I informed her, all out of patience now. "So you can either open that door or I'll kick it down. Either way, I'm coming in there for you."

A few seconds passed and then the sound of a lock

clicking filled my ears. Opening the door inward, Teagan greeted me with a fake as fuck smile and two huge, swollen eyes.

"What happened?" Was my immediate response to her tearstained face, followed quickly by, "who the fuck upset you?"

"No one," Thorn replied, sniffling. Using the back of her hand to wipe her eyes, she stepped around me, moving through the bedroom to her closet. "I'm fine."

I watched as Teagan removed a gray, sparkly dress from a hanger in the closet. Whipping off her shirt, she quickly pulled the dress over her head before shimmying out of her jeans.

"Okay," she announced after she'd slipped her tiny feet into a skyscraper pair of heels. Shaking out her long blonde hair, she adjusted her dress against her slender frame. "I'm ready."

"Well, I'm not," I shot back, gaping at her. Did she think I was going to just forget about her meltdown in the bathroom? "Christ, Teagan," I growled, stalking toward her. When I reached her, I gestured my hand toward the bathroom door. "What the hell was that?"

"I was just having a moment," she replied. "I'm over it now."

"Some moment, Thorn," I countered. "You all but stopped my fucking heart in my chest." I exhaled a shaky breath. "I thought something serious was wrong."

"Nothing's wrong, okay?" She countered in a tone that was far too bright considering less than five minutes ago she'd been crying her eyes out in the goddamn bathroom.

"Bullshit. You're a wreck." I walked straight up to her and placed my hands on her shoulders. "I know something is wrong." I could see it in her eyes. "You're keeping something from me." I begged her with my eyes to open up and let me in. "Tell me."

"I'm just upset about all those female fans," she finally whispered. "It's hard having to watch them leer at you all the time."

"What?" Sagging in relief, I ducked my head and pressed my forehead against hers. "You little fruitcake. You know I only see you." Wiping her cheeks with my thumbs, I kissed her forehead. "You have nothing to worry about, Thorn."

She didn't.

The girl owned me.

Heart and soul.

36

TEAGAN

I didn't want to be here tonight.

Even though I had no doubt that my husband would win, his was the main event which happened to be the last fight of the night, and the thought of sitting around watching men pummel each other into the mat caused my stomach to churn inside of me.

I had never suffered from a sensitive stomach before, but for some reason, I just couldn't bear to watch another damn fight.

Even now, as I sat on a bench in the far corner of Noah's changing room with Lewis beside me, I felt...off kilter.

I felt wrong.

I knew that was a weird thing to say, but it was the truth.

Dozens of people on the other side of the room fawned over my husband; some reporters, others were fans begging and screaming for some pre-fight photographs, and all I could do was sit numbly on this shitty bench and breathe slowly.

"What's wrong with you?" Lewis grunted.

"I'm not sure," I whispered quietly. This was the first time

I'd spoken to Lewis since we'd arrived at the arena. Usually I sat in the stands with Lewis and watched the other fights, but tonight I simply wasn't feeling it.

I was still reeling over what I'd overheard Noah's team saying about me, and the reason it hurt so bad was because deep down inside, I knew that some of what they had said made sense.

Some of it had been true.

I was screwing with Noah's future; unintentionally, but I was.

He was constantly watching over his back because JD had hit the nail on the head when he decided to use me to hurt Noah. I was a weak point for my husband – Noah had said as much to me once – and I didn't like it one bit.

"Are you going to throw up again?" Lewis demanded, looking at me with an appalled expression on his face. "Because if you are then go and do it in the bathroom. I'm not paid to attend to sick women."

"No," I said wearily. I didn't want to speak to him. I didn't even want to look at him. Any of them for that matter, but I was feeling too damn bad to put up a wall. "I'm just tired."

"You look...out of sorts," he added, staring down at me.

"I feel out of sorts," I whispered, agreeing wholeheartedly with the big ape for once. "Can you just..." I paused and looked over at Noah who was still surrounded by a mob. I could tell it was going to be a long night. "Can you take me back to the hotel, Lewis?"

His brow set in a deep frown. "Don't you want to watch your husband's fight?"

I shook my head. "I just want to go." Forcing back a sudden bout of nausea and tears, I choked out, "Please take me home."

"I'll have to run it by Noah first," Lewis said and, without waiting for a response from me, he quickly got to his feet and trudged over to Noah.

"Of course you do," I muttered under my breath, even though I knew Lewis was out of earshot. "My opinion means sweet fuck to any of you guys."

"Thorn!" Instantly, Noah had barged through the crowds and was by my side. "Lewis said you want to go home?" His brown eyes were full of concern as he studied my face. Crouching down in front of me, he cupped my cheek with his bandaged hand. "Are you sick?"

I could hear the announcer calling Noah's name out over the microphone.

He was up next.

"I'm tired," I admitted, flinching when a spasm of pain panged inside of my lower belly. "I'll be fine though," I quickly amended.

"Noah!" Quincy repeated, tone furious. "You need to get out there *now*."

Reaching up, I covered his hand with mine, "Go on," I encouraged. "You have a fight...ouch!"

"Are you okay?" He asked, panicked when I grunted as a sharp pain jolted through me.

"Yes," I spluttered. "Go, Noah."

"What?" Noah shook his head as if I'd spoken a foreign language. "No goddamn way." He stared up at my face in horror. "I'm not going anywhere, Thorn."

"Noah," I said, a little firmer this time, as I clutched my stomach. "I want you to go out there and kick his ass." I wasn't going to be responsible for Noah losing everything he'd worked so hard for. "I'll be fine."

"But you're sick," he whispered, looking at me like I was about to disappear at any moment.

"Noah, you need to get out there," Quincy roared from

somewhere nearby. "You're going to get yourself disqualified, boy."

"Fuck off, Q." Noah snarled. "I'm not leaving her." He turned his attention back to me. "How the hell am I supposed to fight knowing you're in here..." His voice broke off and he looked me up and down again. A strangled noise tore from his throat. He looked truly conflicted.

"If you don't get your ass in that ring you'll be disqualified and automatically lose your title shot," Quincy added.

"Are you deaf?" Noah roared, livid. "I said I'm not leaving her."

"I'll be fine," I added firmly. "I just need to lie down for a little bit.

"I can't..." Noah stared hard at me for a long moment before saying, "I'll come home with you."

"I'll take her back to the hotel," Lewis, who was hovering nearby, interjected in a calm tone. "I'll wait with her until you get back."

"Go on," I urged, seeing Noah's resolve weakening. "I swear I'll be okay."

Standing abruptly, my husband ran a hand through his hair in obvious agitation. "I'll be there as soon as I can."

I felt myself sag in relief when Noah turned around and walked out of the changing room with Quincy.

I knew he didn't want to leave. I knew it was going against everything inside of him to walk away, but I was glad.

I didn't want him to wreck his career over me.

37

NOAH

*I*t went against everything inside of me to walk away from Teagan tonight.

I wasn't stupid. I knew my title shot with Cole was on the line and would be pulled if I put a foot out of line, but she was so much more important to me.

I was disgusted with myself all the way to the cage and that self-loathing only escalated when I was faced with my opponent.

In my fucked up state of mind, this asshole was the reason I wasn't with my wife right now.

Goddammit, she had some special sort of hold on me.

I was raised hard. I grew up with mother fuckers ten times worse than JD Dennis. I was taught the tricks of the trade, the keys to surviving in a gangster's world, but fuck me; my emotions for that woman were blinding my survival instincts.

When the bell rang, I left it all in the cage.

Every frustration, every worried thought and notion.

My anger and fear was overpowering me, and driving me to inflict more pain than necessary on the poor bastard fighting me. I put every ounce of tension and angst into pummeling the poor bastard, not caring about giving the crowd a decent show.

My desire to get back to my wife was overriding all professionalism inside of me and I knew they would have to drag me off his body tonight.

38

TEAGAN

I felt better the moment I stepped into the shower back in our suite. The spray of boiling hot water on my body had instantly made me feel a little better and a little less icky. Sinking to the shower floor, I wrapped my arms around my knees and bent my head forward as my mind continued to torment me about what I'd heard earlier tonight.

There was nothing I could do, I thought to myself sadly.

Nothing I said or could say was going to change Beau, Tommy, and Quincy's opinions of me.

Suddenly, I missed Lucky desperately. He was my only friend out here and I wouldn't see him until the final leg of the tour in Vegas.

I was going to miss that strange guy fiercely.

The sound of male voices rising from outside the bathroom dragged me from my reverie, alerting me to my first sign of trouble.

The sound of a door slamming was my second.

Scrambling to my feet, I switched off the shower before reaching for the towel I had hung over the glass door. Wrapping the fluffy white towel around my body, I stepped out of the shower and padded over the bathroom tiles, stopping when I reached the door.

Curling my fingers around the brass knob, I held my breath and listened to the conversation taking place in our bedroom.

"What are you doing here?" That was Lewis – the same Lewis who had *never* come into our suite before without permission. His voice rang loud and clear through the air when he said, *"Who's this prick?"*

The very first thought that popped into my head was that Lewis McGowan was a spy and I was about to get my head blown off by JD Dennis.

Fear gripped hold of me so tight in that moment that I thought I might faint.

With my back to the door, I remained exactly where I was, heart in my mouth and my eyes clenched shut.

Praying to god for a miracle, I blessed myself repeatedly.

I didn't want to die tonight.

Please don't let me die tonight...

"...None of your business..." a strange voice said, drawing me back to the present. *"...things to discuss..."*

I strained to hear the person Lewis was talking to, but I could hardly make out the voice with the sound of the contractor fan over my head and I couldn't very well stick my arm around the door to switch it off without being seen.

Releasing the door knob like it had burned me, I curled my fingers around the lock and, as slowly as I possibly could, switched it sideways.

The tiny click it made was barely audible and I sagged in relief.

"In here?" That was Lewis' booming voice again, piercing the air. *"Are you fucking with me?"*

"...I don't answer to you...." Definitely a man's voice, I decided. Whose, I couldn't be sure of, but the other person in my bedroom was one hundred percent male.

"Never said you had to." Lewis' tone was laced with disgust. *"But you sure as shit should have to answer to your conscience."*

Quiet mumbling was followed by the sound of footsteps retreating.

I didn't move a muscle.

The seconds rolled into minutes and then hours, and the longer I stayed behind the bathroom door, the longer nothing continued to happen.

Surely if JD was here he would have killed me by now?

I was in the perfect position to get my brains blown out. He was never going to get an opportunity like this again, so why wait?

It didn't matter what JD was plotting, I decided.

I wasn't going to risk my life by going out there. I knew exactly what happened to the curious kitty, and this cat planned on staying the hell alive.

Nu-uh, I had watched too many episodes of The Walking Dead to even contemplate leaving my safe place.

But that notion sprung to life a new problem for me.

They obviously *knew* I was in here.

I mean, Lewis would have told them.

He wasn't guarding the door for shits and giggles and it was pretty freaking obvious by the steam creeping out from under the door that I was inside the locked bathroom.

On my hands and knees, I crawled across the damp tiles in search of a weapon.

If I was going to die tonight, then I sure as hell wasn't going down without the mother of all fights.

Maybe if I drew blood from my perpetrator the cops would have enough forensic evidence to make an arrest.

Glancing wildly around the room, my eyes landed on... a bar of soap.

What the hell was I going to do with a bar of soap?

Wash my killer to death?

Stupid fucking hotel bathrooms...

I wanted to kick my own ass for being such a girl.

When had I turned into a defenseless princess that hid and waited for a man to save her?

Fuck this...

Scrambling to my feet, I grabbed the metal toilet roll holder in my hand.

Rushing over to the bathroom door, I unlocked it before swinging it open.

My mouth was open, the words *Die Motherfucker* were on the tip of my tongue, but the moment my eyes landed on the broad back of a man sitting on our bed, my voice vanished into thin air.

Shock encompassed my features as I stared in bewilderment at the stranger sitting on my bed – the naked stranger.

Not just any naked stranger, I realized, when my eyes landed on the tricolor green, white, and gold flag tattoo on the top of his right butt cheek.

Liam...

"Liam?" I repeated his name out loud as I stood mere feet away from the bed absolutely shell-shocked. "What the hell are you doing here? And naked?" I squeezed out, mortified.

"Teegs." Liam jerked to his feet. He turned to face me and immediately I felt a deep flush of embarrassment waft through me as I took in his nakedness.

I watched Liam's gaze rake over my bare skin. "Do you

mind?" I snapped, tightening my hold on the towel covering my dignity.

Liam shrugged. "It's nothing I haven't seen before." Resting his hands on his hips, he added, "Nothing you haven't seen either." A cocky smirk lifted his full lips.

"Or ever will *again*," I shot back with a glare. Rushing over to the pile of clothes on the floor, I grabbed the jeans and tossed them at my ex-boyfriend.

"Are you sure you want me to put those on, Teegs?" He purred. "We could go again – for old time's sake."

And just like that everything began to make sense.

Liam's reappearance.

The hushed voices outside the bathroom.

"He might just do that," Beau piped up, voice suddenly smug. "When he sees what I've got planned tonight, Noah might just put her on a plane and send her packing..."

Awareness smacked me straight in the face.

I was being set up.

This room was stinking of betrayal.

I wasn't stupid. I knew exactly how this looked. I was soaking wet and naked beneath the towel I had wrapped around me. My ex-boyfriend was alone with me.

Bending down, I grabbed the rest of Liam's pile of clothes and tossed them at him. "Do you honestly think I don't know what you're doing?" I shook my head in disgust. "Get the hell out of here before I call the cops on your dumb ass."

"I'm here for two things," Liam countered evenly. "Once I get them, I'll go."

I stood, unmoving, on the opposite side of the bed, refusing to speak to him until put his pants back on.

Finally, he did.

"I need you to sign off on the business," he told me as he

dragged the denim up his narrow waist and slipped his feet back into his shoes. Pulling a folded envelope out of the back pocket of his jeans, Liam tossed it toward me.

The envelope landed in the middle of bed and I frowned.

Hoisting myself onto the bed, I reached over and retrieved the envelope before quickly opening it.

"You want to buy me out?"

"No, Teagan, I don't want to buy you out," Liam replied in a clipped tone.

I shook my head in confusion as I reread the paperwork in my hands.

"This says you want to buy me out." I lifted my gaze to his face. "For less than a quarter of what I'm owed."

"Yeah, well, I didn't sign up to run a business on my own, but shit happens," Liam shot back coolly.

"So, you're trying to rip me off because I left, *and* sabotage my relationship with Noah?" I narrowed my eyes in disgust. "I never would've put you down as vindictive, Liam."

"Come home with me and we'll forget about it," he blurted out, stunning me.

"You must be joking," I deadpanned.

"Come on, Teegs," Liam urged, tone gentler. "You don't belong over here with these people." Taking a seat on the edge of the bed, Liam stared into my eyes. "You belong at home with me."

"I belong with *Noah*." My voice was rising like the panic in my gut.

"Are you sure about that?" He countered.

"Liam, why are you making this harder than it needs to be?" I sighed. "Just leave."

"You loved me once," Liam countered with a smirk.

"When we were *children*," I retorted, purposefully

bursting his bubble. "And it was puppy love, Liam. It wasn't real." It wasn't a smidgen of the love I felt for Noah.

"If you hadn't moved to America in sixth year, then we'd still be together!" Liam hissed. "We were supposed to be together, Teagan."

"Well shit on a stick," I shot back sarcastically. "I'm so sorry that my mother's death and my father's imprisonment inconvenienced your plans for the future. If I recall, you found someone pretty fast to make you feel better." My stomach churned inside of me again, but I was too furious to acknowledge the pain.

"You haven't thought this through," Liam argued, meeting my glare with one of his own. "You're spontaneous and reckless so I understand the appeal a guy like Messina has," he added. "I truly do. But it's not permanent, Teagan. *He's* not permanent." Letting out a heavy sigh, Liam twisted his body to face me. "This won't last," he continued to say. "It's lust. It's not *real*."

Shaking my head, I forced myself to rein in my temper. "It's about as real and permanent as it gets," I shot back. "He married me."

"You're kidding?" Liam deadpanned. The tattoo circling my ring finger caught his attention then and Liam yanked my hand toward him. "Teagan, tell me you are fucking joking?"

"You have no right coming here demanding anything of me." Burying my hurt under my sarcasm, I snatched my hand away from him and sneered up at my oldest friend. "You screwed me over years ago when you dumped me and fell into bed with Katie Horgan."

Liam paled and I continued, furious.

"Yeah," I sneered. "You didn't think I knew about her? Well I did."

"I was seventeen," he shot back, tone shakier now.

"You were twenty-five when you allowed a man to sexually harass me for months," I countered, not giving an inch. "What's your excuse for Ciarán O Reilly?" I demanded. "Your age? Or the financial state of our business."

"I didn't allow him to harass you," Liam shot back, clearly disgusted. "It wasn't like that."

"It's always an excuse with you, Liam," I hissed. "You're full of them."

"And you're a fucking idiot!" He roared into my face. "You've made a huge mistake with that one, Teagan."

"The only mistake I ever made was taking you into my bed."

Liam flinched. "Don't."

"I thought of him the whole time I was with you," I continued to taunt him. "It was the only way I could bear your touch – pretending it was Noah."

"You know what?" Liam stood up and sneered down at me. "You deserve him." Laughing humorlessly, Liam ran a hand through his blond hair before retreating a few steps. "Don't say you weren't warned when he loses his temper and uses you as a punching bag or when he comes home reeking of perfume and sex."

"Get out of here," I seethed. He wanted to make me mad. Well, I was burning mad, but I wasn't going to give him the satisfaction of knowing his words were getting to me. Reaching for the pen on my nightstand, I scrawled my signature on the paper he'd given me. Replacing the cap on the pen, I placed it back down on the nightstand. "Take your papers and your pathetic attempts of ruining my marriage and get the hell out of here. Don't ever contact me again."

Liam glowered at me. "You're only a body for that one,

kid," he said, continuing to taunt me. "A hole to get his kicks off."

"Enjoy it, dickhead," I sneered. Scrunching the paper in a tight ball in my fist, I tossed it toward Liam. "Now get the hell out of my life."

Liam bent down and picked up the papers. "I am going to enjoy reading about your life going to shit – because it *will* go to shit, Teagan."

"Burn in hell."

Smoothing the paper against his thigh, Liam shoved it back into the ass pocket of his jeans and glared at me. "Last chance, Teagan. Walk out of here with me now and we can forget this ever happened."

I stifled a scream. "Just get the hell out of here before Noah –"

"Gets back?"

Noah appeared in the doorway of the bedroom, flanked by a baffled looking Quincy and a smug looking Beau.

Dread bloomed inside of me.

I was alone in a hotel room with my ex-boyfriend, and naked beneath the towel I had wrapped around my body...

"Noah!" My voice was strangled as I slid off the bed and rushed toward my husband. "Listen to me." Reaching him, I cupped his face in my hands and forced him to look at me. "This is *not* what it looks like."

"How does it look, Thorn?" Noah asked in a deceptively soft voice. His entire body was trembling. His dark eyes were wild, flickering between my face and the bed. He was breathing hard and I felt like I was holding a bomb in my hands. "Hmm?" Noah was holding onto his self-restraint by the skin of his teeth and the rage emanating from him terrified me.

A bomb that was about to detonate at any moment...

"Bad," I admitted, voice torn. "It looks bad, but it's not, I swear."

"*Yeah, Noah,*" Liam mocked, clearly provoking my husband. "It's *not* what it looks like."

His provocation caused Noah to explode like a firecracker.

Roughly shoving me out of his way, Noah lunged toward the bed, taking Liam to the carpet with a spear to his midsection. "You must have a fucking death wish." Straddling Liam, Noah tortured him with punch after violent punch to the face.

"I didn't touch her..." Liam threw his arms up to protect his face, but it was no use. Noah was destroying him with blow after blow. "Get the hell off me, man..."

"Do something," I begged. Grabbing my hair with my hands, I turned to Quincy and Beau. "Stop him!"

Neither one moved a muscle.

"Don't hurt him," I begged as tears pooled in my eyes. "Noah, please!"

"Hurt him?" Noah roared. "I'm not going to hurt him, Teagan. I'm going to *kill* him."

Petrified of what was unfolding before me, but knowing I couldn't stand aside and do nothing, I raced over to where I was pretty sure my husband was killing my former flame. "He's not worth going to prison for!" I cried out as I pulled on Noah's shoulders, desperate to stop him from making a mistake that could take him away from me again. "Please," I growled. A bead of sweat trickled down my brow from the sheer force of trying to pull my husband off Liam.

"Noah, don't!" Tommy's voice suddenly came from behind me.

Brushing me gently aside, Tommy lunged forward and wrapped his arms around Noah's chest before roughly dragging him off Liam. Lewis, who had followed Tommy, reached down and picked the bloodied heap that was Liam up off the floor. "Get him out of here," Tommy hissed as he struggled to retain his grip on Noah.

Wordlessly, Lewis walked from the room with a battered, but thankfully breathing, Liam in his grasp.

The other two men followed until it was just Tommy, Noah, and myself left alone.

"Are you stable?" Tommy asked.

"I wouldn't hurt *her*," Noah snarled, shoving hard against his friend's hold.

Releasing Noah, Tommy backed away slowly.

"I'll get rid of him," he added, eyes locked on me in pure and utter disgust.

The second he closed the door behind him, Noah went berserk.

Ripping one of the dressers clean off the floor with his bare hands, he tossed it against the wall, cracking the plaster when it landed with a huge bang.

"Fuck!" Snarling, he picked up a vase and tossed it across the room.

I watched the vase smash into pieces in a horrified daze.

What the hell had I gotten myself into?

This man was violent, he was deranged – *dangerous...*

So why did I have an unstoppable urge to comfort him?

To reassure him and calm him down.

When had I become a masochist?

Everything inside of my body was telling me to run.

Get the hell out of here before he does worse.

I didn't move a muscle.

Walking over to the window, Noah kept his back to me as he spoke. "What was he doing here?" His body was shaking violently. Broken pieces of furniture shattered everywhere, fragments of glass sprayed over every surface of the room. His hands were gripping the window sill so hard, his corded arms were bulging with veins. "Why was he *in here*, Thorn?"

I approached with caution. "I know what it must have looked like, but you have to believe me when I tell you I have no idea why he was here." Shaking my head, I racked my brain for a better way of explaining this shit storm and came up empty. "I was in the bathroom and I came out and he was just...there. I've been set up."

Noah laughed humorlessly. "Set up."

"Yes!" I nodded vigorously. "I've been set up."

Closing the gap between us, I wrapped my arms around his waist and pressed my cheek to his back, but Noah wasn't having any of it. He roughly shook me off before swinging around to face me.

"Did you do it on purpose?" He asked, his voice barely more than a whisper. "Pretend you were sick so you could flake out on me and meet up with him?"

"What?" I balked. "Of course not. I told you, I've been set up."

"It's too fucking late to leave me now," he blurted out, as if the thought just entered his mind. "I'm not like Jordan, Thorn. You're not leaving me without a fight."

"I don't want to leave you at all!" I screamed, desperate to make him calm down. "You're my husband."

"I can't..." Running a hand through his hair, Noah grabbed his wallet off the dresser and moved toward the bedroom door.

"Where are you going?" I demanded, appalled.

Noah's tone was clipped. "Out."

"I haven't done anything wrong. You can't just walk away from me." I cried out. "We're not done talking here."

"I'm done talking, Teagan. *I* am," he tossed over his shoulder, not stopping. "But hey, if you get lonely, you can always call *him* over again."

"Noah!" Springing into action, I raced after him. "Don't go." I was making a habit of chasing after this man. The second my eyes landed on the rosewood six string resting on the couch, my feet came to an abrupt halt. "*Martin*?"

I approached the six string like it was an oasis that could disappear at any moment.

Closing in on the guitar, I reached a hand out and trailed my fingers over the strings. My eyes roamed over the body. It looked exactly like the one my mother gave me when I was a child.

"This is..." Pausing, I shook my head and trailed my fingers over the strings. Tears pooled my eyes. "Why would you do this?"

"I ordered it a while back," he said gruffly. "Must have arrived tonight."

I didn't know why I was being so emotional.

I was built from tougher bricks than this.

Crying over men because they hurt my feelings wasn't me.

Crying when a man bought me a gift was even more out of character.

"I couldn't afford to replace it for you back in school," Noah added, tone clipped, jaw straining. "I can now."

"But you didn't break it back then."

He didn't reply.

"Thank you," I choked out. "This means a lot to me."

"Do whatever you want with it." With one final glance, he walked toward the door. "Use it for firewood for all I care."

39

NOAH

"*And* what about *you*?" Teagan roared from the doorway of our hotel suite. "Kissing all those female fans. Whoring and touring like you were god's gift to women. Not telling me about that whore Reese sniffing around the place again."

Stopping halfway down the hallway, I turned to face her and narrowed my eyes in disgust. "Are you honestly going to throw shit in my face after what I just saw?"

"Yes," she hissed. "Because you didn't *see* anything." Slamming the door shut, Teagan stalked down the hallway to where I was standing. "I haven't done a damn thing wrong here, Noah."

I felt my skin heat with anger.

My temper was rising.

Screw rising, I was incensed with anger.

I was fucking raging...

"Then why was he in *our* bedroom, Thorn?" I roared into her face. Teagan had broken that fundamental element of trust inside of me years ago, and what I'd walked in on tonight had just shattered every bit of progress I'd made. "Tell me why he was in there alone with you?"

"I've already told you," she growled. "I was *set* up."

"Stop fucking lying to me." I needed to get a grip, but I couldn't take it anymore. "Tell me the goddamn truth, Teagan." Deep down in my heart, I knew there had to be a logical explanation for this, but logic wasn't coming to me right now and the fucking realism of seeing him in that room with her?

It fucking *killed* me.

And knowing that it was my own goddamn fault he'd touched her in the first place?

Well, that took pain to a whole new level.

"Did you get bored of me?" My pain spewed out of my mouth like fucking poison and Thorn was the victim of my rant. I knew I was being unfairly harsh on her. "I'm training too much so you need a little extra attention?" I knew I needed to stop, but I couldn't. "How was he?" I physically fucking couldn't stop myself. "Was he better than me? Did he fuck you like I fuck you?" I got up in her face. "Did you come harder for him than when you come for me?"

"You bastard!" Teagan screamed. I didn't bother to try and protect myself from the hand my wife suddenly raised. Her palm smacked my cheek with more force than usual and I welcomed the sting.

Holding my hands out, I locked eyes with her. "Go ahead," I sneered. "Fucking hit me again."

"Why?" she cried out. "So you have a reason to hit me back?"

I paled and staggered back. "I would *never* hurt you, Thorn."

"You're hurting me now!" Teagan screamed, crying hard and ugly.

"And you are fucking destroying me," I shot back in a torn voice. "Do you want to break me?" I took a step back from her. I had to. "Is that it? Because you're fucking killing me right now, Teagan. Damn."

"I don't know why he was there," Teagan cried out hoarsely. She was trembling all over, and it was only then that I noticed she was still wrapped in a towel. "I was in the shower and I came out and he was..."

"He was what?" I taunted, furious.

"He was just...*there!*"

"He was just there without a shirt on?" I sneered in pure disgust. "What happened?" I demanded. "Did his shirt just fall onto the goddamn floor?"

"You're not listening to me." Shaking her head in what looked like genuine confusion, Teagan threw her hands up in the air and screamed. "Why won't you listen to me?"

"Because you're not telling me the truth!" I roared into her face.

"I can't. I can't –" Her voice broke off and she swung around and rushed over to where Lewis was standing back, watching our little domestic.

"Tell him," she begged, clutching Lewis's arm. "Tell him I had nothing to do with this."

"Teagan," I snapped. "This is between you and me."

"Shut up," she hissed before refocusing her attention on her bodyguard. "Please, Lewis," she sobbed. "Tell him they set me up." Sniffling, she added, "Tell him what we heard."

Lewis stared down at Teagan for a long time before locking eyes with me. "I was instructed to let him inside when he arrived at the suite," he told me. "Their meeting was pre-arranged."

That's what I thought...

"What?" Teagan's jaw fell open. "Why are you lying about

this?" Turning her attention to me, her eyes were wide and full of unshed tears when she said, "Noah, I'm telling you the truth."

"For what it's worth, it was strictly business," Lewis continued to say to me, ignoring my wife's plea. "I remained in the suite the entire time they signed the paperwork and dissolved their business relationship."

"Paperwork?" My brow furrowed in confusion. "What the hell are you talking about?"

"He's talking about my life's work," Teagan choked out, voice breaking. "The gym," she sobbed. "I gave it all away to him."

"Then why was his shirt off?" I demanded, shaking my head, unable to process everything I was hearing – everything I'd just witnessed. "Why was she in a towel?"

"Your wife was in the shower when he arrived." Lewis replied, without missing a beat. "He made an inappropriate comment about her attire and she responded by drenching him with a bottle of water."

"Why didn't you just say that?" I whispered, feeling like the wind had been knocked out of me.

"Oh, because you know me, Noah," Teagan snapped. Hurt and betrayal were evident in her hazel eyes. "I was hoping to get a quick fuck in before you came home."

I flinched; the harshness of her words ripping through me like a blade through flesh.

With that, she turned on her heel and rushed back into the suite, leaving me reeling.

———

Dawn was breaking outside when I finally went back upstairs to my wife. I'd spent the night in the resident's bar with Lewis, mulling over what I'd witnessed. I should have come to bed earlier, but I needed breathing space. I needed time to digest everything that had gone down.

Lewis had assured me nothing had happened between them, but that wasn't why I was hurt. I was fucking in pain to think that she'd go behind my back like that.

Goddammit, why didn't she just tell me she was meeting him?

I would have understood.

Well, no, I wouldn't have understood, but I could have handled it a hell of a lot better if it weren't done behind my back.

The image of that prick shirtless in my bedroom would forever be imprinted in my memory, no matter how innocent it was or not.

Teagan was sitting on the bed with her arms wrapped around her knees when I walked into our bedroom.

"I wanted to," she whispered, nodding at the empty case lying open beside her, her red-rimmed eyes were puffy and swollen. "But I made you a promise I wouldn't run again."

"Thorn," I croaked out, closing the bedroom door behind me. My eyes were locked on the suitcase. My heart was squeezing so hard in my chest that I thought it would burst.

"I know you don't believe me about Liam," she said quietly. "But I had nothing to do with him coming to our hotel room."

Jesus Christ, why did she have to keep fucking lying to me?

"I'll be real here," I managed to slur. "I'm mad as hell that you didn't tell me he was coming." Clearing my throat, I managed to add, "I'm fucking hurt, Teagan."

Huge teardrops slid down her cheeks, dampening the

sheet wrapped around her body, but she didn't make a sound. She was graceful in her pain, that was for sure.

"Jesus," I muttered, appalled, as I stumbled clumsily over to my wife, stinking of whiskey and cigarettes. Sinking down heavily on the edge of the bed, I reached over and wiped a teardrop from her cheek with my thumb. Letting out a sigh, I wiped another tear from her cheek before dropping my hand to her thigh. "I get why you had to meet up with him, okay?" My tone was laced with pain. This wasn't easy for me. "I...*understand* you had loose ends to tie up."

"Loose ends," she muttered under her breath.

"Stop," I begged her. "Please just *stop* lying about it. You're only making it fifty times fucking worse." I exhaled a sharp breath. "I'm not accusing you of having an affair here," I added, voice torn. "But I'm fucking wounded to think that you went behind my back on this."

"Fine," she ground out through clenched teeth. "I won't say another word about it."

"Teagan..."

"I want to go to sleep," she snapped, clenching her eyes shut. Curling up in a tiny ball, she whispered, "I'm tired. Of all of it."

Of me?

My mind thought the words my mouth would never speak, and fear engulfed me.

"Thorn..." I paused. I wasn't sure what I was trying to say. I knew I needed to say something, but I had no clue as to what.

"Goodnight, Noah," she whispered, turning away from me.

"Goodnight, Thorn," I muttered, feeling at a loss.

40

TEAGAN

This morning, like most others for the past few weeks, I found myself not wanting to get out of bed. Lucky was in Colorado which meant I was completely friendless on this tour, surrounded by a bunch of men that hated me. So instead of accompanying Noah to the gym, I feigned sleep and waited until he was gone before getting up and collapsing in a heap in the shower.

Aside from being completely miserable, I was feeling *off*.

I wasn't sure how to explain it, only that I wasn't myself. My body was aching all over and I felt completely shattered both internally and physically. I felt all *wrong* inside. I was teary and lonely and every morning I woke up, I found myself slipping into the shower to have a good cry.

That shower floor had quickly become my therapist, and each morning, I found myself sitting under a steady flow of piping hot water and reflecting over my life and the mistakes I'd made.

Of course, everything good, bad, and indifferent always fell back to Noah.

It was always *Noah*.

When I'd confronted Lewis the morning after Liam's appearance, and demanded to know why he'd allowed Liam into the suite, he'd simply shrugged and turned his back on me. When I'd accused him of helping Beau to try and ruin my relationship – because I just knew that this had to do with Beau Brady – Lewis had neither admitted or denied it...

"WHY DIDN'T YOU TELL HIM?" I SCREAMED, CLINGING ONTO THE doorframe, refusing to allow Lewis to close the door and return to his post. "I had nothing to do with Liam being here and you know it."

"I covered for you, didn't I?" He shot back, flustered. "I made it right for you."

"Made it right for me?" I shook my head, not understanding any of this. "The only way you can make it right for me is if you tell Noah the truth. Tell him I was set up."

"I'm not getting involved."

"You're already involved," I shot back, seething. "You involved yourself the moment you let Liam into my suite."

He didn't even try to deny it.

"So it was Beau?" I continued to prod. "He's the one you were arguing with outside my room?"

Again, Lewis remained silent.

"You said 'what are you doing back here?'" I gripped the door so hard, chips of paint came away under my nails. If Beau hadn't come so close to ruining my marriage, I would have been impressed with his devious methods. "You meant Beau, didn't you?"

. . .

If I had been expecting an answer from Lewis that morning, then I would still be waiting.

His secret keeping skills were exceptional.

He'd had the chance to defend me once and had let me burn.

Granted, he'd scrambled together some pathetic tale to take the heat off me, but that shit didn't float with me.

Lewis knew I had nothing to do with Liam being there that night and trying to take the heat off me when he could have exonerated me was something I could *never* forget.

Thinking about the way I had been treated made me feel so damn homesick. I was barely hanging in here. I wanted to run. I wanted to pack a bag and get as far away from all these horrible human beings as I could...but I couldn't leave *him*.

I couldn't leave Noah.

I wasn't sure who I was madder with; Liam for being a douchebag, Quincy, Tommy, and Beau, for being the sneaky bastards they were, Lewis for betraying me, or Noah for not believing me.

He was different now. Cooler. Our communication skills were worse than bad and we barely spoke more than four words to each other most days.

Last week he told me that he understood why I had to meet Liam, and that he wasn't mad anymore, but wished that I'd spoken to him about it first.

I'd replied by flipping him the bird and telling him to go fuck himself.

He was hell-bent on not listening to a damn thing I had to say and I wasn't prepared to accept *his acceptance* of an apology I hadn't given.

He was mad at me for lying to him and I was furious with him for not believing me.

Climbing to my feet, I switched off the shower and wrapped a towel around my body before heading back into the bedroom.

Sinking down on our bed, I looked around the room sadly. Noah's clothes were laid in neat piles. His sneakers stacked and paired neatly by the closet. Everything he owned was in order. Everything I possessed, on the other hand, was scattered and thrown around.

We were so different in every possible way and we never seemed to be able to stay on the same page.

It was like Noah had said before, he was either fighting with me or fucking with me. There truly was no middle line between us.

Sex seemed to be the only thing we got right.

Anger, love, sex, and hardcore lust...

I'd fallen in love with a boy who came from a different world than me, and when our worlds collided, sparks flew. Noah tied me up in a bazillion different knots, each one more intricately entwined than the next.

We had moved too quickly, I thought to myself, as I studied the room, its contents, and the hastily maimed tattoo on my ring finger.

We should've taken baby steps, taken it slow, but I wasn't going to run again.

Painful or not, I was going to see this through.

Exhaling a shaky breath, I reached forward and grabbed my cell phone off my nightstand before unlocking the screen and dialing the one phone number I knew by heart.

The moment I heard his familiar voice on the other line, my eyes filled up with tears.

"It's me," I sniffled as I sat cross-legged on the ginormous bed, feeling more alone than I'd felt in months. "I miss you," I added, voice breaking.

There was silence for so long that I thought Uncle Max had hung up on me, but then I heard him say, "I miss you, too," and silent tears that had been trickling down my cheeks turned to full-blown, snot-ugly crying.

Hearing my uncle admit that he missed me caused a dam to burst inside of me.

"I miss you so much," I choked out, cradling the phone in my hand. "I don't want to fight with you anymore. Please stop hating me." My voice was rising higher and higher. "I love you so much." I could hardly talk through my tears. "I'm sorry for being a disappointment." I was crying hard and ugly. "Please say you still love me..."

"Teagan, stop," I heard my uncle say in as gentle a tone as I'd ever heard him use. "I have *never* hated you."

I sniffled. "You haven't?"

"Never," he vowed with a sigh. "I've been disappointed in your choices. Hell, I've been downright furious. I still am. But at no point in time have I stopped loving you."

"I want what we used to have back," I admitted brokenly. "I want a relationship with you again."

I heard my uncle sigh heavily. "I don't think that's possible."

My heart cracked clean open.

What little hope I had inside of me evaporated.

"I suppose I should congratulate you on your marriage," he added after a pause. "I'd like to say that it came as a surprise to read, but I always knew you'd run back into his arms again."

"Please don't start a fight again, Uncle Max," I hated begging anyone, but I needed him. I felt so bad. I missed him so much. All I wanted to do was run home to my uncle.

"I'm not," Uncle Max surprised me by saying in a gentle

tone. "I'm just acknowledging the fact that my niece is a married woman now."

"Please, can't we at least try to get back to the way we used to be?" Swallowing deeply, I added, "We're coming to Colorado – Noah's last fight of this leg of the tour is against Gary Bash in Boulder. After that, Noah gets a month off to rest. Can I see you then?" *Can we spend some time getting back on track?*

"Teagan, I'm actually in the middle of something here," Uncle Max replied. "Can I call you back?"

"Yeah," I sobbed wearily. "Okay."

The line went dead and I tucked my phone under my pillow, knowing it wouldn't ring again.

41

NOAH

*M*y marriage had gone to hell in a hand-basket.

For the last several weeks, my wife had holed herself up in whatever hotel we were staying at. She hadn't shown up to any of my training sessions that she used to sit in on and nothing I seemed to say made a blind shit of difference.

On top of that, she wasn't eating.

She had three bites of toast for breakfast this morning, and even less for dinner last night.

I had no idea what to do.

I was the one who was supposed to be mad - she'd invited her ex into our goddamn hotel room - but she was acting like *I* was the one that had betrayed *her*.

"I'm *not* hungry," Teagan hissed when I asked her why she had only taken one bite of her sandwich. "Don't make an issue out of this," she added before climbing off the bed and disappearing into the bathroom.

Seconds later the motor of the shower running filled my ears.

"How the hell am I not supposed to worry?" I called out over the noise, but she didn't respond.

She was such a little liar.

Didn't she know by now that I could read her like a book?

Fuck, she was about the only thing I read clearly.

Standing up, I followed her into the bathroom.

I had a fight tonight. Hell, I was supposed to be in the cage in under two hours and Teagan looked like death warmed up. She was pale and jittery, and even though she futilely denied it, I fucking knew that she'd been sick earlier this morning.

Stripping off my clothes, I opened the shower door and stepped inside, forcing myself to keep my emotions in check as I stared down at her. "First thing tomorrow, I'm making you an appointment with the best damn doctor in this city."

"Noah, I'm fine," Teagan shot back, firmer this time as she pressed her palm against my chest. "Now, do you mind? I'm trying to shower here."

Water cascaded down her body and I frowned.

Teagan wasn't okay.

She hadn't been okay for weeks now – months.

She had lost more weight.

Her shoulder blades were more noticeable and her hip bones were protruding.

The slight swell of her lower belly was evidence of something darker.

Something I'd seen Ellie do on many occasions growing up.

"Are you doing it on purpose?" I blurted out tactlessly, as my eyes roamed over her naked body.

"Am I doing what?" Teagan replied, not understanding me one bit.

"Are you making yourself sick on purpose?" I probably could have come around this conversation a little better, but I was worked up.

"Wait," she deadpanned, eyes narrowing. "You think I am purposefully making myself sick?"

"I heard you this morning," I shot back. "Deny it all you want, but I know you've been sick, Teagan." I knew what a woman who made herself sick looked like.

Frail. Check.

Thin. Check.

Gaunt. Check.

Swollen stomach from the trauma. Check.

Right about now, my wife was checking every fucking box...

"You're freaking unbelievable." Letting out a growl, Teagan shoved my chest hard before stepping around me and out of the shower. "Sorry to disappoint you, Dear Husband," she continued to say as she wrapped a large fluffy white towel around her drenched body. "But last time I checked, not feeling hungry didn't constitute an eating disorder."

The bathroom door slammed shut behind her and I was left alone in the shower.

Groaning internally, I switched off the water and climbed out.

Grabbing a towel, I hooked it around my waist before heading back into the bedroom.

"You've lost weight," I explained in as calm a tone as I could muster. "I'm sorry if it upset you, but I had to ask."

"Of course you did," she shot back coldly.

Dropping her towel, Teagan walked across the bedroom shamelessly, as naked as the day she was born. "I'm naturally skinny," she told me before throwing open a dresser drawer.

Pulling out several items of clothing, she dropped them on the ground.

She was so damn messy.

Why did women need so much stuff?

I couldn't figure it out. I'd spent half a decade in a cell with Lucky.

We had minimal stuff in prison and survived just fine, but Teagan?

Jesus, that woman had a truckload of shit following after her.

We'd arrived in New York on Tuesday and it had taken me three trips to the bus to bring all her shit up to our suite.

Teagan continued to dump the contents of her dresser drawers on the floor before deciding on a pair of plain black cotton panties and stepping into them. "But thanks for throwing my body insecurities in my face."

Teagan grabbed a matching black bra from the pile of rubble on the floor and dangled it in front of her face.

"See this?" She demanded. "Women with bodies like mine don't need to wear these."

She put it on anyway, much to my dismay.

"Do you want to comment on how tiny my breasts are, too?" She asked. "Or mention the fact that I don't have a big ass like all those girls you used to flaunt around with after every fight you had on the television?"

"I'm sorry, Thorn." I was an asshole. "I love your body," I added, feeling like the world's worst piece of shit.

She was going to cry.

I could see it in her eyes.

Her hazel eyes were tearing up.

"You're perfect to me," I added gruffly.

That did it.

The waterworks started.

She was fucking crying *again*.

"I don't have an eating disorder," she said in a voice thick with emotion as tears rolled down her cheeks. "I feel under the weather, okay?"

"Okay." Walking over to her, I placed my hands on her shoulders and whispered, "Don't cry."

That was a big fucking mistake because she only cried harder.

"Stop crying?" I offered, unsure and nervous as hell.

"I can't help it," she half sobbed, half screamed, using my arm to wipe her nose. Lovely. "I'm feeling under the weather and you think I'm ugly."

"What?" Shaking my head, I pulled her into my arms. "I do not think you're ugly."

Jesus Christ. What the hell was wrong with her?

"I think you're beautiful."

"You like curvy women," she shot back, sobbing harder. "You said I'm too skinny."

No I fucking didn't...

"Thorn, come on, baby, stop this," I begged, helplessly.

Tipping her chin upward with my thumb, I brushed the tears off her cheeks, eyes locked on hers.

"I love you." Cupping her neck with both hands, I pressed my lips to hers, shivering when my stomach twisted inside of me.

My legs shook.

I was fucking trembling.

She had that effect on me.

"I fucking love you," I repeated against her lips, taking her breath with another kiss. "Yours is the only body I think is sexy," I told her, knowing deep down inside that she needed to hear it. It was no lie. Teagan was painstakingly sexy. "You turn me on like no one else," I added.

"I do?" She asked, hiccupping. A small smile tipped her lips upward and I sagged in relief.

"Of course," I said carefully, debating whether or not I should say the next sentence. "It only crossed my mind because Ellie's stomach looked kind of swollen like yours every time she made herself sick."

Oh shit...

I knew I'd said the wrong thing the second the words had spilled out of my mouth.

Teagan's face turned a deep shade of red. "Let me get this straight," she screamed, furious. "First, I'm too skinny, and now I'm fucking fat?" Reaching into the drawer, she grabbed a pink lacy bra and threw it at my head. "You insensitive asshole."

"Fine," I conceded, holding my hands up. "I won't say another word about your body... I won't say another word."

"That sounds good to me." Tears filled her eyes again. "Now turn around so I can dress my *fat* ass."

42

NOAH

"Noah, one of JD's men has been spotted. I'm with Teagan. She's safe and oblivious as usual. I'll be removing her from the arena as soon as the fight is over. Good luck."

I had listened to Lewis' voicemail the moment I arrived at the arena and instantly, my good mood had evaporated.

Sitting on a three-legged stool, listening to the crowd screaming and roaring around me, I had this horrible feeling in the pit of my stomach that I was somehow playing straight into JD's hands.

Twisting sideways, I searched the crowd for Teagan's face.

When I found her in the fourth row, my heart jackknifed in my chest.

She looked fucking miserable.

Her face was pale and her hazel eyes were sunken in her face. Lewis was sitting beside her, though he could have been a million miles away she looked so lonely...

"Did you say something to her?" My words were strained

because of the mouth guard I had on and my heavy breathing.

I'd just gone five rounds with Roy Wicks, who was currently curled up like a bitch in the other corner of the ring.

Tonight's fight was a basic ring match.

Apparently, Wicks thought our last fight had been an unfair one because of my 'specialty' in a cage and had demanded a rematch in a ring.

What fucking ever.

At thirty-eight, Roy Wicks was over the hill.

Yeah, he had a nasty right hook, but I had a feeling that after tonight, the guy was going to start seriously considering retirement.

Rinsing my mouth with water, I spat it into the bucket beside me and inhaled several deep breaths, forcing my heart to slow down to a normal rhythm, as I returned my attention to Tommy.

"Well?"

"Jesus," Tommy grumbled, as he wrapped a towel around my shoulders. "Are you for real?"

Running a hand through his hair, he narrowed his blue eyes at me.

"You're in the middle of a fight and you're thinking about her?" Shaking his head in disgust, he spat, "You need to get your head out of that woman and into the game, Noah."

Leaning backwards against the ropes, I studied my oldest friend. Tommy's brown hair was dusted with premature gray hairs.

His lips were narrowed and set in a straight line.

"What did you say to her?" I repeated slowly, ignoring everything else.

"Nothing," Tommy hissed. Dabbing my left eye with a towel, he wiped away the droplets of blood that were leaking from a reopened cut. "I said absolutely nothing to the girl."

"What about you?" I turned to my right and glared at Quincy.

I was paying these guys to support me, but right now I felt fucking betrayed.

Something had gone down.

I knew it, and if Teagan wasn't going to tell me, then one of these fucker's sure as hell was.

"Now you listen here, boy," Quincy snarled. Cupping the back of my neck with his beefy hand, he dragged my head down to his. "Get your head in the game and off your fucking flower woman or I will give you a fucking reason to piss and moan."

I pressed my forehead hard to his, accepting his challenge. "If I hear you did anything to upset my 'flower woman' I'll put you in a fucking body bag."

The bell rang loudly, signaling the start of the sixth round and I pushed off my coach.

Blind rage coursed through my veins as I moved into the middle of the ring, stalking my opponent.

This round was going to be a quick one.

43

TEAGAN

The crowd went crazy when Noah defeated Roy Wicks in the seventh round of their fight.

Never in my twenty-five years had I experienced anything like the atmosphere in the arena when my husband's hand was raised in victory.

It was so electric – so...extraordinary.

Even now, almost an hour after the fight, Noah was still inside the arena surrounded by throngs of supporters and the media, all vying for his attention.

For my own safety, Lewis had chaperoned me outside to the waiting limousine and, to be honest, I was glad.

This world that I had been thrust into wasn't one I thought I would ever get used to.

I knew what I looked like; dressed in a skin tight, full-length black dress with a plunging neckline and a huge slit right up to my thigh and draped in more diamonds than the local jewelry shop stocked back home.

A gold digger...

My cell phone rang out loudly, dragging me out of my thoughts, and I jumped.

"Shit."

Grabbing my purse, I dug my hand inside and rummaged around for a few seconds before retrieving the cool metal device.

Swiping my finger across the screen, I didn't bother to check who it was and said, "Hello?"

"Teegs, it's me." My blood ran cold the moment Liam's voice filled my ears, followed quickly by, "Please don't hang up."

"Give me one good reason not to," I shot back, furious. Anger swirled inside of me at the sound of his voice. The last time Liam and I had spoken, he'd try to destroy my marriage. I hadn't seen or heard from him since Lewis carted him out of our hotel room that fateful night.

"Because I'm sorry," he offered. "Because I know I fucked up."

"You're a dick," I hissed, unable to contain my emotions. "You're not the guy I grew up with." That was true. "The Liam I knew would have never tried to hurt me the way you did." My voice was rising. My hands were shaking.

"I'm sorry, okay?" Liam groveled. "I handled everything horribly." There was a pause and then I heard him sigh heavily. "I'm miserable without you, Teegs."

"Good," I hissed, refusing to allow my heart to simmer up any amount of sympathy for the conniving bastard. "You know there was a time when I actually loved you," I spat, clenching my eyes shut. "You were my best friend for half of my life and I would have done anything for you – ahhhhh..."

The sound of a car door slamming startled me.

Screaming, I all but jumped out of my own skin, dropping my phone in the process.

The moment my eyes landed on Noah's face, the air expelled from my lungs in a heady gasp.

He looked like a god, dressed in worn light blue denim jeans and plain red t-shirt. He smelled like soap and man. His hair was wet and falling forward, brushing his brow. He was bruising – badly. The entire left side of his face was colored purple.

"Sorry for interrupting," Noah said coolly as he settled down on the seat opposite me. "Please," he added sarcastically, holding a cloth covered ice pack to his jaw. "Continue telling some other guy how much you love him." Sitting back with his legs spread open, he never took his eyes off my face, as he tended to his wounds. "I'm fascinated."

My heart plummeted in my chest.

With my back pressed to the leather of the seat, I forced myself to breathe, all while my heart thundered in my chest as I watched him watch me.

Our relationship was tempestuous enough without adding more drama to our fucked up equation.

"It's not what you think," I finally acknowledged in a quiet tone, not knowing what else to say, but knowing that I had to say something. I could have smacked myself for saying something so cliché.

Tossing my hair over my shoulder, a knee-jerk reaction to intimidating situations, I reached down and grabbed my phone off the floor.

"Not what I think," Noah spat, tossing the ice pack down on the seat.

"Obviously," I snapped, red-faced, as I slipped my phone back into my purse.

Noah's eyes darkened.

The vein in his neck ticked as his eyes roamed over my body.

"What fucking ever," he muttered under his breath.

He sat rigidly on the opposite side of the limousine, with one arm flung casually over the back of the seat.

His black hair was all mussed up and sexy and his dark eyes were intense, heated, and unwaveringly focused on me.

The only thing that gave me comfort in this moment was the black circled tattoo on his left hand.

"You fought well," I told him, feeling the burning in my cheeks all the way down to my toes as I tried to clear the air with a compliment.

"I know," Noah replied in a low, gruff tone, his angry eyes locked on mine, hard and unforgiving.

A shiver of fear rolled down my spine mixing with the pent-up lust inside of my body at the sight of the man before me.

Not sure what to do, I decided rummaging in my purse was a good place to start, and while I was at it, I decided to pray for the ground to open beneath me.

Hell had to be a better option than being the sole recipient of Noah Messina's bad mood.

Ducking my face, I unzipped the bag and pulled out a tube of lipstick.

I felt Noah's heated gaze on me as I smeared my lips with the tube.

Suppressing the urge to close my eyes and shiver at the feel of having his eyes on me, I quickly snapped the lid back on the tube of gloss and tucked it back into my purse.

"You miss him," Noah accused.

This time I did shiver.

It was an unstoppable reaction.

"No."

Noah studied me with cool, perceptive eyes. "You love him."

Again, it wasn't a question – just a barefaced statement.

"No." Shaking my head, I sagged back in my seat, finding comfort in the feel of the cold leather against my skin. "I don't." Snapping the clasp of my purse shut, I stared back at him. "*He* called *me*."

Noah laughed harshly. "And you *answered*."

Several more bodies piled into the back of the limo then, breaking the unnerving tension. One of those bodies belonged to Lewis and I sagged in relief when he sat down beside me. Don't get me wrong, I was burning mad with him, but in a car full of men who despised me, Lewis was the safest bet.

Another one of the bodies belonged to Tommy – who claimed the seat to Noah's right.

Quincy and Beau also joined us, choosing to sit on Noah's side of the Limo.

Like I cared...

It wasn't easy to act aloof when everyone hated you.

In fact, sitting in this limo was like being back in a high school classroom.

For years I'd struggled to fit in until the day I decided to stop trying.

But just because I didn't try didn't mean it didn't hurt...

It was safe to say that with the exception of Noah, I hated every single person in this limousine.

Actually, hate was too kind a word for the bastards I was surrounded by.

I *loathed* them.

Yes, loathed.

I was losing myself in this world and I fucking hated it. After all I'd sacrificed, I was still being tested – punished.

"Screw this," I growled, finally cracking under the tension.

Reaching forward, I grabbed a very expensive bottle of

Don Perignon from the nearby ice bucket and popped the cork.

"What?" I said daringly, eyes locked on Tommy as he frowned at me. "It's not like he can't afford it."

With that, I pressed the bottle to my lips, not removing it until I had the majority of it consumed.

44

TEAGAN

*C*limbing out of the limousine first, Noah turned around and reached out his hand to me.

"Think you can love me more for tonight?" He growled, helping me out of the car. "Or is that impossible for you, *wife*?"

"Don't be a dick," I hissed, taking his outstretched hand. "You know how I feel about you, *husband*."

He cocked a brow and smirked cruelly. "Do I?"

I didn't have a chance to respond before Noah was swamped and pulled away by a mirage of people, some were clearly reporters, others undeniably fans.

"Noah, we love you!" His fans were screaming. *"Look at him! He's enormous."*

"Noah...Oh my god, he smiled at me!" A particularly zealous blonde squealed in delight. *"He smiled at me – Noah, please. Fuck my brains out!"*

Startled and, quite frankly, overwhelmed by the media, I stepped away from the madness happening around me, hugging myself in dismay as I studied the hordes of fans blocking the sidewalk to the club entrance.

People jumped in front of me, shoving me out of the way, desperate to get closer to Noah.

Cameras and microphones were thrust into his face and I lagged behind, backing away from the circus show, feeling completely out of my comfort zone, not to mention wounded from his words.

Watching numerous women touch and grab at my husband wasn't helping with my jealous tendencies either.

I felt inferior.

I didn't look like any of these women.

I wasn't tall or curved or big breasted; I was short, skinny, and flat chested and apparently, I wasn't the only person to recognize my shortcomings.

Somebody knocked against me then, throwing me off balance and knocking me off my feet.

Stumbling backwards, I flailed my arms out helplessly, braced for an impact I was sure would sting like a bitch.

It never came.

My body was all but parallel with the sidewalk when a tanned hand came through the crowd and caught onto my arm.

Slinging me up from the pavement like a slinky toy, Noah yanked me roughly toward him.

One huge, muscular arm came around my waist, pinning me to his side.

Another hand splayed across my stomach protectively.

Eyes dark as coal stared down at me causing my heart to flutter and my breath to seize in my throat.

Flustered, I said the first thing that came to mind. "I think a little pee came out." In all honesty, I had come very close to peeing my pants, and his angry eyes freckled with those nasty bruises was doing nothing to ease my frazzled nerves.

Noah stared at me for a long moment, unblinking, his gaze intense as if he was trying to solve a puzzle.

"Get out of the way," he growled after an age. Turning his attention to the crowd around us, he roared, "I said move!"

And just like that, the crowd backed off, clearing a path for us.

Their loud screams and cries turned to hushed whispers as Noah took me by the hand and led me into the club.

"Mr. Messina," a tall, silver-haired man acknowledged when we stepped inside. "Rick D'Angelo. Congratulations on your win tonight. Welcome to The Jungle." He turned his attention to me and nodded curtly. "Mrs. Messina."

"Hey, Noah, I bet they've got fun and games," I tossed out, trying to lighten the mood between us. "It was a Guns N Roses reference," I explained when Rick D'Angelo looked down at me with an unimpressed expression. "Ugh...Never mind."

D'Angelo cleared his throat and said, "Let me show you to your booth," before gesturing us toward the door at the far end of the corridor with a sign stating **VIP ACCESS ONLY.**

"Next time, make damn sure you have more security out there," Noah snarled, striding off toward the VIP access area. "My wife could've been trampled."

"Duly noted," Rick replied, cheeks staining red as he fell into step alongside Noah.

Meanwhile, I was being dragged along like a rag doll toward our booth.

"Can you slow down?" I asked, a little breathless. Noah was walking so fast I was struggling to keep up with him. "Noah, I can't walk that fast."

Noah didn't slow down.

When I tried to pull my hand out of his, he squeezed it tighter.

In fact, I was pretty damn sure he upped his pace on purpose, not stopping until we were standing in front of a large tabled booth with a fancy looking black and neon pink tablecloth on top.

Noah ushered me into the booth before taking a seat beside me, and within seconds, two waitresses were at our side placing bottles of champagne and jugs of what looked like sex on the beach on the table.

Lewis hovered nearby, silent as usual, as a third waitress arrived with a fancy plate of nibbles in each hand.

Shoving away from Noah, I sat on the very edge and as far away from him as I could.

Folding my arms across my chest, I glared at his battered and bruised face.

"You almost pulled my arm out of its socket."

His face softened slightly for a brief moment before he remembered he was mad at me – for what, I had no idea – before quickly morphing back into anger.

Big surprise there...

Quincy, Beau, and Tommy arrived at our table then, bringing with them a few stragglers – five females and two males.

They all sidled into the booth alongside us, leaving me on the edge of the side with Beau to my right.

I groaned internally.

I could see where this night was going and it was straight to hell.

"Can we get you anything else, Mr. Messina?" One of the waitresses purred – the blonde one with the huge rack.

Stroking Noah's arm, Big Tits proceeded to uncap one of

the champagne bottles with relish before filling the glass in front of Noah.

To give him credit, Noah didn't even look in her direction.

His focus was entirely on me and that made me feel a little less stabby.

"We're good," he told the waitress as he shoved the glass toward me. "You want something else?"

Never one to refuse a drink, I grabbed the glass and tossed it back, draining it dry within seconds. "Yeah." Wiping my mouth with the back of my hand, I pushed my glass toward him. "A refill."

Noah cocked a brow but didn't reply and I felt the last piece of my self-restraint slip away.

"I'm his wife, not his ward. I don't need his permission, you know," I snapped, glaring up at the waitress who seemed to be in a semi-comatose trance as she held the champagne bottle in her hand and looked down at my husband with her big doe eyes, waiting for him to give her the go-ahead.

"Ugh." Rolling my eyes, I reached forward and swiped one of the other bottles of champagne on the table.

A hand snaked out and grabbed the rim of the bottle just as I went to lift it.

"You're embarrassing him – *again*," Beau hissed under his breath. "Can't you just behave yourself for one night?"

"And you are pissing me off – *again* - so if you value your left ball sac then I suggest you let go," I snarled through clenched teeth, daring Beau to push me. "*Now*."

The loud chattering that had been going on around me quickly depleted as all eyes landed on me and Beau. Thankfully Beau, or Dick Three, as I liked to call him – Dick One and Two were reserved for Quincy and Tommy – valued his testicle and released the bottle to my trusted care.

It was a small victory, but one I would cherish.

Noah continued to glare silently across the table at me, and the more alcohol I consumed, the more I met his glare with one of my own.

"Why are you doing this?" I finally demanded, losing all tact and patience.

My body was swaying without my permission and tiny little stars were dancing around in front of my eyes.

I was drunk, I realized, but drunk or not, I was having this out with Noah.

"Doing what?"

"Being a bastard to me," I yelled in frustration, not bothering to lower my voice when silence fell around us.

I didn't care that everybody was listening.

Fucking let them.

Any one of these people could look at my vagina if they clicked on the right website.

I had nothing left to hide.

"I should leave you high and dry," I added, hurt.

"If I'm keeping you from where you really want to be, then by all means go, Teagan," Noah shot back, furious. "But don't expect me to come after you again, because I won't."

"I am not taking this shit from you," I warned him. "I mean it."

"So what, you're just going to run again?" He ran a hand through his freshly washed hair. "Then do it, Thorn, fucking leave me hanging again. It wouldn't be the first time."

"I'm done apologizing for the past, Noah!" I screamed heatedly.

"You said you *love* him, Teagan!" Noah roared, losing his cool. His chest was heaving. A vein in his temple bulged.

"Which is something I find really fucking hypocritical considering you were screaming that exact sentiment to me the other night when I was eating your pussy."

"Jesus Christ," I hissed, mortified. "I said *loved* – as in past fucking tense."

"It's all the same to me," Noah shot back, fuming.

Looking around at the several red-faced people sitting around us, I climbed unsteadily to my feet.

"You know what?" Wobbling over to Noah's side of the table, I grabbed the cocktail pitcher. "Cool the hell down, Noah." With that, I tossed the contents over his head before turning to Lewis. "Take me back to the hotel."

I was mad, not crazy.

I knew well enough not to go anywhere without my big, bald traitor.

"Don't you dare, Lewis," Noah barked before turning his attention back to me. Jerking out of his seat, Noah wiped the front of his soaked shirt. "Now I get that you're a raging bitch," he growled, turning his attention to me. "But if you could rein in the violent outbursts for one fucking second, or at least while we're in public..."

"Oh, I'm a raging bitch now, am I?" Swinging around, I stalked toward him. "Well, how's this for a violent outburst, you big bastard."

Reaching my hand back, I smacked Noah across the cheek as hard as I possibly could.

He didn't even flinch so I smacked him again.

Harder.

"Fuck you," I added before turning on my heel and staggering away from him.

Screw Noah Messina.

It would be a cold day in hell before I allowed myself to be treated like a piece of shit on his shoe.

Shoving my way through the crowd, I made a beeline for the bar, mentally patting myself on the back for tucking that twenty into my cleavage before leaving the hotel tonight.

Jostling against several other patrons at the bar, I stood up on my tiptoes and waved my hand in the air, trying to catch the barman's attention; not an easy feat considering I was the shortest person at the bar.

Finally, I caught the barman's eye and he came over to where I was standing.

"What can I get you, sir?"

"*Sir*?" I snapped, furious when I realized he was talking to someone behind me. "I was here first."

"Don't serve her," an achingly familiar voice said from behind me and I groaned. A strong arm came around my waist, pulling me backward into a familiar chest of muscle. "She's been cut off."

"No problem, Mr. Messina," the barman said. His eyes flickered to mine and he gave me a look that said 'Oh well,' before wandering off to serve someone else.

Swinging around, I glowered up at Noah. "You are, by far, the biggest son of a b–"

"Yeah, yeah, I'm scum of the earth," Noah interrupted, unaffected. Taking me by the waist, he walked me toward the dance floor. "Shut your mouth Thorn, and dance with me."

"Over my dead body," I hissed, trying to scramble out of his embrace.

It was no use.

Noah had a death grip on me; his arms were like tree trunks wrapped around me, and short of a bomb going off, I knew I wasn't getting away from him.

Admitting defeat, I stopped fighting him and let my body sag against his. Leaning backward, I rested my head against his hard chest. "I thought you said you weren't going to chase me again."

Ducking his head, he buried his face in my neck and sighed. "I thought you said you weren't going to run again."

"I lied," I begrudgingly admitted.

"Me too."

The heat of his breath on my bare skin caused me to shudder violently in his arms.

"I'm so angry with you, Noah."

"The feeling's mutual, Thorn." He pressed a kiss to the skin covering my racing pulse. "Save your anger for the bedroom. I know I am."

"I'm never having sex with you again," I argued, rocking my ass against the rising bulge in his jeans.

Noah chuckled and the low rumble in his chest caused everything south of my navel to clench in anticipation.

I had no idea how we'd gotten here and I cared even less.

The alcohol currently running through my bloodstream was making my brain think up all kinds of slutty things to do to the sexy god of a man pressing his dick against me.

God...

Closing my eyes, I gave myself up to the music, to the feel of being with Noah.

Fighting or not, we were here.

We were together and we were trying.

Running the palms of my hands down his thighs, I slipped one hand behind my back.

Flicking the top button open, I slipped my hand inside, biting down hard on my lip when his erection fell heavily into my hand.

Noah was more than a handful – he was huge – but I happened to have the magic touch when it came to his cock.

Keeping my back pressed to him, I squeezed him tightly,

knowing exactly how he liked me to touch him. Trailing my thumb over the head, I felt the small drop of pre-cum and grinned in victory.

Noah grunted as my hand flexed between our bodies.

He hissed out a sharp breath when I slipped my hand lower and cupped his balls.

I wasn't being as discreet as I should and I didn't care, but Noah did.

"Thorn," he growled in my ear. "Stop, baby. We're on a... fuck..." Thrusting himself against me, Noah groaned deeply...

And then we were moving through the crowded dance floor quicker than my legs could keep up.

My legs aren't keeping me up, I thought hazily to myself.

Looking down at my dangling feet and then at the two strong arms clamped around my waist, I realized Noah was taking my full weight as he walked us through a doorway at the far corner of the bar.

The moment we stepped inside the dimly lit room, Noah dropped me onto my feet and turned me around.

"You opposed to fucking in a janitor's room, Thorn?" He said, panting. Reaching down, he grabbed the hem of my dress and dragged it roughly over my head before casting it away. "Because I need you badly right now."

Hooking his fingers in the waistband of my panties, he tugged hard, grinning when my red lace thong came away in his hands.

I was trapped in an internal battle of whether or not to be mad at him and his brown eyes were winning me over. "You have a piece of paper stating you can have me anywhere," I replied breathlessly.

My hands dropped to his jeans and I quickly freed him from his denim restraints.

My back slammed against cold tiles seconds before Noah's body was covering mine.

The smell of disinfectant and chemicals was so strong it was stifling, but it didn't stop me.

Wrapping my arms around his neck, I climbed up his body like ivy, desperate to feel him inside me, to feel the pressure of his hard cock inside my body, making me come.

Making me whole...

"Fuck," Noah hissed when I aligned my pussy with the head of his cock and pulled him inside me. Cupping my ass with his hands, Noah steadied himself. "Slow down or I'm gonna ruin you."

"Ruin me hard then," I moaned, thrusting my hips against him, crying out loudly when his erection slid deep inside me.

He was so deep it felt like he was touching my spine.

Groaning, Noah plunged himself hard into me at an unyielding pace.

I welcomed his relentlessness. He suckled on my puckered nipples, coaxing me with his tongue, biting down on my sensitive buds.

Making me cry out for more...

Grabbing his face with my hands, I plunged my tongue inside his mouth, reveling in his hard fucking. I was drunk and Noah was halfway drunk which made our kisses sloppy.

We were all teeth and tongue and viciousness.

He kissed me like he wanted to hurt me and I bit down so hard on his lip that he froze inside me and his head reared back in surprise.

A tiny crevice of blood appeared on his bottom lip.

Dragging his face back to mine, I swiped my tongue over his reopened cut before pulling his lip back into my mouth, suckling hard.

Noah groaned loudly and reclaimed my lips.

His dick thickened inside me as he slammed himself into my opening, making me weak with want and pleasure.

His lips never left mine as he fucked me hard and rough. It was the rawest, most primal experience of my life and I lapped it up like I couldn't get enough.

In this moment, I wanted him to break me.

My clit throbbed like a pulse as every nerve in my body knitted together.

Every thrust of his cock sent shockwaves rippling through me.

Each plunge of his tongue intensified those shocks until I was both clinging to him and arching away all at once.

Nodding my head quickly in approval, I whimpered into his mouth as my fingernails dug into his shoulders, urging him to take me harder.

My orgasm hit me so hard and so suddenly that I screamed out, jerking violently in his arms.

Noah continued to rock inside me so deep, the veins in his neck strained from the pressure.

I could feel him filling me up with his hot release and it prolonged my orgasm until I was a breathless mess in his arms.

45

NOAH

I had my wife pressed up against a wall in a fucking janitor's closet.

She was naked, spread wide open, and I was buried to the hilt inside her.

I knew I needed to put her down, but I was having a real hard time making myself do it.

Her body was trembling around mine. Her tight little pussy was still clenching with aftershocks.

It was the truth. The mere thought of that blond prick even speaking my wife's name caused my blood to boil in my veins. Even though I fucking promised myself I wouldn't let that rat bastard get under my skin again, I couldn't help it. Hearing Teagan speaking to him made me want to rip something apart – *slowly*.

I finally had everything I'd ever wanted and I was jeopardizing it.

I didn't need a shrink to know why; it was because I was scared.

I was fucking petrified of a tiny little woman because she could still go.

She could still leave me and take it all away again.

It was a fucked up attribute of a broken human; to push the one you love most away to see if they love you enough to keep coming back.

And when we were fighting and screaming at each other, all I could think was the sooner I put a baby in her stomach, the better. Marriage wasn't enough. I needed to cement her to me. I needed to fucking tie her down with so much baggage that she wouldn't contemplate leaving me twice.

I knew for a fact that Teagan wasn't on birth control, and my desperation and fucking insecurities meant that knowledge thrilled me. Every night I took advantage of the fact that she was desperately trying to show me her commitment. I rarely used a condom, even though she'd asked me to, and I made damn sure that I came inside that woman at least three times each night.

I mean, how messed up was that?

I was the illegitimate, not to mention practically illiterate, bastard of David Henderson. I was a convicted felon who'd been raised by drug addict parents. What in the hell did I know about marriage and raising families?

The only thing I did know was that losing my wife would kill me, and I was willing to do anything to stop that from happening twice...

"You need to stop doing this to me." I let out a shaky sigh and buried my face in her neck.

"Doing what?" She whispered, trailing her fingers through my hair.

"Making me weak," I admitted gruffly. Lifting my face to look at her, my heart hammered in my chest. "I'm trying so hard to move on," I forced myself to say. "But I'm fucking drowning in jealousy. Because I know he's been with you."

My jaw clenched. "He touched you." My jealousy was irrational and ridiculous, but I couldn't help it.

I could feel her body trembling as she slowly climbed down and stood on her own two feet. "Noah, it was one time." Exhaling a shaky breath, she added, "One, forty-five second mistake that I will spend the rest of my life regretting."

"Me too," I tossed out gruffly. "And I know I can't judge you for anything you did when I was away – hell, it's not like I was celibate or anything – but for me, those women sated a need. A hole to put my dick in. For you, Liam represents a lot more than that. You have a past with him. A better past than the one you have with me. And I fucking hate the thought of you with *him*." *Because I know it's my own damn fault...*

"I can't keep doing this, Noah." Reaching down, Teagan picked up her dress from the floor. "I can't keep going over the same thing time and again," she choked out as she slipped her dress back on. Sniffling loudly, she wiped her eyes with the backs of her hands. "I am so *tired* of fighting and defending myself."

I was an asshole.

She was crying.

Fucking again.

I never knew women cried this much.

Correction, I never knew *Teagan* cried this much.

I was used to angry Teagan –the one who got revenge and if you hurt her she came back at you twice as hard.

Not tonight...

My usually steel spiked, prickly Thorn was turning into a fucking flower and it was all my fault.

"Come on, Teagan, don't cry," I whispered, placing my hand on her tiny shoulder. "I hate seeing you upset, okay? It *kills* me." That was a big fucking mistake because she only cried harder.

"I waited for you," she said against my mouth. "Without even knowing I was doing it." Pulling back, she wiped her eyes with the back of her hand. "All those years?" She shook her head. "I *never* touched another man."

"You're the *only* thing I've ever had that was *mine*," I told her, desperate to explain myself. "You were my choice. Mine. And watching you go was the hardest thing I've ever had to do. And now you're back. I have you, but I just..."

"Can't trust me?" She offered.

I opened my mouth to answer her, but she didn't give me a chance.

"I am here," she growled, marching straight up to me. "With you." She pushed me in the chest. "Taking all of your crap." She shoved me again. "Not to mention your *team's* crap." Harder this time. "Because I love *you*." Teagan let out a hiss of frustration. "But if you can't get over the fact that I had sex with another man when we *weren't* together, then I'm not hanging around to be your punching bag."

"I am over it," I told her. A nervous shock rippled through me. The thought of her leaving almost too much to bear. "I'm trying, Thorn."

"You either want me or you don't," she said wearily, tears once again dripping down her cheeks. "You either believe me or you don't. Because honest to god, Noah, I can't keep doing this with you – going head to head and taking an ass kicking. It's too much and I'm worn out."

"I want you," I told her, knowing deep down inside that she needed to hear it. It was no lie. "I do."

Teagan was the only person I'd ever loved.

Ever.

Making her cry wasn't something I went out of my way to do.

Fuck, it was something I tried to steer my asshole mouth away from as often as possible.

But she was so damn emotional lately I couldn't seem to help it.

I couldn't pretend I wasn't hurt over the past.

It was a hard pill to swallow.

Anxiety was flooding me.

The look in her eyes was causing that anxiety to fucking soar.

Tipping her chin upward with my thumb, I brushed the tears off her cheeks, eyes locked on hers. "I *only* want you." Moving my hands to cup her neck, I pressed my lips to hers, shivering when my stomach twisted inside of me.

"I should've come back sooner, Teagan," I admitted, laying it all out there for once. "If I had, then things would have been different."

The truth was I loved Teagan more than any man should love a woman.

I loved her more than was safe for me and loving her brought to the surface feelings that before her, I'd never had to worry about.

Jealousy. Inferiority. Fear. Obsession.

Before Thorn walked into my world those emotions were a myth to me.

Now, they were my reality.

She challenged me. She pushed me out of my comfort zone. She pushed me to the brink of insanity and then dragged me back again. She stuck it to me regardless of where we were or who we were with. She had the ability to ruin me and heal me with one breath.

It was unnerving, the amount of power she held over me.

Reaching up, Teagan cupped my cheek with one of her hands and sighed. "We won't let this break us," she promised before drawing my mouth down to hers. "I love you more than you hate me," she whispered before covering my lips with hers.

46

NOAH

I screwed up.

I was a big enough person to admit that I'd overreacted.

Hell, I'd done more than just overreact; I'd behaved like a fucking tool toward my wife.

Almost a week had passed since the incident in the janitor's closet, and Teagan was acting like everything was fine. She hadn't chewed me out over my behavior the next morning or held a grudge.

In fact, her latest approach to handling our problems was to brush them under the mat and cover them up with a fake assed smile.

But I knew she was upset with me.

The fact that she wasn't sitting with me proved that.

I was at the back of the bus and Thorn was sitting up front all on her own with her headphones on, staring out the bus window.

She looked so lonely that all I wanted to do was wrap her up in my arms and hug the hell out of her.

Refusing to allow the wedge between us to push us

further apart, I stood up and walked up the aisle of the bus, not stopping until I was sitting down on the seat beside her.

Teagan didn't look away from the window, but I knew that *she* knew I was there.

Her breathing hitched in her throat and she removed one ear plug from her ear and handed it to me.

Without a word, I took the ear plug from her and popped it in my ear before reaching for her hand and pulling it onto my lap.

I couldn't stop the smile from spreading across my face when the lyrics of Kate Nash's *Dickhead* filled my ear.

Just like earlier, Teagan never spoke a word as she entwined her fingers with mine and rested her cheek on my shoulder.

"I'll do better," I whispered before pressing a kiss to the top of her head.

She nuzzled against me. "I know."

We sat side by side in silence as she studied the scenery outside and I studied her face.

She looked deep in thought.

"What are you thinking about?" I asked her after a while, when my curiosity got the better of me.

"The first time I saw you," Teagan replied. Turning her face toward me, she smiled softly. "And how you made me feel back then."

"Great," I muttered, feeling a bead of sweat trickle down my brow. It was bad enough that I'd been a tool the other night, but Thorn was dragging up old memories of me being an even bigger one.

"I was a dick that night," I added, thinking back to the night I'd smashed her car windshield. "I overreacted." Teagan had overreacted worse than I had, but I was trying to get back in my wife's good books so I aptly left out that particular piece of information.

"You were," Teagan agreed. "But that's not the night I'm thinking about."

My brows furrowed in confusion as I waited for her to explain.

"You took the air clean out of my lungs the first time I saw you," she continued to say, looking up at my face. Biting down on her lower lip, she smiled. "I can still remember the way my heart fluttered in my chest when I saw you standing there, watching me play Martin."

Now I remembered.

The summer before senior year. I'd been seventeen years old, with little hope, and a lot of attitude. Angry and full of hatred, I hadn't been expecting her. I hadn't wanted her, but she arrived regardless.

Without my permission, the girl next door had forced herself into my heart with that song...

HER BLONDE WAVY HAIR LOOKED LIKE IT HADN'T BEEN brushed in days. The denim cut-offs she had on were worn to a thread and the white t-shirt she wore was at least five times too big for her, tied into a makeshift belly-top with a hair clip.

Her skin looked like ivory silk, she had a cut on her left knee and a bruise on her right elbow and I'd never seen anything so fucking beautiful.

She wasn't intentionally sexy... she just was.

I watched her intently as she stretched her arms and legs out, clearly basking in the summer sunshine – I couldn't turn my face away.

"You were all beat up and bruised," Teagan said, drawing me back to the present.

"Yeah," I replied, tone thick with emotion. "I'd been in a fight the night before." Actually, I'd been in several fights. I'd had the broken ribs to prove it, but again, I refrained from telling her that.

"You looked so closed off, so... separated from your surroundings," Teagan said softly. "I'd just moved in and I was lonely and scared. I didn't want to be there..." Pausing, she stared hard at my face. "And when I looked into your eyes, I realized that you didn't want to be either." Shrugging, she added, "It was one moment – one brief, flittering moment in the grand scheme of things – but in that moment, you looked into my eyes and I felt a little less lonely."

"Thorn," I croaked out, not knowing what else to say. She confounded me. The way she could be. Her mood swings. Her memories. The way she saw me. I was a better person in her mind. She saw good in my darkness and hope in my despair.

The pull toward her was relentless. I didn't even have a life of my own anymore. Everything was blurred and mixed up with hers.

Fuck...

"Of course, then Ellie came out and ruined the moment." Teagan smirked knowingly. "And then we had that huge fight a few weeks later and I buried that moment we shared under a mountain of grudges," she whispered. "That small space in time, on a long summer afternoon when the boy next door looked into my eyes and saw right into my soul."

47

TEAGAN

*N*oah blew the roof off the place in NYC last weekend, making Daniel Cortez submit in the third round, breaking pay-per-view records and continuing his undefeated MFA record of 38-0.

We had arrived back in Denver, Colorado late last night in preparation for Noah's last fight of this leg of the tour against Gary Bash on Friday.

We were doing better since our altercation in New Orleans. There was still a Liam-shaped wedge between us, but Noah was trying harder with me.

I was trying, too; trying to pull myself out of the semi-comatose funk I'd been in but knowing that The Hill would be our next stop wasn't helping matters. Knowing that we were less than an hour's car ride away from where we'd been ripped apart all those years ago petrified me.

I wasn't really feeling up to going out and exercising this morning – I didn't want to leave the hotel room – but Noah had pestered me all through breakfast until I caved and gave in to him.

To be honest, I really didn't feel like doing anything

lately – well anything but sleep. Exhaustion had finally caught up with me and after four months on tour, I was completely beat –and overheated.

It was only ten o'clock and the heat was already too intense for me to handle, but the sight of my semi-naked husband, draped in ink and tanned like a god was causing my body temperature to spike to epic proportions.

I wasn't sure if I was hungry or horny as I watched Noah lick an ice-cream cone – strictly forbidden ice-cream, I might add.

He was on a strict diet, and the both of us knew damn well he wasn't supposed to be eating it. His shirt was off and tucked into the waistband of his gray sweats as he strolled alongside me with a baseball cap slung backwards.

"I called Max last week," I admitted, needing to get it off my chest, as we strolled through the Rocky Mountain Lake Park.

"Okay," Noah replied calmly.

Emotions flooded me at the thought of my uncle.

"I... I..." Pausing, I cleared my throat before saying, "I miss him."

Tossing the end of his ice-cream cone into a nearby trash can, Noah reached for my hand. "Was he...*nice* to you?" He asked, entwining our hands

I nodded slowly. "Yeah, he actually kind of was." Snuggling into his side, I sighed heavily. "I asked him if he wanted to meet up."

"What did he say?"

"He said...he said he was busy and he'd call me back."

"Stubborn fucking man," he muttered under his breath.

"Are you nervous?" I blurted out.

"No."

I frowned. "You don't even know what I'm referring to."

"Doesn't matter," he teased. "I'm never nervous."

"Everyone gets nervous at some point in their lives, Noah."

"Why?" Cocking a brow, he looked down at me. "Are you nervous about something?"

"Yeah." Nodding stiffly, I repressed the urge to shiver.

"What?" Noah frowned.

"Going home," I whispered.

Home.

Was University Hill my home?

It was Noah's home, but could I actually call it mine having only lived there for ten months?

"Is that where we'll stay for the month you're off?" I added. "The Hill?"

"It depends."

Depends? "On what?"

Pulling me to a stop in the middle of the sidewalk, Noah turned and faced me. "On whether Boulder is somewhere you'd like to stay." Reaching up with one hand, Noah cupped my cheek and said, "Thorn, I meant it when I said I'd take you anywhere that would make you happy." He sighed heavily. "We can leave, baby." Lifting his hand, he gestured around vaguely. "The minute the final bell rings on Friday night, we can get out of here."

I'd left a lot of demons behind me when I ran away from The Hill eight years ago.

Coming face to face with said demons wasn't something I relished the thought of.

The Hill was JD Dennis's playground and just because we hadn't heard from him, I wasn't naïve enough to believe that he'd forgotten about us, but I trusted Noah.

"I'll come home with you," I whispered, leaning into his touch. I trusted Noah with my life and I knew that he would never take me somewhere potentially dangerous. "If you think we'll be safe there..."

"You'll *always* be safe, Teagan," he assured me, voice gruff. "I fucking promise you that."

"Then we'll stay."

"What's wrong, Teagan?" Noah blurted out suddenly. Holding my face between his hands, he studied me with worried eyes. "Talk to me."

"*Nothing* is wrong." I forced a smile. It was fake, unnatural, and Noah saw straight through it.

Noah cocked a brow. "You're a horrible liar, Thorn."

"I'm just tired," I whispered, feeling horrible for lying to him.

"Is that it?" he asked, eyes locked on mine.

No...

I wanted more than anything to open up to Noah and tell him everything.

How unwell I was feeling.

How upset I was over what I'd overheard Tommy and the men saying.

How insecure I was feeling on this tour.

In fact, I wanted to kick the ground and scream at Noah to wake up and see how those bullies he called his team were treating me, but Lewis was right.

I needed to put him first for once in my life.

He needed to focus.

He was riding a high wave to the top of the league and I wasn't going to be the one to screw that up again.

"Yes," I lied.

48

NOAH

*I*f Teagan knew I was calling Hope behind her back she would flip the hell out, but I was desperate.

Not only was I desperate, but also after last night, I was worried sick...

I FELT SOMETHING DAMP TRICKLE DOWN MY BARE CHEST.

"Teagan?" My voice was thick from sleep as I rolled onto my side, taking her with me. Tipping her chin up, I stared down at her tear stained cheeks. Using my thumb to capture the tears rolling down her cheek, I brushed them away. "What's wrong?" Had she been crying all night?

"I'm just sad," she whispered, sniffling.

"Why? Are you scared or something?" It couldn't be the dark. I'd left my lamp on when we went to bed – same as every night. "What's on your mind?"

Clenching her eyes shut, Teagan wriggled closer to my body. "Nothing," she sobbed, burying her face in my chest. "Forget I said anything." Her small hand sought mine, entwining our fingers.

She let her tears fall onto my bare chest and that's when I lost it. "Tell me," I begged. "Tell me how to fix this for you."

Tears fell like big, fat raindrops from her eyes. "I'm tired," she whispered. "Of fighting. Of clinging on and hoping for happiness. I am bone weary and at the end of my tether..."

My wife was clingy and needy and teary and I was running out of options on what to do and how to help her.

Dialing my niece's phone number, I walked into the changing room in the gym and sank down on the bench.

I wasn't sure if I was even calling at an appropriate time for her.

Hope was seven hours behind us in Ireland and it was just gone two in the afternoon here.

"Noah," Hope's sleepy voice filled my ear and I sagged in relief. "What's going on?" I heard her shift around. "Is everything okay?"

"No," I muttered. Dropping my elbows to rest on my knees, I bent my head and sighed. "Not really."

She was moving around, I realized, and I heard the slight murmur of a male voice seconds before Hope's voice filled my ear once again, clearer this time – more alert.

"Okay," she said in a pissy tone. "What have you done now?"

"Who's with you?" I heard myself demand. "Is that a man's voice I can hear?"

"I'm five months older than you, douche nozzle," Hope shot back. "Now, are you going to tell me why you're calling or can I go back to sleep?"

"It's Teagan. I don't even know what's wrong with her," I admitted in a torn voice. "I think she's homesick or something." I threw it out there, hating that I couldn't be enough for Teagan. "I think she's...lonely."

"She is," Hope shot back without remorse. "You carted her off on a tour with a bunch of assholes. She has zero friends over there. You're always training and Teagan's always on her own. How do you expect her to feel?"

"What the fuck do I do?" I ran a hand through my hair and resisted the urge to pummel something. "How do I fix this?" Panic seared me. "I can't let her go." It was out of the question.

"I don't know, Noah," Hope said quietly. "You married the girl."

"She was crying last night," I choked out. "She doesn't *cry*, Hope."

"Everyone cries, Noah," Hope corrected. "Even the strongest people break down sometimes – if they've got a good enough reason to."

I didn't.

I couldn't remember a day in my entire life where I'd shed a single tear.

What the hell did that make me?

"Aren't you due a break or something?" Hope asked, drawing me out of my reverie. "Like, don't you guys get some time to rest when you're on tour?"

"Yeah. My last fight is Friday night," I told her. "I get a month off before the second leg of the tour kicks off in the fall. Why?"

"Well that's good," she replied thoughtfully. "Maybe you could take her away or something. Spend some alone time together?"

"That really doesn't help my cause right now, Hope." Teagan was miserable.

"I'll call her," she offered. "See if I can figure out what's bugging her."

"Thanks." I sagged in relief. "Oh, but don't let her know that I called you."

"Oh yeah," Hope teased. "Because keeping things from your wife is a *great* way to start married life."

"Yeah," I choked out. If Hope knew half of what I was keeping from Teagan, she wouldn't be cracking jokes.

Like that fact that JD had people watching us everywhere we went – our every move had been tracked since we arrived back to the states.

Or the many notes Lewis had intercepted these past few months. Or the thorough room sweeps he performed in each hotel we stayed in before my wife put so much as a foot through the threshold.

Yeah, Thorn didn't know about any of that...

49

TEAGAN

"*H*ope called me this evening."

I watched Noah as he sat with his back to me at the table in the living area of our suite, inhaling a humongous portion of skinless chicken and green veg.

"She did?" Noah replied between mouthfuls, breaking me out of my thoughts.

"Yeah," I shot back, studying the bunched-up muscles on his back. "She did."

I debated whether or not to torment him before coming right out and saying, "She told me you called her last week, Noah."

"Hmm." Dropping his fork down on his plate, Noah turned around and frowned. "Guess I should've known she'd rat me out."

"She's my best friend," I told him. "Her loyalty is with me."

"Fair enough." Picking up the large glass of milk beside his now empty plate, Noah slugged it back, draining every drop before setting the glass back down on the table. "I only called her because I'm worried."

"I know and I love you for caring, but I'm fine." I was a liar. A huge one. But I wasn't going to be the one to throw Noah's title shot off track. One fight. One more win and he got to rest for a month. One more fight and I got a break for a month from his team.

"Bullshit." Shoving his chair back, Noah stood up and walked over to where I was lying on the couch. Reaching for my hand, he pulled me to my feet and walked me into our bedroom. "You don't get weepy, Thorn. That's not you." Pushing me down on the bed, Noah laid down beside me, our bodies facing each other. "Something is wrong."

He was right.

Something was wrong.

Everything was wrong.

"Are you worried about tomorrow?" Noah offered out of nowhere.

We were supposed to leave for Boulder Colorado tomorrow morning and I wasn't ready for it.

I didn't think I ever would be...

"I think I'm going to make an appointment with a clinic when we get back," I said instead, choosing not to tell my husband about how terrified the thought of those mountains made me.

Noah's brows furrowed in immediate concern. "You're still feeling sick?"

All the time. "Only sometimes," I offered. Tucking my hands under my cheek, I sighed. "But I'd feel better once I get the once over."

Noah didn't have a chance to respond because the sound of a door banging followed by a male voice saying, "I'm here, bitches" filled the room, distracting us both.

"What the..." I turned and gaped at Noah, who had

jumped off the bed with fright. "Did that sound like who I think that sounded like?"

"Maybe," he offered, grabbing the metal lamp on his night stand. Wrapping the cord around his wrist, he wielded the lamp like a weapon. "If I had the faintest clue of who you're talking about."

Scrambling off the bed with excitement, I rushed over to the bedroom door and flung it open.

"Teagan," Noah hissed, rushing after me. "Don't..."

"You!" I couldn't stop myself from grinning as my eyes took in the tall, handsome man standing in the middle of the living area, flanked on either side by two identical men.

"How's my Galway girl?" Cam Carter purred. Dropping his duffel bag on the floor, he held his arms out and said, "What? No hug for your favorite nephew-in-law?"

I didn't think twice about it.

Squealing with excitement, I lunged for the eldest of the Carter triplets. "My god, you're a sight for sore eyes," I choked out as I squeezed the life out of the man I hadn't seen since boyhood.

"Don't lie to yourself, brother," a familiar voice teased. "We all know I'm the favorite."

"Colt!" I cried out.

Breaking out of Cam's hug, I threw my arms around Colton Carter's waist, completely overwhelmed to see him.

"Hey, Beautiful," Colt chuckled. "See, Bro. I told you our *auntie* loved me best."

"I see you're as full of shit as ever," I shot back happily. My best friend's brothers had always been like family to me. "I've missed your egotistical ass."

"And I've missed that precious mouth," Colt shot back in amusement before looking behind me. "Uncle Noah," he squealed in a fake, high-pitched tone as he released me and held his arms out in front of himself. "It's me. Your favorite boy."

Noah grinned widely. "You fucking idiot," he chuckled before grabbing Colton Carter and squashing him in a massive hug – a hug that was quickly interrupted by the addition of Cameron.

The two boys – now men – looked like over-excited Labradors as they fussed over my husband. I stood back in a state of shock and unexpected happiness. "What are you guys doing here?" I couldn't stop grinning.

"What?" Colt laughed. "Did you honestly think we wouldn't come visit when you're only a city away from us?"

Just then the door of the hotel swung inward and in walked Logan Carter. Noah was instantly by his side, his love for baby Carter as obvious as the day is long.

My eyes roamed nervously over the youngest triplet; the deep one, the brutally honest one – the one with those lonesome gray eyes – as he hugged it out with my husband. The one who, when he was disappointed with you, could make you feel like the worst type of human.

The last time I'd spoken to Logan Carter, it had gone down like a lead balloon...

"...HE'S GOING THROUGH HELL INSIDE, TEAGAN," LOGAN ADDED. "And you checked out on him. Imagine how he feels."

"Logan, he cheated on me," I cried out in defense. "He fucked that girl right in front of me and he didn't bat an eyelid doing it. What am I supposed to do? Run back to him and wait for it to happen again?" I shook my head and wiped my cheeks with my free hand. "He broke me, Logan."

"He knew they were coming for him," Logan hissed in a tone of pure disgust. "And do you know the only person Noah

was worried about? You. He could've been killed in there, and the only thing that concerned him was getting a fucking message to you. You don't deserve him, Teagan," Logan hissed and I paled.

I tried to find the words to defend myself but Hope's younger brother continued before I had a chance.

"This is on you," he added in a deathly cold voice. "If you hadn't come around and fucked with his head, Noah wouldn't be where he is today. He was protecting you that night, to keep you safe from JD and George, and you betrayed him, Teagan. You fucking buried him and you bailed when it got tough..."

I MOVED TO GIVE HIM A HUG, BUT QUICKLY CAME TO A HALT, unsure whether it would be well received or not.

"Come here, you little dope," Logan chuckled, noticing my hesitance. "Water under the bridge, okay?" He whispered in my ear when he had me wrapped up in his arms.

Nodding, I tucked my face into his chest and sighed.

"What the hell are you three stooges doing here?" Noah chuckled.

Stepping out of Logan's embrace, I moved quickly to Noah's side. "Yeah," I added, feeling happier than I had in months. I hadn't seen these boys for years. And even though they'd been here less than five minutes, things seemed better already.

"We are at your disposal." Colt added. Throwing himself down on the couch, he folded his arms behind his head and sighed happily. "At the request of your big brother."

Noah's cheeks reddened. "Huh?"

"Dad sent us," Logan interjected in that calm voice of his. "He wanted us to remind you that you have a family and a home waiting for you when you come off this leg of the tour." He turned to me and winked. "He wanted you to know that you *both* do."

Noah's face turned an even deeper shade of red as he listened to his nephews' ramble on.

"Basically, the old man knows you wrap up tonight," Colt explained. "He wants you home."

"Home?" Noah's tone was gruff and one of embarrassment. "Why?"

"Because you're his brother," Cam piped up. "And he loves you."

"We all do," Colt added with a chuckle. "And he's planning a family get together."

"So when Colt says Dad wants you home, he means tonight," Cam chuckled. "As in after the fight."

"Here." Logan reached into his jeans pocket, pulling out a set of brass keys and tossed them at us.

Noah caught them mid-air. "What's this?" He asked, examining the set of keys in his hand.

"The keys to South Peak Road," Colt offered up.

"You should see it, man," Cam muttered with a pout. "Fucking beautiful."

"To think of the parties we could have had there," Colt added with a sigh.

"Could have?" Cam snorted. "Speak for yourself, dude."

"Can you two shut the hell up for a second?" Logan commanded before letting out a heavy sigh. "Our parents own several properties across the state," he explained in a calm tone. "The house on South Peak Road is one of them." Shrugging, Logan shoved his hands back into his jeans pockets. "They want you both to consider it their wedding gift to you."

"Are you shitting me?" I blurted out tactlessly. "They want to give us a *house* as a *wedding gift*?"

"We shit you not," Colt shot back with a grin. "The old man takes his family seriously. It's important to him. He wants to keep you guys close."

"Not to mention the fact that he's a control freak," Cam muttered under his breath. "With more money than sense."

"Why didn't he come here himself?" Noah asked, tone gruff and thick with unshed emotion.

"And scare you off?" Colt offered. "You've been absent from our lives for years, Noah, and the old man's tactlessness." Shrugging, Colt added, "So he sent us to sway you."

"The three stooges?" Noah shot back with a smirk.

"I prefer the term *three musketeers*," Colt was quick to respond.

"Yeah," Colt snickered. "And consider Hopey-Bear *Dogtanian*."

"Bottom line," Logan interjected with a roll of his eyes, clearly unimpressed with his brothers. "He wants you home and has sent us here to make sure you do just that."

"I can't..." Noah's voice broke off and he shook his head. "You're all fucking crazy," he added with a chuckle. He dropped his gaze to my face. "Are you hearing this, Thorn?"

"Hearing it?" I shot back, jaw still hanging open. "I haven't heard a word since *free house*."

"With a pool," Colt snickered.

"And a hot tub," Cam added.

"And a built-in, top of the range gym," Logan filled in swiftly.

My jaw fell even further open.

"We're not taking it," Noah was quick to respond – respond and ruin my hopes and dreams. "It's too much."

"But they said there's a *pool*," I pouted. My voice sounded whiny, but I didn't care. "Don't kill my dreams, Noah," I begged, the thought of turning down a house with a pool, hot tub, and gym almost brought tears to my eyes. The prospect of going home to Boulder was looking more appealing already. "*Please.*"

"Yeah, Noah," Colt teased. "Don't kill your new wife's dreams."

Noah looked down at me with a smirk. "Fine," he conceded. "We'll stay there."

"Yay." I clapped and squealed like a girl. Finally, an actual house instead of a hotel. I could hardly contain myself. I was so excited.

"But we're not keeping it, Thorn," Noah warned me. "This is just temporary."

"Of course," I muttered flippantly, even though I knew full well that Noah would have to pry my cold, dead body from the house before I gave it up.

50

NOAH

"So, why are you really here?" I asked Logan when Teagan had walked on ahead with the boys. I'd hung back, pretending I'd forgotten something in my room, when in truth, I wanted to talk to Logan alone.

"What do you mean?" he asked, confusion etched on his face.

"Kyle didn't really send you guys here, did he?" I'd been around the block enough times to know bullshit when I heard it.

"You're as paranoid as always." Logan smirked. "Why is it so hard for you to believe that people actually care about you, man?"

Because they didn't.

At least no one had before.

"So you're seriously telling me that your father sent you three here to coax me home?"

"Yes," Logan replied calmly as we jogged down the back stairwell. I was running late for my fight – nothing new there.

I shook my head when we reached the ground floor "I don't get it."

"You don't have to," Low chuckled, falling into step beside me as we walked through the foyer. "You just have to accept it."

"Yeah," I muttered, holding the door open for him. "Because I'm really good at accepting shit."

"Does she look pale to you?" Logan blurted out when we reached the street, interrupting my train of thought, as he pointed toward Teagan who was climbing into the awaiting limo.

"Yeah," I noted, as my thoughts quickly turned to worry. "She's been off for a while now."

Logan frowned. "How long's a while?"

"I don't know." I shrugged uncomfortably. "Teagan had severe food poisoning back in May. She hasn't been herself since."

"Have you guys been to a doctor?" I knew from Logan's tone that he was concerned.

"She said she was going to make an appointment when we get home."

"She should," he agreed, eyes narrowed in concern at my wife.

"What about you?" I asked quietly. "How are you doing?"

Logan never met my eye as he said, "I'm still here."

51

TEAGAN

*M*y head was spinning.

The crowd screaming around me was causing my brain to throb like a drum.

The scent of sweat mixed with tobacco and alcohol around me meant inhaling through my nose was out of the question. Using my cardigan as a shield, I breathed through my mouth, managing to tolerate the lavender scent of laundry detergent. My stomach was up in a heap, and I knew if I smelled the stench in this arena one more time, I was going to barf.

Cameron and Colton, who were sitting to my right, were so engrossed in the fight taking place just a few feet from us that they didn't notice my horrified expression, but Logan, who was on my left, did.

Leaning closer to me, Logan whispered, "Are you okay?"

"I don't think so, Low," I choked out as my stomach twisted inside of me.

Just then, Noah's opponent – the young red headed guy in the blue trunks – landed a left hook to my husband's face.

Blood splattered everywhere.

I was pretty sure I heard bone crush and the crowd went wild.

Slapping a hand over my mouth, I closed my eyes and held my breath, hoping the wave of nausea would pass.

It didn't.

"Come on," Logan said in a surprisingly gentle tone. Standing abruptly, he took me by the arm and led me through the crowd. "Let's get you out of here."

Like a magnet, Lewis stood and trailed after us.

With my hand covering my mouth, I allowed myself to lean against Baby Carter. Right about now, he was the only thing keeping me upright.

Noticing my weakness, Logan wrapped his muscular arm around my body, taking my weight for me.

"Nearly there," he said as he hustled us through the crowds toward the out of access area that led to the changing rooms.

"Surprise!" Lucky chanted the moment we stepped inside Noah's changing room. His smile quickly morphed into a concerned frown. "Teegs, what's wrong?" His gaze flickered to Logan and he frowned, clearly puzzled. "Who's this?"

"I think I'm going to be sick," I whispered weakly.

Everything was spinning.

The ground.

The walls.

The ceiling was closing in on us.

I could hardly breathe...

Knowing I wasn't going to make it to the bathroom, I broke out of my burly bodyguard's arms and dropped to my knees just as the contents of my stomach spewed out of my mouth.

"Jesus," I heard Lucky say from somewhere behind me and then a pair of strong arms were around me.

"Good girl," Logan's voice was in my ear, praising me in a rare, soothing voice as he knelt beside me and pulled my ponytail out of the firing line. "Get it up."

I wanted to say 'welcome home' to Lucky and tell him how much I'd missed him, but I couldn't. Retching, I continued to vomit, right there in the middle of Noah's changing room, and there wasn't a damn thing I could do to stop myself.

"Go and find a doctor, Lewis," Lucky ordered. I could hear the concern in his tone. I could feel the tension emanating from him. "Hurry up."

"I'm on orders not to leave her," Lewis was quick to reply.

"Fine," he snapped. "I'll get one."

Lucky opened the dressing room door, letting in the screams and bellowing roars of the crowd. Thankfully, when he closed the door behind him, the sound died down a little.

"Sounds like the boss man won," Lewis mused from somewhere behind me.

I wanted to give him a thumbs up, but I was too busy dying on the floor at his feet.

"Good girl," Logan continued to coax, holding onto me as I threw my guts up.

"I'm...sorry for puking on you," I managed to squeeze out through fits of heaving when I noticed the condition of his jeans.

Logan chuckled softly. "I've had worse, Teegs," he comforted me, rubbing my back with one hand. "Don't worry about me."

The screams and cheers from the arena grew louder and louder until they were almost deafening.

"What's happening – ugh, Christ," Colton's voice filled

my ears followed by the roar of the crowd. The door closed behind him, muffling the crowd some. "Hey, Beautiful." The middle triplet approached me with caution. Dropping down to his haunches, Colt patted my shoulder with his hand. "Are you alright?"

"What do you think, douchebag?" I heard Cameron sneer seconds before he entered my peripheral vision. "There's more of her on the floor than inside her body."

I had a feeling Cameron was right.

Even though I'd left everything inside of me on the changing room floor, I continued to dry heave, unable to regain control of my upchuck reflex.

"Not helping, Cam," Logan hissed through clenched teeth.

"You're right, Low. You're right," Cam muttered, tone panicked, as he disappeared from sight once again. "I'll go... ah...get Noah."

The door opened again as Cameron exited the room and an African American woman entered with Lucky hot on her heels.

"I'm Doctor Reinhart," she announced to Lewis who had decided to play guard dog around my barely breathing corpse. "I'm here to help."

Obviously, Lewis decided he could trust the doctor, because he stepped aside.

"How long have you been sick, Teagan?" Dr. Reinhart asked.

"Just today," I whispered, as Logan, Lucky, and Lewis continued to hover nearby. "But I've been feeling...off...for a while now."

"How long is a while?"

"A month," I offered, gawking. "Maybe two."

My whole life...

Setting a black leather bag down beside her, she proceeded to feel my face, asking me a string of questions I had a hard time answering when my mouth was heaving uncontrollably.

"Where is she?" The sound of Noah's booming voice filled my ears. "Thorn!"

"I'm here," I called out weakly, searching the room for him.

The minute Noah's eyes landed on me, he visibly sagged in relief and he quickly closed the gap between us in three long strides.

With another man's blood on his hands, my husband knelt beside me, head bowed, looking both vulnerable and indestructible. His face was all beat up. His body was drenched in sweat, and with the exception of a pair of black fighting shorts, he was completely naked.

"You good, Thorn?" He croaked out, tone gruff, as his hands wandered over my face and neck.

I shook my head weakly and forced myself to smile, hiding the blusterous emotions inside of me. "I'm not too good, Noah," I whispered. "I think you're kneeling in my vomit."

Sighing heavily, Noah wiped the corner of my mouth with his thumb before dragging me onto his lap. I groaned in pain. Moving made everything inside of me twist and churn.

"Shh," he whispered, wrapping me up in his arms.

Sagging against my husband's body, I buried my face in his chest and forced myself to breathe through my mouth.

The smell of vomit was making me feel queasy.

"Mr. Messina," Dr. Reinhart acknowledged kindly. "My name is Doctor Aubree Reinhart." She held out a blood pressure monitor. "Do you mind?"

Reluctantly, Noah nodded and released his hold on me so the doctor could check my blood pressure.

"I assume you're sexually active, Mrs. Messina?" Dr. Reinhart asked as she examined me.

I nodded weakly, way too sick to feel any embarrassment at having this conversation in front of Lewis, Lucky, Colton, and Logan who were still present and hovering over me like four guard dogs.

"And birth control?" She asked as she administered a shot into my arm. "Are you using any specific method?"

"Just..." I empty reached again.

"Condoms," Noah filled in for me, holding back my hair. "Only some of the time."

I tried to scramble out of his arms, not wanting him to see me like this, but he wouldn't let me go.

"Uh-huh... and when did you last menstruate?" She asked. "Do you have a regular twenty-eight-day cycle?"

"My periods are all over the place," I groaned weakly. "I've been irregular since my teens."

"Aaaand that's a rap," Colton groaned from somewhere behind me.

"Yeah, hold the door for me," Lucky added queasily. Lewis was the last to leave, after Logan, announcing in his deep barrel of a tone that his job didn't include delving into the female reproductive system.

"Sorry about them," I muttered sheepishly as I wiped my mouth with the back of my hand. "They're not used to...women."

Whatever the good doctor had stuck me with was working at a rapid rate because I was able to straighten up without heaving.

"I'm used to it," Dr. Reinhart chuckled. "Men are such fickle creatures." Picking her bag up off the ground, she approached the bench. "You can help her up, Mr. Messina."

Noah immediately stood up, taking me with him.

Walking over to the bench, he gently sat me down beside the doctor.

"Are you okay?" He asked in a panicked tone when I grunted.

"Yes," I whispered, clutching my stomach.

"Okay, give me the bad news," I choked out. Her silence was telling and panic flared inside of my heart. "There's something really wrong with me?"

"On the contrary." Reaching into her bag, Dr. Reinhart pulled out a rectangular shaped box and handed it to me. "I don't think there's anything wrong with you."

I stared down in horror at the box in my hand.

Nine letters to terrify me to my very core...

"I'm not," I whispered, feeling sick all over again. "No fucking way."

My eyes immediately went to Noah's face.

He was standing stock still and frozen to the spot, staring down at the box in my hands.

"Well you could be suffering from a bad stomach flu," Dr. Reinhart offered kindly. "However, given your age and sexual status, I would strongly urge you to take a test to rule out pregnancy."

There was that word again... that scary nine-lettered word that crawled over my heart like a tarantula.

"And do you think taking a test will rule...it...out?" I choked out as I desperately tried to count my dates, but I couldn't think straight.

I'd had a period...last month, or was it the month before? I was never regular.

In fact, I was used to going three months at a time

without a period, which was why I didn't panic when Mother Nature didn't arrive.

Dr. Reinhart smiled. "Possibly."

"You don't, do you?" Groaning, I dropped my head in my hands.

"Do it in your own time," Dr. Reinhart said kindly.

Standing up, she retrieved her bag and said, "But do it," before leaving me on my own with my mind going ninety to the dozen and my husband doing a fantastic imitation of a statue.

"I'm calling a doctor," Noah announced, bursting to life. Pacing around the changing room like a deranged lunatic, he hissed, "I'm taking you home and I'm calling a goddamn doctor."

"I've already seen a doctor," I offered weakly.

"Well, another one then!" Noah snapped. He disappeared into the bathroom, returning moments later with a handful of wet paper towels. "Put those on your forehead," he ordered before dropping to his knees in front of me. "If you've got a fever, it will help cool you down."

"I don't have a fever," I shot back, though I kept the paper towels pressed to my brow. "I'm *okay*," I added. "Dr. Reinhart said I'm fine."

Actually, she'd said I was more than fine...

"Are you going to take it?" He asked me, tone gruff, eyes wild and panicked.

I knew what he was talking about and I wished like hell he understood that I *couldn't* talk about it.

"Don't," I begged, clenching my eyes shut. I needed a minute. I couldn't take it all in.

"Thorn," he argued. "We have to deal with this.

"No." I shook my head. "We don't." Not right now. "Not tonight."

"We need to know."

"And if I am, then where do you propose we raise it?" I cried out, frantic. "In a different hotel room every bloody night?"

"Stop panicking," he replied in a passionate tone. Clamping his hands down on my thighs, Noah looked deep into my eyes. "Whatever happens, I'll take care of you, Thorn."

"So in other words, you'll dump me in a mansion on my own to bring up your spawn while you live the high life?" I shot back, red-faced and irrational. "I'm not starting a family – not until you're finished fighting." Noah opened his mouth, no doubt to protest, but I quickly carried on. "I'm not bringing a child into this world who could become fatherless."

It was a very real possibility.

My husband was a professional MFA fighter.

He put his life on the line every time he stepped into the cage...

"You don't get to decide this, Teagan," Noah shot back, losing all patience and tact with me.

"I'm scared to find out," I admitted.

"The doctor as good as told us that you are," he shot back, tone just as panicked as mine. Shoving his wallet and phone into the jeans he'd just pulled on, he walked over to where I was sitting and crouched down in front of me. "So stop being a fucking baby and take the damn test."

A sudden knock on the door startled me and broke the tension between us. Scrambling, I managed to stuff the box into my purse just as Lucky slipped his head around the door.

His eyes landed on Noah first and then me. "Hey you," he said with a crooked smile. "Feeling better?"

I nodded and forced a bright smile. Physically, I was feeling better. Emotionally, I was a wreck. "Welcome home," I added after a moment. "I missed you."

Letting the door close behind him, Lucky ambled over to where I was sitting and Noah was standing over me, glaring. "Everything okay?" He asked cautiously, eyeing my husband with concerned blue eyes.

Noah shook his head and opened his mouth to speak.

"Everything's fine," I blurted out, interrupting, not wanting to air my private turmoil with anybody else just yet.

Like a cruel twist of fate, the triplets walked into the changing room then, all three loaded down with questions, all three sharp as razor blades, followed by Noah's team of asshats.

"What the hell is going on in here?" Quincy's loud voice boomed through the room and suddenly everyone was talking at once, giving their two cents on what had gone down – well, everyone except for Noah.

Sinking down on the bench beside me, Noah continued to stare hard at my abdomen, so much in fact that I was beginning to feel extremely self-conscious. Every once and a while he would shake his head before resuming his staring.

Surrounded by eight men and a mute husband, I managed to drone their voices out until Cam's broke through my resistance.

"So, you must be the convict," he announced without an ounce of tact or shame, as his eyes roamed over Lucky's ink-covered skin. "I was expecting someone..."

"Bigger?" Lucky interjected good-naturedly.

"Who looked less like a boyband member," Cam corrected with a grin, revealing that devilish dimple in his cheek. "You don't look like a killer."

"Smooth, Cam," Logan said with a heavy sigh. "Real smooth, bro."

"Whatever, Low," Cam grumbled before refocusing his attention on Lucky. Moving toward Lucky, he held out his hand. "It's good to finally meet the man who kept Noah sane inside."

Lucky grinned crookedly and shook Cam's outstretched hand. "The pleasure was all mine."

"We need to leave," Noah announced out of nowhere.

Jerking to his feet, he grabbed my purse and stalked toward the changing room door only to halt halfway and turn around when he noticed I wasn't by his side.

"We need to leave *now*, Thorn," he repeated in an emphatic tone, eyeballing me. "We have things to do." He not-so-subtly shook my purse in my face.

"Right," I whispered, wanting to do anything except that. Hell, I was contemplating staying right here with Tommy, Quincy, and Beau.

I really was afraid...

"You guys can't go," Colt piped up. "Mom and Dad are expecting you both at the hotel."

"Tonight?" I squeezed out.

"Yeah," Logan was the one to reply this time. "He has a car waiting outside for us. He has this family dinner organized."

"Speaking of..." Cam muttered as he checked his watch on his wrist. "We should get going."

"At ten o'clock at night?" I asked, puzzled.

Logan's face reddened and Colton whistled as if he hadn't heard me.

"What are you guys up to?" I demanded, smelling a rat.

"No," Noah snapped, interrupting me. Reaching for my hand, he pulled me up. "We have things to do."

"Come on, Noah," I pleaded, desperate to delay the inevitable. Even though I had stopped dry heaving, I still felt weak as dishwater and rested all of my weight against my husband's huge frame. I didn't want to find out. I wasn't ready. "It would be really rude not to go."

Noah balked. "Thorn," he hissed, glaring down at me.

"Please," I whispered, shaking my head ever so slightly, imploring Noah not to push me on this.

I needed time to comprehend this.

I needed a minute to myself to think this through.

I was reeling, I was petrified, and I refused to be bullied into doing this until I was ready.

"Fine," Noah growled after a long pause. "We can do that *thing* at the hotel."

52

NOAH

I wasn't in the mood to make small talk much less entertain a roomful of people, but that's what we were met with the moment Teagan and I stepped foot in the function room of the Henderson Hotel. Balloons, confetti, and more people than I name surrounded us, all smiling, all creeping me the hell out.

"Congratulations, you two," an elderly lady, who vaguely resembled my high school biology teacher, announced as she ambled over to Teagan and me and squeezed on our cheeks. "You two were made for each other," she added with a raspy chuckle before pottering off, leaving us both confused as hell.

"What's going on?" Teagan whispered in a small voice, tightening her hold on my hand, eyes locked on mine

"I have no fucking clue," I shot back, equally stunned.

"Surprise," Colton announced, slinging an arm around me. "Happy engagement/shotgun wedding party."

"You're joking," I deadpanned as I stared in horror at the roomful of people.

"Oh my god, oh my god!" A familiar came from behind

me, breaking through the noise. "Cash, go get your daddy. Tell him Noah's here!"

Swinging around, I froze to the spot when my eyes landed on Lee Carter – the woman who, for all intents and purposes, had been the mother I never had throughout the course of my teenage years.

She was smiling up at me and this feeling of warmth hit me straight in the chest.

Memories bombarded me.

Some of them good.

Most of them bad.

"Noah Messina," she said in that soft southern drawl of hers. "Aren't you a sight for sore eyes?"

"It's good to see you, Lee." I was careful with my brother's wife, the same way I'd always been, letting her initiate the hug first – knowing she was as jumpy as a slippery fish.

Her gaze flickered to Teagan and her gray eyes shone with sheer delight. "Teagan," Lee gushed, releasing me only to throw her arms around my wife. "Look at you," she gasped. Holding Teagan's shoulders, Lee took a step back and looked my wife up and down, gray eyes sparkling. "You are glowing, Teagan."

"I am?" Teagan squeaked, blushing beetroot red.

"Absolutely," Lee said gleefully. "Married life obviously agrees with you."

"Yeah," Teagan whispered, flashing me a sideways glance. "I guess it does."

"Noah!"

Kyle's voice penetrated through my mind, and I turned slowly, taking in the sight of my oldest brother – the man who, along with his wife, had stepped in and raised me throughout my teenage years. The respect I had for my half-brother was the only reason I was here enduring this *party*.

Especially since I knew my wife was sitting beside me with an unopened pregnancy test in her purse.

When I saw her curled up in a heap on the changing room floor earlier tonight, my heart had all but stopped dead in my chest.

That woman meant everything to me and knowing that there was a possibility she had my baby growing inside of her – well, that took my love for her to a whole new level.

She'd been so sick lately that I was praying for that test result to come back positive.

A baby I could handle.

Something seriously wrong with her health, I could not.

God, I needed to know.

I couldn't understand why Teagan was stalling.

Why was she trying to delay this?

We needed to know.

Christ, if my wife was pregnant then what hope did our kid have?

What the hell kind of father would I be?

I was a convicted felon.

I could only imagine my kid's shame rolling up to school with me on one of those *what does your daddy do* days.

Shuddering, I forced myself to concentrate on Kyle and not the fear threatening to take me over.

"Did you get my gift?" He asked, casting a wink at Teagan. "Blondie," he acknowledged.

"Kyle," Teagan bit out with a stiff nod.

"We did," I replied. "And we can't accept it."

"I can," Teagan piped up, holding her hand up. "I can accept...I...I...Noah, I'm going to kill you...ugh."

Her threats and words of violent promises were cut off as her stomach rejected everything inside of her for what had to be the fiftieth time tonight.

Teagan dropped to the floor in the middle of the room and heaved mercilessly.

"It's okay," I soothed, dropping to my knees beside her. "You're okay, Thorn."

"Oh my god," Lee exclaimed in delight. "I *knew* it."

"Knew what, Princess?" Kyle asked, sounding both curious and horrified.

"She's pregnant!"

"She's what?"

"No!" Teagan wailed, waving her hand in the air weakly. "I'm not...ugh."

"Oh, she so is," Kyle chuckled. "You were the same with the boys."

"Why is this happening to me?" Teagan sobbed between heaves.

"Congratulations, brother," Kyle said proudly.

"Jesus," I muttered. *What a fucking conversation.* Looking up at Kyle, I asked, "Is there somewhere I can take her?"

53

TEAGAN

I was dying and it wasn't an exaggeration.

Every breath I took caused the nausea inside of me to rear its ugly head, resulting in me projectile vomiting.

Clinging to the toilet bowl in the hotel room Kyle had graciously given us after I decimated his pretty carpet, I heaved loudly.

"Get it up, Baby." Noah encouraged, holding my hair out of the firing line of my mouth. "That's it," he soothed, rubbing my back with his large, calloused hand. "Good job."

"This is all your..." More vomit. "Fault." Dizziness engulfed me and I sagged forward, slapping my chin against the porcelain rim of the bowl. "You and your..." Tears stung my eyes as the ripping sensation in my throat intensified. "Fertile dick."

"I know, Thorn," Noah agreed, wisely accepting my jabs and proclamations of blame. "I'm sorry."

"Sure you are..." My words transformed from a muffled groan into a huge heaving gawk. Clutching the toilet bowl with a death grip, I breathed through my mouth, not daring to smell my own funk. "I mean it," I added in a weak tone. "This is all your fault, you big bastard..." my words broke off once more as the remaining contents of my stomach projected out of my mouth and into the toilet bowl.

"I know, Baby," Noah cooed, as he crouched behind me, holding my hair back, his fingers gently brushing my bare shoulder.

I couldn't see him, but I could tell he was smiling.

Panting in relief, I remained positioned over the toilet bowl for a few more minutes, until my brain was convinced my stomach had decided to stop screwing with me.

Feeling empty and violated, I leaned back and snuggled into his chest, shivering in comfort.

"I think I'm dying," I whimpered.

"You're not dying," he assured me. Pulling me into his arms, Noah stood up swiftly, taking me with him. "You're pregnant."

Carrying me out of the ensuite, Noah sat down on the bed in the adjoining bedroom, keeping me wrapped up in his arms, and pressed a kiss to my damp forehead.

"We don't even know for sure," I countered weakly, sagging against him, wanting nothing more than to fall asleep and stay there. I was so desperately tired and my body wasn't playing ball with me.

"There's only one way to find out," he countered calmly.

"I..." I shook my head and felt the blood draining from my face. "I..."

"You can't hide from this, Thorn," Noah told me. Reaching over, he grabbed my purse off the bed and dug inside it. Retrieving the pregnancy test, he handed it to me and said, "We've got this, Thorn. Whatever the result is. We've got this."

54

TEAGAN

*M*y uncle was going to kill me.

That was the one structured thought that found its way through the muddled up notions of my mind as I gaped down at the piece of plastic between my fingers and the two pink lines that were staring me in the face.

Fear like I'd never known before enveloped my heart as I sat on that toilet seat and then, weirdly enough, Michael Jackson's *Billie Jean* reverberated through my mind followed swiftly by Uncle Max's furious voice screaming at me.

Flushing the toilet, I arranged my clothing and tossed the traitorous stick in the trash can, all the while strangling down the panic threatening to choke me.

Well, that was that.

At least I knew.

There was an explanation for the nausea.

This was not good.

Not good at all.

What the hell were we going to do with a baby?

I was pretty sure I was still a baby myself.

A mother?

No... No freaking way.

Exhaling heavily, I forced myself to calm down, but it wasn't coming easy to me.

I was pregnant.

Oh, sweet baby Jesus.

Shaking my head, I closed my eyes and inhaled a deep, calming breath.

You can do this, I told myself over and over again.

But how can you? The sensible side of me demanded.

Noah and I were still adjusting to life on the road while being together.

We were still going through teething problems – big, jealous, trust issue teething problems.

Adding a baby to the mix would be catastrophic.

And the team?

I groaned loudly at the thought.

Noah's staff couldn't stand me at the best of times and they didn't try to hide it. I could only imagine what they would have to say when they heard the news.

The words *on purpose* sprang to mind.

This was the least on purpose and most irresponsible thing I had ever done in a life full of reckless choices.

Suddenly, I felt less like a twenty-five-year-old woman and more like a terrified teenage girl.

I needed my best friend, Hope.

I needed my mom...

Noah and I didn't have a stable environment.

Hell, we never stayed in one place long enough to leave fingerprints, let alone make babies.

JD's face and the imminent threat he represented to us flooded my mind and my entire body began to shake violently.

I couldn't do this...

In a daze, I walked over to the sink and sagged against it.

I was pregnant.

I had Noah Messina's baby growing in my belly.

Resting one hand on the sink, I covered my tender stomach with the other and allowed my mind to wander...

"Shit," Noah growled, stilling inside me.

"Wh-what?" I mewled, continuing to grind my body against his. My skin grew warmer with every move and I knew I was close.

"The condom," he ground out. A vein bulged in his neck. "Split."

"So?" I was too horny to care. "Don't stop," I begged as I writhed beneath his hot, naked body, desperate to feel his weight on me. "Please..." Thrusting my hips upward, I grabbed his hips and tried to drag him back down to me.

"Thorn, please," Noah hissed through clenched teeth. "I'm trying to be good here..."

"Don't be good," I purred, pulling hard on his hips. "I like you better bad."

His eyes fluttered shut and he sank into me once more before letting out a groan that sounded like he was in genuine pain. "I...can't..."

Pulling out of me, Noah climbed over to the driver's seat of his Lexus and sank down.

Disappointment floored me as I lay naked and needy on the reclined passenger seat. "You suck," I growled, twisting my head to glare at my boyfriend. "Big, fat donkey balls."

Noah cleared his throat. "You'll be glad I did that when you're not on your back in nine months."

"Okay," I muttered, appalled. "You just killed my girl-

erection."

"I'm not going to be reckless with you," he told me. *Rubbing his hands over his face, Noah muttered a string of curse words under his breath. "You're too important to me. I won't be selfish with you, Thorn. I won't..."*

"THORN?" NOAH'S VOICE INFILTRATED MY THOUGHTS, AND I jumped.

The door flew inward then and Noah stood in the middle of the bathroom, eyes wild and full of questions.

He must have changed his clothes while I was in the bathroom, because he was clad in jeans and a plain white shirt now, sleeves rolled up, that sexy arm-porn on full display.

This man is the father of my unborn baby...

The thought penetrated my mind and it was all I could think about as he took a step toward me.

This is the man, my heart whispered as it hammered furiously against my ribcage. *The man who walked through a ring of fire to save your life... the man who covered your body with his all those years ago,* my heart continued to torment me with harsh truths. *He took the brunt of the force when the car plummeted into the mountains. He went up in flames to keep you safe...*

He was my partner in crime, in life, and very soon my partner in parenthood.

"Well?"

One word.

One simple question.

And I couldn't verbalize an answer, so I did what I usually did when I felt under pressure.

I screamed.

*W*aiting for Teagan to come out of that bathroom was the longest five minutes of my life.

Shit, it was only supposed to take three minutes.

She knew.

She knew what our future held and she was hiding in that damn bathroom, leaving me sweating buckets out here.

Unable to cope with another second of not knowing, I charged into the bathroom, all guns blazing.

"Thorn."

She was standing in the bathroom with her head bowed and one hand curled protectively around her belly.

Unsure of what to do next, I hovered by the door and asked, "Well?"

Teagan stared at me for so long that I wasn't sure if she had actually heard my question, but then she did something so typically *Teagan* that relief flooded through me.

"You bastard!" She screamed at the top of her lungs. Teagan stormed over to the trashcan and bent down to retrieve the test. "Congratulations," she hissed, as she stalked back into the bedroom, waving the pregnancy stick in the air like it was some sort of evidence of my crime. "I'm pregnant and it's all your fault."

She *was* pregnant.

With my baby.

My Thorn had *my* baby growing inside her belly.

"How many?" Teagan demanded suddenly, breaking me out of my thoughts.

Taking aim, she flung the stick at my head before grabbing her purse off the bed and tossing that at my head, too.

"How many?" I asked calmly, because god knows one of us had to be, as I caught the bag midair.

"How many babies did you implant in my uterus?" Her gaze dropped to her stomach and she let out a howl. "What if the whole litter thing is a gene you got from your biological father?" She bit down on her fist. "I'm not built to breed *multiples*, Noah."

Holding my hands up, I approached my wife with great caution.

"Okay, you need to calm down." I wasn't sure if the whole littering was a genetic thing or a Kyle thing, but I sure as fuck wasn't telling Teagan that right now. The look in her eyes showed me that I would be wise to sleep with one eye open tonight...

"Noah, I am so scared," Teagan blurted out and suddenly all the fight and aggression seemed to deflate out of her.

There it was...

That vulnerability she always tried to hide with harsh words and raised voices.

Sinking down on the edge of our bed, Teagan dropped her head in her hands. "Please don't leave me on my own."

Claiming the space between us, I sank down beside her and hauled her onto my lap. "You ain't ever getting rid of me,

Thorn." With my hands on her waist, I turned her to face me and stared into her fearful, hazel eyes. "And you have nothing to be scared of," I told her, trying to remain calm, even though my body was in flight mode. Suddenly it was all starting to make sense.

The mood swings.

The abnormal amount of crying.

The nausea.

The swollen abdomen.

"Noah, you've seen my vagina," Teagan sobbed, clinging to me like a baby monkey. "How am I supposed to push a baby out of *that*?"

Fuck if I knew...

"You just will," I soothed, pretending that I knew about shit I didn't. "And I'll be with you the entire time."

That was the truth.

I wasn't going to let this woman out of my sight ever again.

"Every step of the way," I added.

She was invaluable to me before.

Now she had my kid inside her...Jesus, she was my beating heart walking around outside of my body.

"What if we're no good at it?" She whispered. Lifting her face up to mine, her large hazel eyes were glossy as she spoke. "What if–"

"Thorn," I interrupted, clamping her lips shut between my fingers. "We *can* do this." Pressing a kiss to her temple, I cradled her fragile body to mine, gentler now that I knew what was growing inside of her.

My kid...

"I'm going to take care of you." I had no fucking clue of what to do or how to raise a baby, but I wasn't going to let her down. I wasn't certain of a lot of things in this crazy world, but one thing I never doubted was the lengths I would go to in order to provide for and keep this woman safe. I was scared, too.

Fuck, I was petrified, but I had to be strong.

I had to give my wife the strength she needed.

I couldn't stop myself from staring down at her abdomen. It was *swollen*.

God, I was fucking clueless.

I'd missed all the signs – thinking she had a goddamn eating disorder. The woman who could eat a twelve-ounce T-bone steak down to the bone quicker than I could.

"How far along do you think I am?" She whispered, eyes locked on my hand covering her stomach.

"I don't know." The part of her stomach my hand was cupping was hard as rock. Was it supposed to be that hard? "When did you last...you know.... bleed?"

Ugh.

I was fucking tactless, but I didn't know the proper etiquette when dealing with this.

"Your period," I added in a gruff tone. "When was your last one?"

"I don't know," she sobbed, burying her face in my chest. "I can go for months at a time without having one."

Well *that* didn't help the cause.

"Try and think," I urged her in as gentle a tone as I could. I didn't want to get all up in my wife's female business, but we needed to know how many weeks along she was. The mere thought caused a tremor of fear to run through my body. "Have you had a period yet this month? Or last month?"

"No." She blinked back her tears. A huge, heaving sob racked through her. "I had one for like three days." Sniffling, she added, "Back in March."

"March?" *Jesus Christ...* Over five months had passed since Teagan's last period. "Why didn't you say something sooner?" I ran a hand through my hair in frustration. "It's August, Teagan. How the hell could it slip your mind?"

"Because it's nothing out of the norm for me, Noah," Teagan cried out.

"You're twenty-five years old," I argued. "Surely women your age keep track of that sort of thing."

"Why would I?" She screamed, voice breaking with emotion. "I was a virgin. And then there was you. And when you went down I was on my own again."

"That's not strictly true." Liam's face entered my mind and Teagan seemed to read my thoughts almost simultaneously.

"Don't you dare," she warned as she scrambled off my lap and climbed shakily to her feet. "Don't even think about throwing that one time with Liam– *that one protected time* – in my face." Betrayal and pain crossed her features and I stifled a groan. "It was *months* before you came back into my life."

"I wasn't," I was quick to reply.

I was such a dick.

Standing up, I held my hands out as I approached her. With every step I took toward her, Teagan took a step backwards.

"I'm not your mother, Noah," Teagan cruelly tossed out. "I wouldn't lie about who the father of *my* child was."

"I know," I replied calmly, letting her cruel remark sail over my head. She was frightened and I had unintentionally insulted her in one of the worst ways a woman could be insulted. "I'm sorry...hey." Tipping her chin upward, I stared down into her wild, fearful eyes. "I'm sorry."

I dropped my hand to her stomach and my heart fluttered in my chest. "*We* made this." She had a bump and I'd put it there. A baby inside my wife. Pride, fear, and adoration floated inside of me. I wasn't sure what to do. I didn't know how I'd cope or if I'd make a good father, but I wasn't going anywhere. "I'll do my best for you – for both of you."

"A baby is a blessing," she sobbed, hiccupping, my slip of the tongue seemingly forgotten. "That's what my mother always used to say when I came home from school with the latest gossip on who'd gotten themselves knocked up from school."

"Your mom was a smart lady," I agreed, hoping I was comforting her, or at least calming her down. "I feel... blessed," I added gruffly. I wasn't religious. I didn't have a god I believed in like Teagan had, but in this moment, I felt truly *blessed.*

Sniffling, Teagan nodded her head slowly. "Me too, but I'm frightened."

"It's okay to be frightened," I told her. *I'm fucking petrified...* "But you need to know that you're not alone in this, Teagan. You're not." Looking down at the only person I'd ever cared about, I found myself desperate to reassure her. "You have me." *Not that I was worth much, but still...* "I *will* take care of you, Teagan."

"We're in this together," she whispered, with a little too much uncertainty in her voice for my liking.

"I don't have any plans to let you down, Thorn," I promised. I'd finally gotten myself a little family of my own. Seeing her in my bed, all vulnerable and beautiful, and knowing she had life growing inside her...

Jesus, it made my heart squeeze so tight in my chest I could barely breathe.

"Nothing's going to take me away from you," I whispered. "You can depend on me.

"I just wish..." Shaking her head, Teagan swallowed deeply and swatted her hand in the air. "Never mind."

"Tell me."

"I can't," she squeezed out, eyes wide and fearful. "Lewis said –" Slapping her hand over her mouth, Teagan froze on my lap.

"Lewis said what, Thorn?" Reaching up, I caught her chin gently in my hand and forced her to look at me. "Did he say something to upset you?"

Teagan shook her head slowly. "It wasn't him."

"One of the others then?"

Her nose scrunched up and that was all I needed to know.

"Who? I'll fucking kill him." Furious, I lifted her off my lap and placed her gently down on the bench before jerking to my feet. "You know what, it doesn't matter. I'll kill them all."

"Noah, wait." Teagan snaked out a hand and circled my wrist. "I was set up that night. I know you don't want to talk about it, but you *have* to believe me. The guys were in on it," she added in a passionate tone.

I shook my head. "Who? Q, Beau, and T?"

Teagan nodded. "I'm not saying they set the whole thing up, but I know one of them brought Liam to the hotel and forced Lewis's hand."

"Tommy wouldn't do that, Teagan." I refused to believe Tommy was capable of being so fucking vindictive. "I know you two have issues, but he wouldn't go that far..."

"Wouldn't he?" Teagan stood up shakily and padded over to where I was standing. "Noah, I had *nothing* to do with Liam coming here. I was as shocked and ambushed as you were." She placed her hand on my forearm and rested some of her weight against me. "Tommy hates me, Noah. He blames me for throwing you off track. He thinks I'm a huge pain in your ass and as for Beau and Quincy? They think the same way."

Fear crawled through me as Teagan's face turned an even lighter shade of white. "Come here." Taking her by the arm, I led her back to the bed. "You need to sit down, baby." Gently, I forced her back down.

Sinking down on the edge of the bench, Teagan exhaled a shaky breath. "They all want me off this tour, Noah." She kept her hand on my forearm as she spoke. "It was bad enough before, but now that I'm..." she choked on her words. "Now that I'm pregnant it's even scarier."

"Teagan, I..." I didn't want to shut her down – not when she looked so sincere. "Are you sure?"

"If you don't believe me about Liam, then go and ask Lewis." Folding her arms across her chest, she stared straight up at my face. "Go ahead and ask him."

"Alright," I told her. "I will." And if I found out they had been fucking with my wife, I was going to raise hell.

Grabbing my cell off the bed, I stashed it in my pocket and moved for the door only to halt in my tracks when I noticed Teagan standing up. "What are you doing?"

"I'm coming with you," she told me. "Don't even think about asking me to stay here because I won't."

This was the first time in weeks that I'd seen fire in my wife's eyes and I sure as hell wasn't going to be the one to quench it.

56

TEAGAN

I'd been around Noah during many meltdowns down through the years, but not a single memory from our past compared to the anger that was emanating off him tonight.

"You're a son of a bitch," Noah snarled as he dragged me down the corridor of the Henderson Hotel toward the elevators with Lewis and Lucky trailing behind us.

Slamming his palm down on the keypad, Noah finally let go of my hand and began to pace. "A fucking Judas traitor bastard," he added, furious, as he ran his fingers through his spiked up hair.

Lewis remained silent and I was glad.

One word would be too much right now.

I should have known that telling Noah would cause the mother of all rows, but in the frame of mind I was in right now, I didn't care anymore.

I was done covering for those assholes.

They'd done me wrong.

They'd done Noah wrong.

And I was feeling too emotionally unbalanced to keep a handle on it.

To give him credit, Lewis had confessed immediately when Noah straight out asked him what had gone down, which only made me angrier because he should have done that for me months ago when I'd begged him to.

I guess the old saying was true; *he who pays the piper gets to call the tune...*

Noah was paying Lewis, which meant he called the shots.

The elevator opened and all four of us stepped inside.

I chose to sidle closer to Lucky, the one calming soul in a barrage of turbulence and anger.

Noticing that I had shuffled closer to him, Lucky winked down at me and held out his fist.

I discreetly fist thumped him before putting my hands behind my back. I watched Noah as he continued to pace the small space, nostrils flaring, and hair standing up on the top of his head.

"I should have been told about this sooner," Noah continued to rant, rage emanating from him. "Not weeks goddamn later."

"Who would you have believed?" Lucky drawled calmly.

"Her!" Noah roared, visibly shaking. "Always *her.*"

"I tried to tell you," I couldn't stop myself from saying.

"I know," Noah confessed, jaw clenched. He turned his face to look at me and I could see the emotions churning in his brown eyes. "I'm so fucking sorry."

Stepping toward Noah, I reached out and wrapped my hand around his bare forearm.

The elevator pinged open on the ground floor and we were on the move again, stalking through the foyer of Kyle Carter's hotel.

The party was in full swing in the function room and that was exactly where Noah was leading us.

57

*L*iars.

Fucking Judas bastards.

Betrayal was an understatement for how I was feeling right now.

Disgust didn't compare either.

I'd been a complete dick to Teagan. I'd been unfairly harsh on her. I'd held a grudge.

Because of these pricks.

Lewis had confirmed to me what Teagan had tried to make me believe.

She'd been set up.

We both had.

They had organized for Liam to come to our fucking room.

Beau and Quincy, I didn't give two fucks about. I didn't trust them and I cared about them even less, but Tommy?

Fuck, that hurt like nothing else.

My *best friend*.

My *only* fucking friend for a long assed time had betrayed me like that?

I was reeling, barely holding onto my temper.

I owed Teagan an apology for all the shitty jibes I'd thrown her way since we'd started the tour.

Hell, I owed her a hell of a lot more than that.

Every drunk person I bumped into in my bid to find my so-called team and every congratulatory message I heard only caused the anger to rise inside of me. My gaze flickered over the crowd surrounding us as I searched for the sorry ass fucks that called themselves my team.

Yeah, not anymore.

"Noah!" Lucky called out from my left and I turned to see him pointing in the direction of the far corner of the room.

I turned and marched in the direction Lucky was pointing. I could barely stop myself from breaking into a run.

I hadn't felt anger like this in a very long time.

Lewis came up beside me and placed a hand on my arm. "Would you like me to take her outside?"

Until that moment, I'd forgotten Teagan's hand was still in mine and I'd been dragging her along like a fucking rag doll.

Jesus Christ, she was pregnant...

Turning around, I glared at Lewis. "I'd have liked it if you'd told me the goddamn truth!" I roared. "No, I don't want you near my wife. Fuck!"

Nodding stiffly, Lewis took a sensible step back, cheeks stained red.

Good.

He should be embarrassed.

I was fucking embarrassed.

I was disgusted with myself.

All this had been going on under my goddamn roof and I hadn't known.

I'd sat back and watched Teagan getting bullied in high school.

I sure as hell wasn't going to watch it happen again...

Barreling through the crowd, my eyes honed in on the three men in the corner of the room with the partially naked women cozied up with them.

"Nice," Teagan growled in disgust, obviously spotting them, too. "Real classy."

"Come on, Thorn," I snarled, tucking her into my side. "These bastards owe you an apology."

And by the time I was done with them, they would be groveling at her feet...

"Noah?" Tommy's voice was thick from arousal as he jerked away from the women he'd been sidling up to, sporting a confused look on his face. "Are you alright?" Rushing straight up to me, he placed his hand on my shoulder. "What's happened?"

"What do you think?" I snarled, not bothering to explain myself.

I was done.

I was fucking through with this shit.

Shoving past Tommy, I stalked over to the booth he had vacated, reached across the table, and grabbed Beau by the scruff of his neck.

"Noah," Beau hissed as I dragged him out of the booth. "What the fuck?"

"What the fuck is right, asshole," I roared, shoving him roughly onto the white carpet. "Did you think you were clever?"

"What the hell is this about, boy?" Quincy snarled, jerking to his feet.

My attention turned to Quincy, who was out of the booth and slowly backing away from me.

Smart man.

"I told him," Lewis announced calmly. "About the Harte boy."

"Yeah," I snarled. "Now, all I want to know was which one of you geniuses' idea it was to fuck with my wife?"

"It was mine," Tommy announced and my heart shriveled up in my chest.

"No," Teagan countered coldly. "I heard Beau say..."

"It was *my* idea," Tommy repeated slowly.

"Why?" I whispered. The air felt like it had been sucked out of my lungs. "I *trusted* you." I fucking trusted him more than anyone else. "Why would you do that to me?"

"I did it *for* you," Tommy replied hoarsely. "Noah, you've worked so hard and I've been by your side throughout everything..."

"Which is why I *trusted* you," I hissed, feeling like I'd been stabbed through the back.

Holding my hand up, I forced myself to calm down and breathe, but I couldn't.

All I could see was my oldest friend and the knife he'd driven into my back.

"I *trusted* you, Tommy."

"She's going to take you down, Noah," Tommy shot back in a passionate tone. His gaze flickered to Teagan and then back to me. "I had to at least try and stop it from happening."

I knew I sounded like a broken record, but I couldn't stop myself from repeating the same three words over and over again. "I trusted *you*."

I'd never had much faith in the human race, my upbringing had only cemented that notion, but I had never tarred Tommy with the brush I used for everyone else.

I had always held him above the others...and he'd proved me *wrong*.

I knew there was a crowd gathering around us, but I didn't care.

Words I never thought I'd hear myself say fell out of my mouth with a finality that surprised me. "I want you off this tour." Turning my attention to Beau and Quincy, I steadied myself before saying, "I want all of you off this goddamn tour."

"Noah..."

"You're all fired!" I roared. "Don't fucking be here in the morning."

"You can't fire me, boy," Quincy snarled, getting up in my face. "I made you what you are today." Shoving a fat finger into my chest, he hissed, "You'd be a jumped up little prick on parole if it weren't for me."

My lip curled up in disgust. "Is that so?"

"Damn straight," Quincy sneered. "I turned you into an athlete – a star. You ain't nothing but a jumped up, street-fighting convict without me, boy!"

"Well this jumped up, street-fighting convict is going to take his chances without you," I shot back. "Fuck you, Q."

"Exactly," Teagan growled, jumping to my defense. "Noah has been kicking ass for years – *real* ass, not the kind you have to get cleared to fight!" Narrowing her eyes in anger, she walked straight up to Quincy and poked him in the chest. "You can't claim you made a self-made man."

"What the hell do you know about it, girl?" Quincy snarled.

"Don't speak to her like that," I snarled, furious.

"No," Teagan interrupted, putting a hand on my arm. "It's okay, Noah." She turned to face Quincy once more. "I know a lot more than you've ever given me credit for. And here's another thing I know. I hope you've enjoyed hanging off

Noah's coat-tails these past few years, because it ends tonight."

"You can kiss that belt goodbye in December without me in your corner," Quincy was quick to reply, eyes locked on my face. "Without a team behind you, you don't have a chance in hell..."

"Who says he doesn't have a team behind him?" Lucky drawled. Stepping forward to stand beside me, he tipped his head to one side and smirked. "He's got me."

"And me," Teagan piped up, backing up against my chest.

"A homicidal convict and a deranged woman," Beau, who had come to stand beside Quincy, said. "That's some team." He laughed humorlessly before adding, "You're finished, Messina."

"We'll see," were the last words I heard Quincy say before the sound of a single firework exploding filled my ears.

BANG...

Within seconds, a piercing pain ricocheted through my shoulder – a pain so fierce it took the air clean out of my lungs and my feet from beneath me.

Dropping to my knees, I did the only thing I could think of doing at that moment; I grabbed my wife's arm and dragged her roughly to the floor just as another explosion went off nearby.

BANG...

I couldn't feel my arms as I shoved Teagan under a cloth-covered table and out of sight.

Hell, I couldn't feel anything as I scrambled under the table and covered my wife's body with mine, just my own heartbeat hammering in my chest.

I could hear it above all the carnage as it thundered in my ears.

"Your arm," Teagan choked out as she lay on her back, looking up at me with wide, fearful eyes. "Oh my god, Noah, look at your arm. You've been shot!" She cried out. "He shot you, Noah!"

"I'm fine," I whispered. My gaze drifted to my right shoulder to where blood was soaking through my shirt. "It barely nipped me."

"Noah!" Teagan screamed frantically. "You're bleeding out."

"Shh." Clamping my hand over her mouth, I lowered my forehead to hers and exhaled shakily, struggling to rein in my emotions. "Quiet."

Keeping my hand over Teagan's mouth, I turned my head to the side and peeked out from under the full-length tablecloth that was cloaking us from sight.

"You're okay," I whispered over and over again, desperate to comfort her.

Teagan was shaking so badly beneath me that I felt it reverberating through me, but I didn't dare move my hand.

Keeping her safe was my only priority at this moment.

"Come out, come out, wherever you are, *Messina*!"

I felt Teagan stiffen beneath me as the voice I recognized from the past boomed like a drum from somewhere close by.

"Don't you know by now that you can't hide from us?" Gerome Javi continued to taunt. "Your pretty little bitch can't hide from us either. We've got a really nice homecoming gift for you, boy."

"He's not here, asshole!" Tommy's voice penetrated my ears and my heart plummeted into my ass. "But the cops are,– or at least they're on the way, and you've made it so much easier for them to lock your ass up."

"You'll do just fine, Moyet," I heard Javi sneer and I jumped into action.

"No," Teagan hissed, grabbing the front of my shirt with both hands, pulling me back from the tablecloth I was moving towards.

"Don't," she mouthed, tears streaming down her cheeks as she clutched my shirt in her fist like it was her last lifeline. Taking my hand, she placed it on her stomach before mouthing the words, "You promised."

58

*P*eople around us were screaming and running for their lives, but I couldn't move a muscle.

I had been knocked to the floor and was buried beneath an insufferable amount of weight.

Frozen with fear, I remained on my back, barely daring to breathe. Noah had somehow managed to drag us both under a cloth-covered table.

We were out of sight, but he continued to lie on top of me, covering me from view, protecting my body with his.

He had his hand over my mouth and I was glad.

My fear was spiraling out of control and I didn't trust myself not to scream.

Never in my life had I felt fear like I had when I noticed the red blood spreading across Noah's white shirt.

He looked unfazed.

Adrenaline.

It had to be.

Nobody moved around like he had after getting shot.

"You're okay," he continued to whisper in my ear and I

continued to sob against his hand and point to his shoulder in horror.

I closed my eyes and prayed.

Please don't let us die here.... Lord, please don't let anything happen to my baby...

My eyes sprang open the second I registered what I'd prayed for.

My baby.

Mine.

Suddenly, this overwhelming feeling of possessiveness rolled through my body, bringing with it an indescribable feeling of protectiveness.

It was a feeling I'd never experienced before.

A feeling of unequivocal love and desperation.

I dropped my hand to cover my stomach once more and every nerve in my body came to life inside me. My heart began to drum a battle cry of its own accord.

And just like that, the course of my life took a sudden turn.

Motherhood.

This was my baby.

Noah's flesh and blood growing inside of me.

My heart hammered against my chest as excitement, fear, uncertainty, and unadulterated love washed through me. An almost crazed urge to defend and protect the child inside my womb possessed me. The child that only an hour ago I hadn't known existed, but now couldn't see a future without...

"I didn't know you were in there, you little intruder," I whispered in my mind. *"But I won't let anything happen to you."*

I clenched my eyes shut as an abundance of emotions threatened to spill over.

Please, keep my baby safe...

My heart swelled so big I thought it would burst.

"Come out, come out, wherever you are, Messina!"

Everything inside of my body stopped moving the second that man's voice filled my ears.

My heart.

My muscles.

Everything.

"Don't you know by now that you can't hide from us? Your pretty little bitch can't hide from us either. We've got a really nice homecoming gift for you."

My eyes were locked on Noah's face as I watched him battle an internal fight with himself.

Whoever this man was, he was baiting him, and Noah was desperately trying not to take it.

"He's not here, asshole, but the cops are, or at least they're on the way, and you've made it so much easier for them to lock your ass up." Tommy's voice filled the room and Noah's body seemed to jump to alert.

"You'll do just fine, Moyet," the man gloated and just like that, I felt my husband's self-control snap. "You can give your comrade a message from me."

Noah lunged for the tablecloth at the same time I lunged for him.

"No," I begged, voice strangled, as I managed to catch a hold of the front of Noah's shirt and pull his body back down on mine. "Don't."

I was crying big, fat, ugly tears.

Fear was imploding inside of me and the thought of Noah going out there was driving me close to hysteria, so I used in that moment the only tool at my disposal.

The child growing inside my womb.

Taking Noah's hand, I placed it on my stomach. "You promised."

I wasn't sure if I was speaking the words to him or mouthing them, but I had his attention.

Noah was still *here* with me and that was what mattered.

BANG!

The sound of another gunshot going off cut through the air, followed moments later by several police officers shouting, "freeze," and commanding, "Put your hands in the air."

Their threats and orders had come too late, I realized, as my gaze drifted toward the blood-stained carpet and then to the limp frame of a man hunched face down on the floor.

"No!" Noah roared as he scrambled out from under the table. On his knees, he crawled over to where the man was lying on the floor. "No, no, no.... God, T. *No!*"

Climbing out from under the table, I staggered to my feet and made to go after Noah, but a pair of strong arms came around me, holding me back.

"Don't," Lucky whispered in a tone I found oddly comforting. "Just... stay back. Give him some space, okay?"

"Is he?" I felt my body weaken and sag against Lucky as I watched my husband slam his hands down on Tommy's chest before covering his mouth, frantically trying to resuscitate him.

"Is he..." I couldn't say it, not out loud, not while the maniac who'd caused all of this was still in the room, snickering at my husband's agony.

Guilt rushed through my veins as my eyes confirmed what my mind refused to acknowledge.

"Yeah Teagan," Lucky whispered. "Tommy's dead."

"And you're next," the man taunted, smiling cruelly at me as the officers led him from the room. "We've got something special in place for you, bitch."

With the threat of a deranged man in my ears and the

image of a slain man in my mind, everything became too much.

The fear, the guilt, the throbbing in my head.

"Teagan," Lucky cried out in a frantic tone. "God, Teagan."

Confused and dizzy, I followed Lucky's line of sight to where he was staring.

I was bleeding.

Blood was trickling down my legs, pooling at my feet.

"Why am I bleeding?" I stared at Lucky's face.

The horror in his eyes caused a ripple of fear to run through my body.

Shivering violently, I grasped at my stomach. "Noah," I whispered, staggering forward. "I..." All of it became too much for me then and my legs gave away beneath me moments before I collapsed into a blanket of darkness.

I didn't cry.

Not a single tear spilled from my eyes when the coroner zipped up the body bag with Tommy Moyet inside of it.

Even now, as I sat in the waiting room of the hospital, having been stitched up, I couldn't feel a thing.

Nothing.

His face; blue, bloodied, and marred with a bullet hole in the center, haunted me, just like my father's had when I watched first hand when George Dennis took his life away, and still I didn't weep.

Emotionless, I kept my eyes locked on the door of the room the doctors had rolled Teagan into over five hours ago.

This was on me.

All of it.

Tommy was dead.

Teagan was... I didn't even know what was happening with Thorn.

They'd taken her away from me the moment the ambulance doors had opened and I hadn't been allowed to see her since.

And the baby?

I didn't know a damn thing.

The cops had come and gone, several of them. All asking the same fucking questions with their tiny notebooks and beady eyes.

I'd answered all their questions.

I had nothing left to hide and only one thing left to lose – she was currently behind door 203...

"Did you recognize the man that shot you, Mr. Messina?"

"Yes."

"Do you know his name?"

"Gerome Javi."

"Several witnesses said they heard him mention you personally. Did he have some sort of vendetta against you?"

"Yes."

"Why would that be?"

"I beat him to within an inch of his life eight years ago and served a five and half year sentence for the privilege."

"And Tommy Moyet? Do you know of any bad blood between Mr. Javi and the deceased?"

"No. The only mistake Tommy Moyet made was befriending a guy like me."

Tommy was dead and the last words I'd spoken to him were on bad terms.

Tommy protected me when I should have been the one protecting *him*.

He could have told Javi I was there, but he *didn't*.

I could have come out from under that table and stopped it, but I *didn't*.

I did absolutely nothing as my oldest friend in the world had his brains blown out by a man after *my* blood.

All because I loved my wife too much.

Because I chose to put her life and feelings above everything and *everyone* else.

The worst part was knowing that if I had to do it again, I would choose her *every damn time*.

What kind of a heartless monster did that make me?

Knowing that I would rather watch the whole world burn before losing my wife?

Knowing that even though I was heartbroken my friend was dead, I wouldn't change a thing because Thorn got to live.

From the age of seventeen, I'd been obsessed with her.

The girl next door.

The thorn in my side.

She was my best friend – then and now.

She was strong.

She was opinionated.

She annoyed the shit out of me back then and she challenged me on everything.

She was my biggest weakness and having her love me was my proudest accomplishment.

She was the only reason I'd had to keep my nose clean in prison.

She *had* to live.

"How's the arm?" Lucky, who was sitting beside me asked, stirring me from my reverie.

"Still there." I reached up to touch the part of my arm just below my shoulder where the bullet had gone through. "Doc said the bullet went straight through." It stung like a motherfucker, but I wasn't going to lie down on a gurney for the night and feel sorry for myself, not when my wife was inside that room. "It didn't hit anything...important. Just muscle." The countless x-rays I'd had confirmed that. "He gave me antibiotics and called it a flesh wound."

"You were damn lucky you didn't lose your arm, Noah," Lucky continued to say, eyes locked on the sling holding my right arm up. "That bullet could've ended your career."

Lucky was telling me the same damn thing I'd heard from the doctors earlier...

"You will need to undergo an intense rehabilitation and therapy program to get that arm functioning again, Mr. Messina," the doctor told me as I sat on the hospital bed, trying to take it all in. "Absolutely no fighting for the next three months..."

"I'm a fighter, Doc," I shot back. "It's what I do. You said the bullet went straight through, so just give me some antibiotics and let me get back to my wife."

"The muscles in your arm have been severed," the doctor countered. "This isn't some playground wound you can treat with an icepack and painkillers."

"What are you saying?"

The doctor sighed heavily. "I'm saying that even with rehabilitation and intervention, there's a possibility that you may never regain full mobility in your right arm..."

"Do you think I give a damn about my career anymore?" I choked out. "When Tommy's dead and Teagan's..." My voice broke off. I couldn't say it. I couldn't even bear to *think it*. Shaking my head, I continued my silent vigil by watching her door.

"Teagan will be *okay*," Lucky countered quickly. "It's shock." He nodded his head, but his hands were shaking. "Just shock," he repeated quietly.

"The blood," I choked out. The thought of Teagan hemorrhaging on the floor caused a spike of adrenalin to rush through my veins. Clearing my throat, I continued to stare at the door. "She's pregnant, Lucky."

"Shit," he let out a heavy sigh. "How far along?'

"I don't know." My voice was flat. Empty. "We just found out."

"It'll be okay." Lucky muttered under his breath. "Have a little faith."

"Faith is for the optimists." I cleared my throat again, hating the sound of my own flat voice. "I'm a realist."

"I don't know what to say except that I'm here, man," Lucky replied, nudging my uninjured shoulder with his. "I'm right here, man. Whatever you need..." He looked at me with a murderous glint in his eyes. "Whatever comes next? I'm all in."

"Mr. Messina?" A small, female doctor, clad in purple scrubs came to stand in front of me, distracting us both. "My name is Dr. Hardy. I've been taking care of your wife."

Immediately, I was on my feet. "Is she okay?"

"Yes, she's stable," Dr. Hardy replied. "Her blood pressure dropped significantly and it took a while to regulate due to the fact that she was severely dehydrated, but we've managed to stabilize her temperature and blood pressure, and we've administered an IV line with fluids."

"And the baby?" I managed to squeeze out. I was afraid to ask about the baby. She'd had no prenatal care. She'd consumed alcohol. She'd roughhoused around a goddamn gym and had jetted around the country for the past five or so months. I was afraid of what that doctor was going to tell me. "We...I -I don't know if she's still ..."

"Your daughter is just fine, Mr. Messina," the doctor replied with a smile. "Strong heartbeat and perfectly proportioned for twenty weeks gestation."

"My..." My head began to spin. *A daughter...* "Twenty weeks?" Every emotion I'd been holding back impaled me in that moment. *Daughter...*

I felt my legs buckle beneath my weight and if Lucky hadn't been standing beside me to lean on, I would have collapsed.

"Hear that, man?" Lucky chuckled, wrapping his arm around my waist. "Your *daughter*."

"My daughter," I repeated slowly. "My...daughter."

I had a daughter.

Teagan was carrying my daughter inside of her.

I knew at that moment that whatever the future held for me, I was going to protect her.

I'd heard Javi's threats. He'd said they had something special planned for my wife.

There wasn't a doubt in my mind that they would have to kill me dead before I allowed anyone to lay a hand on my wife or my baby.

THANK YOU SO MUCH FOR READING!

Noah and Teagan's story continues in Torment, available now.

Please consider leaving a review on the platform you purchased this title.

Carter Kids in order:
Treacherous
Always
Thorn
Tame
Torment
Inevitable
Altered

OTHER BOOKS BY CHLOE WALSH:

PLAYLIST FOR TAME

Music is one of the most important parts of my writing process.
I create playlists for each individual character.
If you want to check out my playlists you can find me on Spotify.

Check out my Spotify where I make all my playlists for my stories
https://open.spotify.com/user/215l6ymtg7ulpype2otbeseji

These are just a few songs that inspired me during writing Tame:

Ultrabeat – Elysium
Styles and Breeze – You're Shining
Safety Suit – Never Stop
Rita Ora – Poison
Zedd, Foxes – Clarity
Lera Lynn - Ring of Fire
Nickelback – Far Away

Halestorm –Here's to Us

Adele – Sweetest Devotion

Ed Sheeran – Small Bump

Taylor Swift – Out of the Woods

The Script – Walk Away

Ron Pope – In my Bones

Imagine Dragons – Warriors

Roy Jones – Can't be Touched

Tyler Hilton –Picture Perfect

Max Schneider – I'll come back for you

Charlie Daniels Band – The Devil went down to Georgia

Tenacious D – Fuck her Softly

ABOUT THE AUTHOR

Chloe Walsh is the bestselling author of The Boys of Tommen series, which exploded in popularity. She has been writing and publishing New Adult and Adult contemporary romance for a decade. Her books have been translated into multiple languages. Animal lover, music addict, TV junkie, Chloe loves spending time with her family and is a passionate advocate for mental health awareness. Chloe lives in Cork, Ireland with her family.

Join Chloe's mailing list for exclusive content and release updates.
http://eepurl.com/dPzXMi

Made in the USA
Las Vegas, NV
03 December 2024